Happy MAN

Rebecca Skovgaard

WP

Whimsical Publications, LLC

Florida

Happy Man is a work of fiction. Names, characters, and incidents are the products of the author's imagination and are either fictitious or are used fictitiously. Any resemblance to actual events or persons, living or dead, is entirely coincidental.

To purchase the authorized electronic edition of *Happy Man*, visit
www.whimsicalpublications.com

Cover art by Traci Markou
Editing by Brieanna Robertson

Published in the United States by
Whimsical Publications, LLC
Florida

ISBN-13: 978-1-940707-58-7

Will wondered if his friend, lacking certain expert detective skills, knew just how "taken" Sadie was. Still, his point was a good one, and well timed, as nearly six feet of redhead joined them. She wore a little black sheath that hugged all her curves just so. She carried two whiskey glasses filled with generous shots of deep amber. She handed one to Sadie and clinked them together.

"Cheers."

Will switched glasses, passing the soda back to Sadie and taking the whiskey. "Thanks," he said, and lifted it to the redhead. "I'm behind."

She arched a brow, but then followed his movements and tossed back the shot. No pink umbrella drinks for this one.

Will felt the smooth burn all the way down his throat—at a guess, Joe had broken the wax seal off a bottle of Maker's Mark. He met the amused green eyes watching him and refused to cough or clear his throat.

When it was safe to speak, he nodded. "I'm Will."

She put a hand out. "Katherine."

He set the whiskey glasses aside and took her hand, not so much shaking it as holding it. "Dance?"

She smiled as though that were a normal, expected question—little did she know. But she stepped into his arms and he moved his feet to take them out onto the dance floor. He hoped a little more foot shuffling would pass for dancing and gave a silent thanks to the DJ for slowing the tempo. No need for hip swiveling here.

In just a few steps, he relaxed. The whiskey had warmed him, the music was soothing, and the woman in his arms felt exactly right. She wore heels that put her eye to eye with him. He'd kept one hand holding hers and the other was on her back, making him keenly aware of the heat of her skin through the silky fabric of her dress.

Her gaze was on his, her eyes a clear, perceptive green. And inquisitive. "So—is she pregnant?"

Will looked back at her, hoping for an air of innocence.

She wasn't satisfied with it. "She's told you and not me?"

He lifted a shoulder. "I'm not sure she's told anybody. Maybe not even clueless over there. All I know is she's drinking club soda."

Katherine glanced over at Sadie and Leet. "She could have gin in it."

"Could have. Doesn't."

She raised an expectant brow.

He shrugged his shoulder again. "I checked it."

"So you drank her whiskey."

"I *was* behind."

"You were watching out for her." She used those perceptive eyes on him again. "You take care of people, don't you?"

"You know I'm a sheriff's deputy, right? That's what I do."

"Hmm."

"Hmm?"

"Not every law enforcement sort I've known takes that approach. Often, they just like to boss people around."

"I've been known to boss."

She lifted one corner of her very pretty mouth. "But that's not your usual approach, is it? You'd rather—nudge."

"I nudge?"

"Yeah. You'd prefer to prod people off in the direction you'd like them to go without their being entirely aware of it."

He didn't see what was wrong with that. "You're some kind of shrink, right?"

She arched her brows, but answered the question. "I have a doctorate in psychology."

"You nudge."

She smiled, fully now. "I do indeed."

He used the hand on her back to draw her closer. He lifted his thumb just a little and reached the edge of her dress. Then he stroked it over the bare skin of her back. "I've been looking forward to meeting you."

"Why?"

"I was pretty sure I was going to like you."

"Have I met expectations?"

"Exceeded."

$\mathcal{A}$CKNOWLEDGEMENTS

In my work as a midwife, I'm surrounded by remarkable women. They are working women—midwives, physicians, nurses, patient care techs, and staff. They show up every day for something more than a paycheck. We're on a shared mission—to do our best for the women and families we care for. It's my honor to work with them, laugh with them, and, when it comes to it, cry with them.

So here's to you. Sit down. Put your feet up. Take a rest, because you deserve it. Find a little light reading. (Hint, hint.) Love you.

PROLOGUE

35 years ago

"I have two things I'd like to ask you." Truman Hunter rowed them gently around Lake Fairlee, his shoulder strong enough now for this mild workout. Earlier in the summer, Elyse Fergus's eyes had sparkled as she took the oars, knowing that it tweaked his sense of manhood just a little to sit there while she rowed. But he was healing, in more ways than one. Soon, he'd be able to go back to work. If he decided he would go back to work.

A lot depended on how she answered his questions.

The lake was still now, the sun just falling behind the mountains. She no longer had to lift a hand to shade her eyes to look at him, to *see* him in that deeply perceptive, accepting, and somewhat unsettling way of hers. He'd gotten used to her way. He'd gotten to like it.

She was pretty as a picture, sitting there in her faded homespun dress, with the green of the mountains and the blue of the water as her backdrop. Her arms and legs were bare, tanned from a summer spent outdoors, toned from the work on her parents' simple farm. Her hair, a lush, rich brown, was loosely restrained in a thick braid that fell to her waist. Her eyes were a deep blue that matched the lake, pure and innocent in a way he'd no longer even considered possible.

Her lips were full and soft in the gentle smile she gave him now. They were sweet and welcoming when he kissed her, as he had, just once, last night when he'd walked her back up to her cabin after dark. For there were no motors on Fergus Mountain. No cars or tractors. No electricity either.

She waited for him to speak. And would wait, he knew, silent and content, for as long as it took him to choose his words. The families who'd come to play at the lake were on their way home now for dinner. The silence was deep, broken only by the occasional creak of the rowlocks, the small splash of water as the oars dipped below the surface, and, from the trees on shore, the rasping hum of cicadas as they signaled the drop in temperature.

"First, I'd like you to let me show your work to my mother. She owns an art gallery in Washington."

"My work?"

"Your weaving."

She wouldn't see it as art, but it was. She made scarves and stoles, cloths for tables, and light blankets. They were works of beauty.

He hadn't been to these Vermont mountains in the spring or fall or winter, but he knew what they would look like. He'd seen them represented in her work. Her summer weavings lovingly illustrated what he saw now—deep greens and blues with the occasional sparkle of white water or yellow sunlight. From her work, he knew what he'd see in autumn—the deep brown of the earth and the red, orange, and gold of falling leaves. In winter—the blue-white of the frozen lake and streams, the dark of night with a twinkle of stars shadowed by the skeletons of bare trees dolloped with snow. And in spring—bright yellow-green of new leaves, the pink blush of dogwood blossoms, and the jewel colors of hyacinths.

They were nothing short of incredible works of art, and his mother would owe him forever if he brought them to her. And she'd like it even better if he brought Elyse to her, as his wife.

"And I'd like you to marry me."

"Truman—"

He'd been named for the president, the sponsor of the Marshall Plan that had his father working in France to help re-build post-war Europe. The war had interrupted his mother's study of art history at the École du Louvre, but the recovery had brought her a love that had lasted his father's lifetime. And a son whose name honored the man whose policies had brought them together.

But the word sounded different when it passed Elyse's

lips—not so much a name as a declaration, a statement.

"Yes." That, too, a declaration.

"You know I don't leave Fergus Mountain."

"You do, a little. You're here on the lake with me. You've taken me into the village. But it doesn't matter, Elyse. I can stay here with you."

Her smile was just a little sad. "Oh. I didn't realize the FBI was opening a branch office in Fairlee Village."

He grinned at her tease. "I had a chat with the dean at the college across the river. I've begun to think maybe teaching suits me better."

She shook her head. "That's too much for you to give up, Tru."

He shook his head right back. It wasn't, and he knew it. He'd come here in June, determined to spend his medical leave poking around a bit. He had a theory about a serial killing. It was a thought that had risen out of his prior case. That one had taken a particularly nasty turn.

He'd needed to recover from injuries in the line, but more, he'd needed to recover his, *well*, his soul. That seemed too solemn a word for it, too laden with a concept of religion he wasn't sure he'd been able to preserve, but it was the best he could do.

An essential part of himself, of his humanity, had been left in the bottom of a mineshaft down in West Virginia. And he wouldn't be a man unless he got it back.

He'd found it, here, in these mountains, and with this woman. A certain salvation.

She was wounded, too, in her way. Or constrained, at least, left unable to grow and blossom as she should. It was partly her nature, perhaps, to be hesitant in her approach to life, to be shy of folks. It was reinforced severely by the extreme isolation of her upbringing. Her parents were the only humans she'd seen until they first took her into the village when she was seven or eight.

She hadn't had a friend until, when she was fifteen, a girl named Melissa Hancock, also fifteen and vacationing with her family at a lake cabin, wandered onto Fergus Mountain.

Melissa disappeared forever that summer. And Elyse hadn't had another friend until three years later, when Truman came looking for the missing girl. He had a theory that

Melissa had been a serial killer's first victim, the kill that had given him a taste for murder. The death that wasn't part of a pattern, because a pattern hadn't been established yet.

Truman had learned that Melissa had made friends with the girl who lived on Fergus Mountain.

He'd climbed the mountain every day for a week before Elyse agreed to see him. On that first day, he sat for hours on the front porch swing, watching the rhythms of the farm, knowing she peeked at him from the dark of the cabin or the barn. He'd spoken with her father, Thomas, and explained what he wanted. Thomas said he didn't think his daughter would want to speak with a strange man, nor talk about Melissa. It hadn't gone well three years before, when the local sheriff had come looking to ask the same questions.

On the second day, he changed his suit for dungarees and work boots. After sitting on the swing for an hour, he went to the barn and, awkwardly, using mostly just one hand, mucked out stalls. That week, by virtue of observation, he learned how to milk cows, prune fruit trees, and clear a field for plowing. On the third day, Elyse's mother set a fourth place at the table. Each evening, before he walked back down the mountain, he took an hour on the swing.

On the eighth day, Elyse came and sat next to him. After yet another hour of silence broken only by the creaking of the swing as Tru idly pushed it with his foot, she let him ask her about Melissa. And, over the next few weeks, she gradually led him around the town, showing him where she and Melissa had gone, what they'd done, and rowing him around the lake, pointing out cabins and describing the families who'd been there that summer three years back.

And in that time, two not-quite-right souls had found some healing, some completion in each other.

"I don't think I can be a wife, Tru."

"You can be my wife, Elyse."

She touched her fingers to her lips. "I'm afraid of...things."

The small boat drifted as he feathered the oars. *Yes.* She was afraid of many things. But she managed to do with him what she'd never done before. She walked alongside and talked with a man. She introduced him to people in the village. She rode next to him in a car. She let him kiss her.

"You're not as afraid when you're with me."

She looked away, to the mountains.

He knew it was the kiss—and more—that she thought of.

"Were you afraid last night, when I kissed you, Elyse?"

She studied him. "You know I wasn't."

"If you want, I'll take you to my room right now, and show you that you don't have to be afraid of anything that happens between us."

Her eyes were open, without guile. "I think I might like that."

Truman grinned. "I think you'll love it."

They married that week, on the mountain. A few days later, Truman left for Washington. He took boxes full of Elyse's work to his mother's gallery and his case notes from the summer to his office.

As he predicted, Isabela Hunter was entranced with Elyse's art and anxious to meet her daughter-in-law. And also as expected, he confirmed his suspicions about the identity of the serial killer. He was writing up his report, his last act for the FBI, when his telephone rang.

It was a voice he'd never heard on the phone before—Thomas, Elyse's father. Elyse had disappeared.

CHAPTER ONE

Will Hunter tied his dog and best buddy, Beowulf, under a tree outside the gym at Oak Mill Basin High, leaving him plenty of rope to move, cool shade, and a bowl of water. With school out for the summer, the pick-up basketball league had added a Friday morning game. He was often coming off a night shift for it, but Sussex County, Vermont, was not such a rockin' place that sheriff's deputies were normally kept busy all night long.

There were enough cars, motorcycles, and bikes outside the gym to guarantee a good number of players. They'd be short two of the usuals, he knew—his best human buddy, Leet Hayes, and Leet's soon-to-be-adopted son Jace were busy. Leet was marrying Jace's mom, Sadie, the next day. Leet had done an enviable job of ducking most of the wedding prep, but this close to the event, there were things even he, artful dodger that he was, couldn't avoid. Sadie and her moms had him corralled, and Jace, too.

Will, as best man, had responsibility for the party that night, but that was hours off. Besides, good music and plenty of beer out on the deck at the Tap and Mallet were really as wild as Leet wanted to get.

The gym was hot with the first hint of true summer weather. He sat down next to a relative newcomer, the man who helped out on Sadie's mothers' goat farm.

"Hey, Cane. I'm surprised the women don't have you hanging the farm with ribbons or arranging flowers or something."

"Yo. I told them I'd take care of the animals for them today, and I did. But I'm staying out of the girl stuff. They're all at Leet's place now, doing it up."

That was really about the first time Will had heard Canaan string together more than a couple words with the occasional grunt. And another first occurred when Canaan, in deference to the heat, stood to strip down to his shorts.

"What the fuck, dude? What the hell is that?"

Canaan stood with his hands on his hips and a mild glare in his eyes. "It's the leg I got compliments of the Taliban."

"Shit, man." Will stood, too, with the same hands-on-hips posture, and eyed the sleek, high-tech metal prosthesis that ran from Canaan's knee to the court shoe that covered the foot. "You should have told me about that. I had you crawling through the woods at Leet's house two weeks ago. With a freaking assault rifle."

"Yeah. And was there something wrong in the way I fulfilled my mission?"

"Nope. Course not. But don't you think I should have known?"

"I don't know. I do know I can't go back and tell you. Anyway, what's it matter?"

Will brushed a hand over his head and noticed other players were showing surprised interest as well. "Doesn't it matter to you?"

"Only if you start calling me Peg Leg. Then I'd have to take you down."

Will rolled a shoulder. "Would that be every time I call you Peg Leg, or—"

The rest of the sentence was lost as Will found himself laid horizontal just a couple inches above the hardwood floor. In some kind of movement too quick for the eye to follow, Canaan had hooked his legs out from under him and put him flat out. He was saved from slamming against the floor when, at the last millisecond or microsecond or something, Canaan grasped his hand and stopped his movement.

With their hands still clasped between their chests, Will looked up at him. "Or just until you understand it as a term of endearment?"

Canaan dropped him none too gently the last two inches. "You use a term of endearment on me, you'll be slow to walk upright."

"We'll see."

Canaan rolled his eyes at that and Will, still on his back, had to give it to him. "We gonna play, or what?"

Canaan pulled him to his feet. Will was a couple inches taller and maybe a few pounds heavier—but it didn't look to cost the man any real effort. "Play."

Everyone in the gym had played with Canaan before. They'd known him as a tough, physical player, and he only had to run roughshod over his opponents a handful of times before they all stopped holding back during this game. It was one thing to give a handicapped player a break. It was another to let him steal the damn game.

Will had been wise enough to team up with him and so hadn't had to struggle with the issue. Victorious, they walked out of the gym together a couple hours later. Canaan owned one of the bikes and he walked it along to the tree to greet Beowulf.

"You'll be at the Tap tonight?"

In a quick second, Canaan was on the ground with Beowulf over him chest to chest, having a good wrestle. "Yeah. I'm Leet's DD, right?"

"If you don't mind."

"No prob. I doubt anyone's really going to tie one on."

"Not likely. We'll be lucky to get rid of the women."

The women were coming early for dinner, in place of a more formal rehearsal event. The original, more complicated plans had been for a May wedding with more of the bells and whistles. That had been put off when Leet's first wife, who for three years had been thought dead, made an unfortunate though blessedly short reappearance. The ceremony set for tomorrow was simpler. Leet had given Sadie and the moms only two weeks to put it together. He was done waiting, he said. Will suspected there was a little, uh, procreative matter cooking that put some urgency behind it, too.

Leet was nothing but happy. Will liked Sadie just fine, so he was all for it, too. It was good to have a buddy testing those waters first, looking out for some of the rough spots. Lately, Will's mother was losing all subtlety about her desire for grandchildren. And he had to admit, Leet's setup with Sadie and her two boys had some appeal.

Beowulf took a breather and Will pulled Canaan to his feet. "And on the subject of women—about the tall, red-headed volleyball player?"

Canaan raised a brow. "Sadie's friend Katherine? What about her?"

"I'm callin' her."

"Callin' her? Like, dibs? We in high school?"

"Just sayin'."

"Sayin' what? You want her to bear your children, or you just want to be the first to ask her to dance?"

"Dance? There's going to be dancing?"

"It's a wedding, you dumb shit. I'm laying the floor for it this afternoon. Wouldn't mind a hand with it either."

"Yeah, sure, but—you can dance, Peg?"

Will was quick enough this time to stop the blow, just barely getting a hand between Canaan's fist and his own chest. Likely that meant Canaan wasn't half trying. Still, he leaned into him, his eyes pretty fierce.

"I can dance, Hunter. And I'll dance with anyone I want to, regardless of hair color." He turned and climbed onto his bike.

"Shit. You've got moves, don't you?"

Canaan chuckled as he pushed off—the prosthetic leg not affecting him at all. "At Leet's, about two. You help me get the floor down, I'll give you a salsa lesson."

Will was left with Beowulf. "Salsa. Shit. What the hell is salsa?"

Beowulf yapped.

"Not that. He's talking about a dance."

Katherine Noble had to put some effort into keeping her red head from turning enough to get a sneak peek at the clock on her desk. She wanted to be in her rental car now, headed up to Vermont in time to join her best friend Sadie, her family, and the groom that Katherine had yet to meet for their pre-wedding party.

Elizabeth Baker's fifty-minute appointment was the last thing between her and a very pleasant long weekend. She was Katherine's only client who'd not been willing to re-schedule when the short-notice invitation to the rearranged wedding had come.

Elizabeth had her issues and Katherine truly was sympathetic. But really, it had to be today? The woman had a husband who loved her pretty well, whose good job allowed her to stay home to care for their two healthy, entirely cute children. Things weren't perfect, and the sense of low self-worth that had colored her childhood was haunting her again, in large part because she'd given up the job at which she was so very competent.

Katherine could help her. It wouldn't take much for Elizabeth to change the patterns of thinking and behavior that kept her from finding happiness in her really quite privileged life. A life that many would envy.

After four years of college and five more getting her PhD in psychology, Katherine had the skills. And she was happy to use them with Elizabeth, especially since clients like Elizabeth paid her bills.

But she believed other aspects of her work—her volunteer job at a battered women's shelter a couple evenings a week, the Tuesdays she spent at a children's center, and her two Mondays a month at a women's prison—really made best use of her abilities. It was at those sites that she saw people who truly needed her help.

In comparison, the Elizabeth Bakers of the world had little to complain about. Still, Katherine enjoyed working with them—enjoyed seeing how the work she did with them could pay off in happier, fuller lives. Appreciated that it led to happier families, healthier children, a better future. All of that was good, and a good way to spend her day.

Just not this particular day.

Finding her discipline, she nodded encouragement as Elizabeth worked her way to a better life.

Will knew he'd be late to the party at the Tap. The owners, Joe and Maura, would have it all in hand, so Will didn't have to sweat it. But he pushed his four-by-four a bit as he drove up Fergus Mountain.

After the game, he'd worked out in the weight room at the school gym. Then he stopped by the office to clean up his desk. He ended up spending more time than expected. His on-duty partner, Paul Weber, asked Will to cover him while he went with his wife for their prenatal ultrasound. That led to a celebratory lunch at the pizza shop in the Basin with Paul and a couple other deputies—it was a boy, after all. Then he'd helped Canaan lay the dance floor out near Leet's pond. Leet and Jace had been let off their leashes in time to heckle when Cane had put on some music and tried getting Will to swivel his hips. They'd had a beer together then, in their last quiet moments with all three of them single men.

So he was later than he'd meant to be taking supplies up to his mom. She'd e-mailed her list to Power's Grocery so they had the order ready. Then he stopped by the post office for the packages that had accumulated over the last week.

Few citizens of Sussex County would recognize his mother if they saw her, but her textile art was recognizable and highly prized worldwide. Her weaving was built on natural wools from Vermont sheep and goats. But she special-ordered unique yarns and dyes from all over the world. Though she hadn't left her mountain in nearly two decades, the world came to her through the Internet.

As always, she heard his truck come up the road and was there in the yard to greet him. The same was true for Beowulf's brother, Spinner, and their mother, Lucy. Beowulf was out of the truck ahead of Will, giving a polite canine greeting to Lucy before running and wrassling with Spinner.

Human mother and son, both tall and lithe, held each other in a prolonged hug.

"Hello, Will." She smooched his cheek.

"Mom." He held her a bit longer, looking her over. She was still beautiful and fresh, with eyes that sparkled and cleared only for him and the occasional visit by his paternal grandmother. For all others, her gaze would be sheltered, downcast. "How are you doing?"

"I'm fine, Will, as always. You know I am."

They both took a bag of groceries, but still held an arm around each other as they walked to the cabin, Lucy sedate at Elyse's side. The answer was always the same and always a partial truth. She was healthy and strong and happy in her limited way. But she wouldn't leave her mountain and rarely spoke with another human being.

Elyse had been gravely wounded, body, heart, and soul. A week of her life was missing—a week of unspeakable terror and torture. A week where her mind had shut the door then locked it tight. She didn't recall what had happened during that time and had given up trying. It was enough that she'd survived it.

Yet, her survival had been a retreat, nearly a defeat. Just married, quickly widowed, she'd been taken in the loving arms of her parents to the sanctuary of their farm, their mountain. Where the small family—expanded nine months later by the birth of her son—secured their safety by maintaining total isolation. No more strangers were allowed on Fergus Mountain.

Elyse had dug for the strength to help her young son's life be as normal as she could make it. When it came time for school, she bravely walked Will down to the bus stop and even made it to parent-teacher conferences the first couple years. The last time she'd left the mountain had been for his high school graduation. She'd watched the procession as he and his classmates filed into the auditorium. She hadn't been able to enter the building.

Will went to college locally so he could live at home. Elyse's mother died his freshman year, and her father, Thomas, two years later. Will helped her bury them on the mountain.

He moved out when he trained at the state police academy. When he was hired into a deputy position in Sussex, he rented the top floor of an old Victorian in the village. But he sent graders up to rebuild the road that had become little more than a footpath to his mother's cabin. And he drove up the mountain three or four times a week, bringing her, like today, supplies and connections to the world.

In the kitchen, Elyse put groceries away while he toted her mail from the bed of his truck. She hummed as she worked—a testament to her acceptance, her simple happiness, which was both a relief and a sadness for Will.

"I have some stew and biscuits to warm up for dinner. But I know you have Leet's party tonight." Elyse knew Leet well. He'd come to the cabin with Will since their high school days, when they'd been best friends and stars of Oak Mill Basin High's football team. Through Will, she'd followed Leet's pro career, as well as his romance with Sadie. "You'll want to eat there, won't you?"

Will rarely missed a Friday night dinner with Elyse. "I'll eat with you, Mom. Maura can't match your biscuits. And I don't think they'll run out of beer before I get there."

Elyse smiled, but Will knew she'd have smiled either way. She was very careful to not be a burden.

She loved him. He was very nearly her only human connection. But she refused to rely on him too much. Her love was always a little cautious, a little distant. As though her wounded heart had never fully healed, had never fully resumed normal function.

Will in no way blamed her. He was quite certain that she'd never been sure if Will was the son of her beloved Truman or of the monster who had killed her husband and stolen her life.

She had every reason to guard her damaged heart.

Joe handed him his favorite Belgian ale as he passed through the bar. The noise from the deck was loud, the music hot. Before he went any further, Will did some deep breathing. A couple good swigs didn't hurt any either.

The umbrella-shaded tables had all been pushed to the edges of the large deck. They were littered with food and drink, and many of the partiers sat in happy groups around them. He spotted Leet's parents—the somewhat formidable Drs. Hayes. They were chatting remarkably amiably with Jocelyn, one of Sadie's moms.

Sadie's midwife friend, Meg, and her husband, Raul, sat with some of their brood at one table, and a couple of Leet's New Hampshire Metal teammates lounged at another. But to a person, all eyes were on the center of the deck that had been made the dance floor.

Will stopped in the doorway and watched, too. And then downed the rest of his beer. Damn Canaan was in the middle of a bevy of hot women—more than one man ought to be able to handle. The women danced with each other as much as with him, but he spread his attention around. He seemed to be keeping them all happy.

Will put his hands on his hips, grunting as Canaan did a slow turn and closed in on a tall redhead. "Dammit. He's got my woman."

He heard a huff of laughter and turned to see Leet at his shoulder. Sadie's younger son, Tino, was propped on his arm. "You haven't even met her yet, have you? She just got here in time for the party."

Will nodded at Leet and gave a fist bump to Tino. "Yeah, but I called her."

"Called her? What is this, high school?"

"Why does everyone keep saying that? And how does Canaan do that?"

"Do what?"

"Look at him. He's barely moving, yet he looks like he should be on stage at the Easy Rider, down to nothing but a G-string. Close your ears, Tino."

"You've seen men dance at the Easy Rider?"

Will's attention drew back and he met the humor in Leet's eyes with a glare. "In an official capacity."

Leet snorted. "The Easy Rider is across county *and* state lines. What official capacity would that have been?"

"I have a duty to protect my citizenry, wherever they are."

"Yeah, well, I'll ask you to protect them tonight. I have a feeling a bunch of these wild women are going to end up there before this is over."

Tino giggled. "My moms are wild women."

Will raised his eyebrows.

Leet nodded his head toward the dancers. "Next to Sadie. Little red dress? That's Seffie—Josefina. She's Tino's biological mom. She's living with my parents now. Has one more year of pre-med at the college, but Mom already has her accepted into med school."

Will looked, then looked some more. "She's—"

Leet finished for him. "A mom."

"Yeah."

"I have two moms and one dad now," Tino piped in. "How many do you have?"

Will looked back at the five-year-old. "Just one mom. No dad."

"Mom says a family is what we make it."

Will leaned a bit into Leet—a man as much family to him as anyone—and nodded at Tino. "Your mom's right. And so that makes you my nephew."

"Wow," Tino said, and looked up at Leet. "I have an uncle."

"Two uncles," Leet corrected. "You met my brother Matt, right? He's your uncle, too. And his girls are your cousins."

"Huh. Do I have to have cousins?"

Leet and Will exchanged grins then Leet nudged Tino, forehead to forehead. "I'm pretty sure a day will come when you'll like girls, dude."

"It's true, baby."

Will had watched as Sadie approached them—she was still mostly dancing, and in a way that belied the trauma she'd experience just two weeks before. A strong, athletic body, a determined will, and a few units of blood apparently were enough to mend the damage of a gunshot wound. Leet's push to get the wedding over and done with might have helped, too.

She'd swung by a table to pick up a tall glass—ice, clear bubbles, and a wedge of lime. She nuzzled Tino before favoring Leet with a long kiss. Then she turned.

"Hi, Will." She went on tiptoes again to press her lips to his. It was nothing like the body fluids-exchanging thing she'd given Leet. Just as well, he supposed.

"Hey, Sade." He took the glass from her hand and had a swallow. Club soda and lime. Evidence to confirm his theory—if she wasn't drinking alcohol at her own wedding party, she had to be pregnant. She smiled, utter happiness shining clearly in her eyes, and let him know that she was on to him. "Congratulations," he said quietly. Then he kissed her again, making a little more of it.

"Thanks," she murmured as she gave his hand a squeeze and held on.

Leet pulled her to his side and gave Will a direct look. "Get your own girl. This one's taken."

Will wondered if his friend, lacking certain expert detective skills, knew just how "taken" Sadie was. Still, his point was a good one, and well timed, as nearly six feet of redhead joined them. She wore a little black sheath that hugged all her curves just so. She carried two whiskey glasses filled with generous shots of deep amber. She handed one to Sadie and clinked them together.

"Cheers."

Will switched glasses, passing the soda back to Sadie and

taking the whiskey. "Thanks," he said, and lifted it to the redhead. "I'm behind."

She arched a brow, but then followed his movements and tossed back the shot. No pink umbrella drinks for this one.

Will felt the smooth burn all the way down his throat—at a guess, Joe had broken the wax seal off a bottle of Maker's Mark. He met the amused green eyes watching him and refused to cough or clear his throat.

When it was safe to speak, he nodded. "I'm Will."

She put a hand out. "Katherine."

He set the whiskey glasses aside and took her hand, not so much shaking it as holding it. "Dance?"

She smiled as though that were a normal, expected question—little did she know. But she stepped into his arms and he moved his feet to take them out onto the dance floor. He hoped a little more foot shuffling would pass for dancing and gave a silent thanks to the DJ for slowing the tempo. No need for hip swiveling here.

In just a few steps, he relaxed. The whiskey had warmed him, the music was soothing, and the woman in his arms felt exactly right. She wore heels that put her eye to eye with him. He'd kept one hand holding hers and the other was on her back, making him keenly aware of the heat of her skin through the silky fabric of her dress.

Her gaze was on his, her eyes a clear, perceptive green. And inquisitive. "So—is she pregnant?"

Will looked back at her, hoping for an air of innocence.

She wasn't satisfied with it. "She's told you and not me?"

He lifted a shoulder. "I'm not sure she's told anybody. Maybe not even clueless over there. All I know is she's drinking club soda."

Katherine glanced over at Sadie and Leet. "She could have gin in it."

"Could have. Doesn't."

She raised an expectant brow.

He shrugged his shoulder again. "I checked it."

"So you drank her whiskey."

"I *was* behind."

"You were watching out for her." She used those perceptive eyes on him again. "You take care of people, don't you?"

"You know I'm a sheriff's deputy, right? That's what I do."

"Hmm."

"Hmm?"

"Not every law enforcement sort I've known takes that approach. Often, they just like to boss people around."

"I've been known to boss."

She lifted one corner of her very pretty mouth. "But that's not your usual approach, is it? You'd rather—nudge."

"I nudge?"

"Yeah. You'd prefer to prod people off in the direction you'd like them to go without their being entirely aware of it."

He didn't see what was wrong with that. "You're some kind of shrink, right?"

She arched her brows, but answered the question. "I have a doctorate in psychology."

"You nudge."

She smiled, fully now. "I do indeed."

He used the hand on her back to draw her closer. He lifted his thumb just a little and reached the edge of her dress. Then he stroked it over the bare skin of her back. "I've been looking forward to meeting you."

"Why?"

"I was pretty sure I was going to like you."

"Have I met expectations?"

"Exceeded."

Her laughter warmed him, as did the sparkle in her eyes. "I got the sense your buddy Canaan was looking forward to meeting me, too."

Will shook his head. "No."

"No?"

He grinned and slid the hand he was holding up along his shoulder. "I'm sure he enjoyed meeting you."

"And dancing with me."

He put his now free hand at her waist, thumb circling front, and pulled her closer. He watched her mouth now as he spoke, his voice low. "Yeah. Definitely that." He took her a few more steps and even moved them into a kind of twirl. "But what he was looking forward to was busting my chops."

"Because?"

"Because I'd do the same to him." He was happy with the effects of the twirl—it had brought her body against his, hip to waist, and so he did it again. "It's a sign of the—affection between us."

She laughed again, throaty now, and he felt her thumb stroke along his shoulder. "I'm going to tell him you said that."

She got it. That made him very happy. "Please do."

For a fact, the women did end up at the Easy Rider.

Will followed them. Sadie's mom Marta drove a van full of them and Meg brought a bunch, too. Will had checked out both of the drivers—sober as nuns, as Marta had said.

They'd left Leet and several of the men getting down to some serious drinking at the Tap.

The Easy Rider was a decades old strip club with a typically raunchy history. Its owner, Hog Newton—named for either his shape or his fondness of Harleys, Will never knew which and would certainly never ask—had mellowed enough into middle age that he'd actually attracted a woman. A whole lot of locals were left shaking their heads when Hog got a high-end real estate agent, Esther Weinberg, to walk down the aisle to him.

Heads shook more when Hog—Esther called him Walter—cleaned up the bar to make it, well, something closer to respectable, and then built a small addition for women. It worked surprisingly well. Old fashioned swinging bar doors separated the men's area from the women's. The doors swung both ways at times, and all sorts of folks left the bar in a happier state—accompanied—than they used to.

It was at those doors that Will parked himself. Sadie's group was getting a bit rowdy, egged on by the famed Bill Blade, who could do things with his ass that Will didn't know were possible. Or it was the other way around, and the happy women were egging Bill on. Anyway, inevitably, they were attracting some attention from next door.

Quite a crowd gathered, peering over the doors, pushing against them, though they were blocked closed by the strategically placed impediment of Will's solid backside. The men couldn't get through, but that didn't keep them from speculating.

"I like the looks of the tall redhead."

Will cast a glance over his shoulder, though it didn't seem

to quell them as it should have. "She's taken."

"How about that little one in the red dress?"

Seffie. She'd been making eyes—and sexy little moves on the dance floor—at Canaan all night. Canaan had looked suspiciously unaware.

"She's too young."

"She must be old enough if she's in here."

"Nope, I'm entirely certain she's too young."

Like a hydra, squash one and another two popped up.

"I'd like a closer look at that blond in the middle there."

"Yeah, me too."

Sadie. "Also taken." Will speared the hopefuls a look. "*Way* taken."

Then an older guy spoke up. "How about that chunkier one with the short hair?"

Will smirked. "Not interested."

But Sadie's mom Jocelyn—Joss—always one to challenge stereotypes, chose that moment to slip a little green into Bill's G-string.

The guy's eyes were popping. "She looks interested."

Arms crossed over his chest, Will leaned toward him and spoke deliberately. "Not interested. *And* taken."

That bounced the guy back on his heels. But others in the group were starting to grumble. Apparently, some were of the opinion that they had the legal right to hear from the women themselves whether in fact they were taken or not. It never ceased to amaze Will what some dumb ass or other would consider to be his legal right.

One of the doors bumped against him with a certain lack of subtlety. So he turned to face them all, solidly planting his feet. Then he took out his wallet and flicked it against his shoulder a couple times, letting it fall open to reveal his star. There'd been some drink taken, so it needed a few flicks to get everyone's attention.

They so didn't need to know that he was out of his jurisdiction.

Gradually, they subsided. The old guy took one last look at Joss, then, all hang-dogged, slunk away. Amid many mutters about legal rights and what was fair, the others followed suit.

When Will turned back, he saw that Katherine had been watching. She held his gaze and moved her lips to say one word. Then she took the shot of whiskey she was holding, downed it, and turned her attention back to Bill.

Nudge.

Bill ended his dance. Apparently, Lance Duguid was up next. The women seemed entirely happy about that.

When Hog Newton finally gave him the nod to clear the bar, it was well after two in the morning. The women looked like they could go another few rounds, but the male dancers had taken to repeating their routines. Not that the women appeared to care—or even notice. They were still very happy.

Hog and even Esther helped round them up. They were divvied into the two DD vehicles. Meg took Aletha—Leet's mom boogieing pelvis to pelvis with Lance was an image he was going to have to work at smudging from his mind—and others going more southward, and Marta had the up county group. He figured there'd pretty much be a pajama party at the farm.

Katherine, at the Arlington Inn, was just across the river and could have gone either way. He grabbed her around the waist when she bent to get into Meg's back seat.

"I've got this one."

A couple too many whiskey shots had apparently turned her legs to rubber. She flopped back against him, and he had to hold her from sliding to the ground.

"Oops," she said.

"Yeah. Oops."

"You're taking me?"

Indeed I am, he thought. "Yup. It's right on my way." It wasn't exactly, but she didn't know that now and wouldn't remember it when she actually learned the local geography. Which she would. In detail. Over the next fifty years.

After hauling her a few weaving steps toward his truck, he gave up and lifted her into his arms. That generated a bunch of whoops and whistles as the women were sloppily calling out goodnights and "luv yous."

Katherine slid her arms around his shoulders nicely, but complained nonetheless. "You can't carry me. I'm too big."

"Evidence seems to be to the contrary."

She looked at his lips as though that might help her follow the thread of the conversation, but she was too slow. "Hmm?"

He boosted her up a little, easily. "I *am* carrying you. Therefore it appears I *can* carry you."

"But..."

He grinned while she worked at it again. She was a pretty cute little drunk.

She found the track of her train of thought. "I'm too tall."

He got her to the truck and set her on her feet again, steadying her body against his with one arm as he opened the door. He looked at her, down four inches now because she'd lost her heels. And one earring. "You're tall, sweetheart. Not too tall."

The other two vehicles peeled out of the lot. Of all people, Marta laid rubber, provoking another round of rowdy cheers and hollers. He shook his head with a chuckle, amused to think this group had left their mark among the many others who'd exited the Easy Rider parking lot in a happy hurry.

His rig was the last in the lot, and Hog put a period to their night by closing down all the lights. It was nothing but dark as he lifted Katherine again and slid her onto the passenger side of his bench seat.

"You must have big muscles."

He laughed again as he reached across her. "Indeed I do, darlin'."

He scoped her out as he secured her with the safety belt. All limp noodle, she stayed where he put her, head flopping back against the rest. But he could see her eyes were open and following his movements. Her lips curved in a small smile, he could hear her thoughts about his caretaking, and he figured she wasn't as much under the influence as she might seem.

So he leaned a little into the cab, face to face with her. Her eyes watched his for a long moment and when the smile finally faded, he touched his lips to hers.

It was just a touch, lips to lips and nowhere else, but it lasted. He felt the warmth of their merged breaths against his cheek, felt the connection as their eyes remained open in that too-close-to-focus but entirely together way.

She shuddered out a little breath and he pressed harder,

not opening her mouth, but still having more of her, making the most of his lips rubbing against hers.

It was a long time before he was done.

Finally, he lifted a little away. They watched each other as he held there, waiting for their breaths to calm. Then he stepped back, closed her door, and walked around to the driver's side.

She was quiet as he drove. He wouldn't be at all surprised to learn that she understood he'd just marked her, claimed her. He didn't really care one way or the other whether she understood it, or even how she felt about it. It was what it was. Sooner or later, she'd have to get on board.

Reluctant to tempt fate, Will parked under the portico at the Arlington Inn. He even gave a moment's thought to leaving the key in the ignition and the engine running. Determined to have more control of himself than that, he circled the truck and opened the door. Katherine was already fumbling her seatbelt off. Arching a look at him, she slid her legs around and brought herself to her feet, more or less steady.

He shrugged and stepped back. She could go on her own power if she wanted, but if she wobbled at all, she was going to be in his arms again. He kept an eye on her as she stepped by him, but took a moment to reach into the glove box for the bottle of ibuprofen he kept there.

Close on her six, he followed her through the lobby. She gave a nod to the sleepy desk clerk, but Will could see it cost her. The clerk, a young college kid, came to attention, all eyes now as she wove her way past. She missed a step and didn't object when Will took her elbow. He followed her lead to the grand staircase and pretended not to notice that she relied a lot on the curved rail for balance.

With fair composure, she walked down the second floor hallway and stopped before what he could only hope was her room. She fumbled with the opening to the sexy little evening purse she carried until he took it from her.

He opened it and savored the sense of intimacy he got when he peeked inside. A credit card and some bills folded into a slim side pocket, a cell phone secured in another. Two lipsticks, a tube of some eye stuff, a compact, a couple tissues. And not one but three little foil packages. *God*, he liked the way this woman thought.

More to the point, an old-fashioned brass hotel key. Leaving the rest of the contents nestled in the purse, and the thought of them in his heart, he took the key and opened the door. He stopped her with a hand on her arm as she began to move through. He stepped past and left her at the door while he checked out the room. He left the lights off, but peeked into the bathroom and brushed aside the lace curtain to get a view of the small balcony.

She must have been rushed when she'd gotten there. The bathroom counter had a mess of makeup and hair fixing stuff tossed around like a tornado had hit, and a couple of used towels littered the floor. She'd dropped a pair of shoes beside the bed, and on it, a T-shirt, a very short pair of cut-off jeans, and a matching set of undies—lacy, red, and skimpy.

He girded his loins, so to speak, and bit down hard on his imagination. If she wore red, skimpy lace to drive a car for several hours, what the hell did she wear under the slinky little black number she had on now?

It didn't bear thinking about. At least, not now, when she was well past the legal limit for participating in consensual sex. Freaking hot, sweaty, mind-blasting sex.

Girding again, he moved back to her.

She watched him, her eyes all too knowing. He was gratified that when she started to speak, she had to clear her throat and start again. "All safe there, sheriff?"

"Deputy," he said. "And, yeah."

Keeping some distance, he took her arm and pulled her in. Closing the door behind her, he shepherded her toward the bathroom. Leaving just the nightlight on, he ran a glass of water and then handed it to her with three pills. She swallowed them down with the same efficiency she used for a shot of Maker's.

He took the glass again and refilled it, then backed out of the bathroom. "Do what you need to do. I'll wait for you."

Will set the water glass on the bedside table and another three pills alongside it. Then he cleared her clothes from the bed—possibly not resisting the urge to breathe her scent from them. He opened the side of the bed nearest the bathroom and waited, trying hard to keep his imagination where it belonged.

When she came out, she walked up to him, right there next to the bed. He liked the little bit of height he had on her now. And the scent of something French on her skin.

She pressed lightly against him and lifted her face to his.

Very manfully, he kept his hands at his sides.

She leaned closer, lips almost touching as she spoke. "You're not going to make love to me tonight, are you?"

Fuck her lights out was more what he had in mind. He moved his head just a little. "No."

He thought he heard a sigh. "Because you're a gentleman?"

"Mmm. Well, and a *law*man."

She tilted her head a little, peering at him. "Ah. But you want to, don't you?"

He teetered, listing a bit toward her, making their contact more solid. "Yes, Katherine. Yes, I do."

She slipped her arms around his shoulders and sagged against him. "Okay then."

Will spent a couple minutes letting the angel on his one shoulder debate with the devil on his other about how to interpret that. But her weight came heavier against him and he knew he was losing her. *Game off.*

Still, he took pleasure in sliding his hands along her arms until he reached the bodice of her dress. He ran his fingers around until he found the zipper hidden along her left side. It took both hands to work it down to where it ended, a bit below her waist. He had to arch a little away from her to let it slip down to the floor.

He made no gentlemanly effort to refrain from taking advantage. He spent a good long time learning the answer to the question of her undergarments. There was a little black triangle that covered—well, not very much. If he was right about what "Brazilian" applied to, it had been applied here. He didn't think he was going to be able to straighten up for a week.

Gradually, his gaze wandered up. She had a little jewelry hung at her navel. Her waist narrowed from her sweetly rounded hips, her belly a small convex curve. Toned ropes of muscle were subtly visible.

And then—the bra she wore was black, and strapless,

and, well, almost missing entirely. From below it cupped her breasts—smallish, but definitely enough to please him—giving support but not a lot of coverage. It ended halfway up so that her nipples—he swallowed hard here, and had to check himself from taking them with his mouth—peeked out above. And *were peaked*, calling out to him. Pale pink, like ripe little berries, looking so sweet and tasty—

Will lifted his head and stifled—mostly, given her smug smile—a groan. He kept his eyes focused over her shoulder—not that there was much he hadn't seen—as he unfastened the bra and let it drop.

He figured he'd better quit there, while he was more or less ahead. So he left her poor excuse for panties where they were and rotated around so he could sit her down on the bed. She slid from his arms and curled over on her side. He brought up the sheet and blankets to cover her, then nudged alongside her hip to sit.

He stroked her hair with his hand, and along her shoulder with his lips. "I'll come get you here about one, okay? That will give you time for coffee and a little food before we have to be at Leet's."

She might have heard that. She might remember in the morning. But she gave every appearance of sleep just now. So he set her alarm for noon and left a note on her bathroom mirror just in case. Then he picked up her clothing from the floor and laid her dress out over a chair, since he couldn't figure how to get it on a clothes hanger.

He spent a couple minutes watching Katherine sleep, in what he hoped was a sweet rather than creepy way. Finally, he bent over her and touched his lips to her cheek. Her hand reached up to squeeze his where he leaned onto the bed and he wondered if that was natural or whether she'd been playing possum.

She kept him guessing. He figured he'd like that, most days.

He checked the lock on the doors to the balcony. On his way out, he used the brass key to lock her door from the outside, then slid it under so it would be there for her in the morning.

Having his woman locked up right and tight, he went out to his truck.

CHAPTER TWO

"I don't know, sweetie. It seems to be what they do."

Katherine *humphed* in her mind. She was still much as Will had left her—curled on her side, tucked under the blankets. But she had her phone to her ear and Sadie on the line.

"He stood over and watched me while he thought I was sleeping."

"Creepy or sweet?"

"Sweet, I think."

"So what's the problem?"

"I don't know. It just feels like he's already made the decision."

"That you're the one?"

"Yeah."

"Any chance he's right?"

Katherine rolled over and raised her voice in frustration. "How would I know? I barely know him. And how would he know? He hardly knows me."

"I think it's a guy thing. Leet knew the first day we met. He was sure."

"Come on. He thought you were hot and he wanted your bootie."

"Apparently, I *am* hot. And he does want my bootie. But also, *he knew*. And you probably shouldn't discount what Will knows. He notices things."

"Yeah, like I have boobs and an ass."

Sadie chuckled. "You surely do and he surely noticed. But more. A lot more, I'm sure."

"Like?"

"Like, I love you and that counts for a lot. To his mind,

I'm a very good reference. You're an athlete and have a doctorate. So he knows you have discipline and determination. You're in a caring profession—that would count for him, too, and also a lot. You shoot whiskey. You can hold your own on the dance floor with Lance Duguid. You're smart and strong—you'll challenge him. He's smart enough to know he needs that, wants that."

"Hmm. And there's chemistry."

"Is there now? Tell me more."

"Well, he can kiss."

"Um-hmm. And?"

"That's it. I believe he didn't want to take advantage of my inebriated state." Katherine knew Sadie would hear the disgruntlement in that.

Her laugh confirmed it. "Okay, so he got that one wrong. We all know you can hold your liquor. But still, that's kind of sweet, isn't it?"

"And straight up."

"That, too."

"So maybe I could like him."

"I'm glad to hear it."

"But I want to take my time about it. I want to get to know him. I'd like a little—"

"Courtship?

"Eeuw. Okay, yes."

"He won't pressure you, Katie."

Katherine smiled. She'd dropped her nickname in graduate school, going with her more adult and professional formal name. But Sadie had the right of long attachment and much affection.

"Yes, he will."

"Do you really think so?"

"Well, not overtly. But yes, with the weight of his conviction. With the—the power of his presence."

"Hmm. He has a powerful presence, does he?"

"Indeed he does."

Sadie laughed in answer.

"You're enjoying this, aren't you?"

"Oh, very much."

"Remember the thing you said about Will noticing things?"

"Yeah."

"He noticed that wasn't gin and tonic you were drinking last night."

"So he did."

"Is there something you want to tell me?"

Sadie hesitated. "I can't. I haven't even told Leet."

Katherine smiled. "I'm very happy for you."

"Me too."

"So, I guess we'd better hurry up and get you married. I'm getting up. I have a wedding to get ready for. Plus, I have to go buy some pink stuff."

"Pink stuff?"

"For my niece. I'm going to be an auntie."

"Ah."

"See you soon, Sade."

"Love you."

Will listened outside her door for a minute before he knocked. All was quiet, so he wondered if she'd slapped the alarm off and rolled over to go back to sleep, or if she was tiptoeing around with the shades down, nursing a thick head.

What he didn't expect was for Katherine to open the door even as he raised his hand to knock. Or for her to look all bright and chipper. And gorgeous. *Well*, that part wasn't a surprise.

She had a lipstick in her hand. "Come in. I'm almost ready."

She looked all the way ready to him. She had a slim little sundress on—white with black polka dots, no sleeves, no straps. Someday, he was going to peel her out of that one, too, so he was going to have to learn how she hung those things up. Her black dress from last night was no longer draped over the chair, so he could check it out in the closet. But right now, he was busy watching her through the open door of the bathroom as she leaned toward the mirror to paint her lips. Bright red.

He could watch that for a good long time, but he was already having to adjust himself, so he forced his gaze away. There were several small bags on the bed. He moved toward them. "You've been shopping?"

He lifted out a little pink baby...*thing*. And jumped some-how guiltily when she spoke from the door.

"Yeah. There are some great little boutiques in the vil-lage."

He lifted the...thing in question.

"For Sadie and Leet's little girl."

"She knows it's a girl already?"

"Nope. But I'm confident." She dug another ridiculously girlie pair of shoes—spiky high heels, black and white straps—out of the closet. He swallowed hard as she sat on the bed and fastened them at the ankle. "Anyway, I'll proba-bly buy some boy stuff, too, just in case. But the girl stuff is cuter."

He looked at her and wouldn't argue. He couldn't in any case, not with his tongue hanging out of his mouth.

She stood, all long and lean, of a height with him again in her heels. And waited in patient amusement, it appeared, while his gaze slowly tracked up from those sexy little ankle straps, taking in every bit of enticing scenery, until they were eye to eye.

He could have stayed there a while, lost in that green.

But she spoke, and after a couple seconds, it registered. "You were going to feed me?"

"Uh, yeah. They have a nice brunch here at the inn. That okay?"

"It's great."

He kept a hand at her back as they left the room.

She glanced over her shoulder at him. "Do you really think Leet doesn't know Sadie's pregnant?"

"He might guess. He's not entirely clueless."

"He wouldn't talk to you about it?"

"He will, sure. But not until Sadie tells him."

"Man code?"

"Man code."

For the most part, Katherine held back tears during the ceremony. It was so sweet—Sadie and Leet's love for each other so obvious, the love and support from their family and friends so manifest—that just a little moisture in her eyes as she held Sadie's bouquet while the two of them exchanged vows was entirely defensible.

What was tougher to accept was the feeling—where? In her heart, her gut?—that was entirely solid, entirely extant, that came whenever she met Will's gaze from across the arbor where he stood at Leet's side. Which she did frequently—every time she looked that way, in fact. Because, apparently, he had nothing to do but stare at her. One might think he wasn't paying attention to the wedding at all. She was surprised he managed to come up with the ring at the proper moment.

The feeling was not a mild suggestion but a blatant declaration, a firm resolve, that it could be, should be, *they*—Katherine and Will—making this commitment.

It was a ridiculous thought. She'd have flashed his hard-assed stare right back at him, and stomped her foot to boot, if that wouldn't have been totally inappropriate at her best friend's wedding. So she put her focus on Sadie and went to great lengths to convince herself that she was reading way too much into the message in the eyes of one tall, strong, attractive in the extreme, best man.

It was a glorious Vermont summer day. The sky was cobalt blue with pure white cotton candy clouds mirrored in the still water of Leet's pond. The trees—natural ones—that surrounded the yard were in full, fresh leaf, rustled gently by the occasional soft breeze. Others—Leet's remarkable sculptures—reflected and refracted light from shimmering metal leaves and crystal prisms that moved with the air and sent out random rainbows of color. Their chimes produced a unique sort of wedding bells.

The ceremony ended with applause and long minutes of joyful hugs. Katherine was caught up in it, filled with happiness for her friend. She shared embraces with bride and groom, then Sadie's boys, then her moms. She hugged everyone, even the very large football players from Leet's team who were strangers to her.

Everyone, that is, except Will. It took a bit of studious effort to dodge him. And even so, she couldn't avoid his heavy, watchful gaze that was patently aware of her evasion.

Figuratively, she sniffed. Or maybe she did so literally. So what if he watched her with amusement? So what if he was there, the implied next in line whenever she left one embrace for another? So what if it took some awkward maneuvering to make sure there was someone else, *anyone* else, she could turn to next?

Finally, the party settled in for a wedding supper. Scattered across the lawn, tables draped in white were beautifully set with crystal, china, and silver. Katherine sat at the head table next to Sadie, with two whole bodies, including Leet's large one, separating her from Will. It was a distance dictated by protocol rather than her own panicky urge to evade. Still, it felt significantly short of enough.

Sadie and Leet sat in sleek dining chairs of burled oak. Gifts from one of Leet's wood sculptor friends, they were upholstered in a beautiful weave of blue and green wool. That, Sadie said, was the magical work of Will's mother.

Katherine did her best to keep her attention on the newlyweds, though she was always conscious of Will's presence. But she couldn't legitimately avoid watching him as he gave a toast, which was expectedly funny and unexpectedly sweet and touching enough to cause tears to threaten yet again. And he was not too small to take advantage of the opportunity to hold her gaze throughout. When he finished, he stepped over specifically to clink his glass with hers. He surely looked fine in a tux.

He was there again when dinner was over and the dancing started. He held his hand at her waist while they watched Leet and Sadie waltz, their first dance as man and wife.

The bridesmaid dress Katherine wore was a blessedly simple, narrow sheath in midnight blue. Its only dramatic elements were a high slit below the bum to allow movement for dancing and a daringly low-cut back that left her spine subject to the caress of Will's thumb. In fact, between the slit and the low back, only a few important inches were covered.

As they stood together, the stroke of Will's thumb provoked a shiver she couldn't suppress. He stilled for a moment, making it clear he was aware of her response. With the next stroke, he slipped his thumb inside and dragged his nail across her back a good two inches below the line of fabric.

She fought a shudder and started to step away. But he corralled her with his wide palm on her back, brought her against him, and moved them out on the floor where others had now joined the dancing. Like he had the night before, he guided her hands up to his shoulders and put both his arms around her.

She braced her hands against him, arching back so their bodies didn't touch except where he clasped her at the waist. His gaze held hers, strong and heated.

"Katherine." He slid one hand up her back, tangling it in her hair until he reached her nape. Bringing her closer, he dropped his head until their lips nearly touched. "Move up here."

"What?" Her feet stopped moving of their own accord and she pushed back against his hold. "Are you kidding? Just because we like each other a little?"

He didn't let her go far. "Like each other a *little*?"

"All right." She didn't have to respond to that, *per se*. "*Know* each other a little."

"I know enough that I want to see you, to be with you."

"Well, then you come to Manhattan to visit me. Or invite me up here to visit you."

"And so we see each other a couple times a month? That's not enough. Something happens and then you don't come. I can't get a weekend off and so I don't go. Then it starts to snow and we don't see each other at all. That's not what I want."

Katherine looked away, shaking her head in wonder. She remembered her conversation with Sadie just a few hours ago. Back when she believed Will wouldn't pressure her with the strength of his feelings. "If it happens like that then maybe that's what's supposed to be. That's how you find out about a relationship. You spend time together, get to know each other, see where it goes."

"That's in the relationship rule book? Guess I didn't read that one. Couldn't we—you and I—do it another way? I want you here, Katie." His arms brought her closer, his hands taut against her skin. "Katie, look at me."

It took her a moment, but she did. She wasn't certain if it was a mistake or not. She did know her heart began to melt.

His gaze was open, undefended. He let her see—desire, feeling, wanting. His awareness that what he asked was no small thing, no usual thing. His own wonder that he was asking, that he was driven to ask.

She saw nothing dark in it, no warning whisper of a need to control, no hint of abusive use of power. She recalled their discussion about nudging and knew this pressure, this urgent desire to compel, was not his usual way. He was surprised by it, too.

Katherine settled a little, softening in his arms. He responded. She could hear the calming of his breath, feel the easing of his body. She laid her head onto his shoulder, her face toward his neck. He began to move, taking them back into the dance.

For a few moments, they were together, moving with the music, moved by feeling. Accepting, sharing the surprise, the sense of wonder in what was there between them.

When the music ended, she lifted her head and stepped back. His arms let her go, and she took both his hands in hers. She looked at him and he waited for her answer.

"I have my own practice, Will."

"We have crazy people up here. I could give you a list."

She almost smiled, but something hurt too much. "It takes years to build a practice."

"You'd have years up here."

For reasons she didn't want to ponder, Katherine's eyes burned. "You could move. You could find a job down my way."

He moved his head, shaking it just once. "Can't."

"Won't?"

He lifted a shoulder and she read the meaning. Same thing.

She took another step back, out of reach now of his hands. He watched her, gaze still open, showing pain now, as she turned and walked away.

Katherine danced every dance. Will watched Katherine dance every dance. He considered the time-honored way of drowning his sorrows. There was probably enough booze in the bar set out on Leet's terrace to do the job.

If he asked everyone else to quit drinking.

But he was determined that, whoever else she danced with—and that seemed to include every male present, old or young, attached or unattached, *breathing* seemed to be the only prerequisite—he would be the one to take her home. Or back to the inn, in this case.

For that, he needed to be sober.

And so he watched. Watched while he stood there alone. Watched while one of his buddies came to visit him while he watched. It was pitiful and inevitable that even Canaan came to watch with him, still breathing just a bit fast after his own dance—a hip swiveling, body shimmying *salsa*—with Will's woman.

They stood side-by-side, arms crossed over their chests.

Canaan waited, apparently needing to catch his breath, before he spoke. "Got it bad, eh?"

Great. Sympathy from Canaan. He really was in a pitiful state. Nothing to do but own it. "Ay-yuh."

Cane looked from him out to the dance floor.

At least she was boogieing with a bunch of women now. That was marginally better.

"Let's have it. What'd you do?"

"I asked her to move up here."

"Dude! You met her, like, yesterday."

With Katherine safe among women, he turned to look—okay, maybe *glare*—at his friend. "What else can I do?"

Canaan met him eye to eye until Will was certain he was seeing a little too much. He went back to watching Katherine, thinking now about the burden of friendship. When you got to know people, they got to know you back.

But he couldn't deny that Canaan's hand on his shoulder was a comfort. They watched some more together.

"She's putting a lot of effort into not looking your way."

"And this strikes you as a good thing."

"Yeah. You've got her on the run."

"On the run is really exactly *not* where I want her."

"Oh, come on. It's the natural way of things. You didn't expect it to be easy, did you?"

"I don't see why not."

Canaan laughed and slugged his arm. Somehow, that felt better. "She's a woman, man. You chase, she runs. You have to chase harder." He shook his head. "It wasn't meant to be easy."

The setting sun had blessed the party with a pure, glow-ing evening light. As night fell, lights placed to illuminate Leet's fantastical trees came on, turning the grounds into a setting fit for faeries. The air cooled, but the dancing kept Katherine warm. That and the constant heat of Will's gaze.

He'd taken up a post between the pond and the dance floor. It should have seemed rude, the way he physically dis-tanced himself from the party. Yet, by virtue of the many people who approached him, standing beside him and, to all appearances, comfortably visiting, he remained a part of it. Leet's parents, Sadie's mothers, Jace and Tino, really every one of the locals, those who knew him, went and chatted with him.

It gave Katherine the sense that this was a common cir-cumstance, with Will among them—these people he knew and watched over, protected—but not quite *of* them, *with* them. She thought it could be simply due to his profession—that he was always a bit on guard, always feeling responsible and alert for trouble.

But there was more.

It almost seemed as if the locals were watching over him, too. Protecting him.

It seemed—very complicated.

It set her psych instincts—honed now with years of train-ing and experience—humming.

Will was very attractive, very appealing, and very, *very* interesting.

He was trouble.

And trouble walked her way now, as the party wound down. Leet and Sadie were saying goodnight to their guests. They planned to spend a few days here, alone, in Leet's amazing home. Then Leet had some plan that Sadie knew nothing about for a wedding trip.

Will gave Sadie a hug—a big one, lifting her off of her feet—and then Leet, too. He left Leet on his feet, but it was a real hug, not the clasp hand, pound once on the back thing that men seemed to think passed for a hug. Then he turned to face Katherine. "You ready to go?"

Katherine bit her tongue. They hadn't reconnected since

she'd left him on the dance floor, hadn't exchanged a word. Yet she'd been certain he would consider that it would be he, and no one else, who took her home.

She nodded, feeling Sadie's gaze. She shared a look with her friend and knew Sadie understood. The look implied another shrug, another "it's a guy thing."

She left it for a moment, putting her whole attention on Sadie and Leet. And then had to fight tears—the same ones welling in Sadie's eyes.

Leet got to her first, taking her up in a warm, sweet embrace. "No tears. She's still yours, too."

His understanding touched her heart and she gave him a lip-smacking kiss. "And now you're mine, too. I'm not losing a friend, but gaining a big lug."

Sadie stepped into the hug. "A very handsome big lug."

Katherine laughed, but it was kind of a teary hiccough. "Just so. Oh, I'm going to miss you."

Sadie slid tears away with her wrist and then gripped her hard in a hug. Katherine knew Will was just over her shoulder, and Sadie was smiling when she looked at her again. "I think we'll be seeing you."

"Hmm." They shared a quick kiss. "I love you."

Leet's supportive arm was around Sadie again and he pulled her close. Her friend had chosen well. Sadie sniffed. "I love you, too."

Katherine turned to Will. "Ready, then."

Will took possession of Katherine's arm and walked her around Leet's massive studio and home of stone, wood, and glass until they reached his truck. He opened the door and gave her a hand up onto the seat.

She shouldn't have been able to walk, much less climb into a truck, with the way the line of her dress narrowed at her knees. But there was this slit in the back—he'd pretty much spent the last several hours watching it. He'd long known that it made a man think that if she would only move just so, he'd get a peek not just of long, lean, lovely thigh, but of heaven itself. He knew now it was a cold-hearted tease, but that didn't keep him from looking again as she climbed up.

He suspected she knew he was looking, too. She took her damn sweet time about it, brushing past him and pretty much wafting her ass in his face as she lifted up and settled in. His suspicion was confirmed by the evil twinkle in her eyes as she pulled her seatbelt across and fastened it.

Apparently, her breasts wanted in on the act too, revealing themselves just a little more with that turn and twist, basking in the way the belt separated and defined them. He didn't move—well, most of him didn't move—for a long moment while he savored the whole production.

She had the nerve to lift a brow, like she was an innocent in the entire deal. That pissed him off a little and he closed the door on her none too gently.

They didn't speak at all as he drove down to the Junction. And this time—*fuck fate*—he pulled into a parking space at the inn.

She got herself out of the truck before he made it around to give her a hand. But there he was again, stupidly hopeful gaze locked on that slit, as he followed her up the stairs to her room.

Katherine managed the key herself this time, but had learned already to step aside while he checked the room. When he came back, they did a little awkward dance around each other until she was inside the room and he was out. Which satisfied him not at all.

"What's your plan for tomorrow?"

His voice was unexpectedly gruff, a fact he chose to attribute to his not speaking to her at all on the ride down. She fiddled, her hand on the doorknob, while he watched the pulse thrum at her neck. He couldn't be sure it was more than his imagination that made him think the beat picked up a little.

"I...thought I'd to just get up and head back." He didn't want to read too much into it, but she seemed a bit regretful. She rallied and took another breath. "There's an outlet mall..." She petered out entirely.

"Well then. Safe journey." And good fucking shopping.

Her eyes scanned his. "Thank you. Goodbye, Will."

He didn't answer as she closed the door.

The obvious thing then would be to turn and walk away.

His feet didn't seem to get the obvious. They stayed put while his right hand lifted to press flat-palmed against the door. And then he leaned forward so his forehead rested there, too.

He stood like that for a long moment, certain as he could be that she stood there, too, on the other side of the door. He imagined he could feel the heat of her palm, mirroring his, through the hard oak.

Finally, he spoke one word in a rough whisper. "Katherine."

She kept him waiting long enough for him to begin to think that his mind's image of her standing there was nothing but a lame fantasy. Then, finally, she opened the door.

He put his hands on her hips and nudged her back a couple steps so he could clear the door. He kicked it shut with his foot and turned back with one hand to secure the lock. Then he grasped her with both hands, pulled her tight against him, and took her mouth.

He knew in the first second it wasn't the gentle, seductive, questioning kiss that he should have used. It was a taking, a possession. And there wasn't a damn thing he could do about it.

His mouth brushed hers open and he was inside, stroking, tasting. He grasped one last moment of sanity to loosen his hold, to lift his head. But she followed him, her body plastered against his, the very gratifying strength of her arms around him, her mouth seeking, pushing to stay joined with his.

In that last moment, he gave thanks.

And then he let go of all restraint.

He did what he'd been dying to do for hours, only hoping she appreciated that he'd waited until he had her alone. He reached behind her and put his hand right into that damned slit. His fingers slid up her thigh, bunching up the silky slick fabric until he had his hand on her ass. He covered one firm globe and squeezed, massaging hard, rocking her against him.

The movement brought her center up against his rock-hard erection. She moaned, then tore her mouth away from his to haul in a real breath. It came out in a ragged keen. She strained against him, rubbing herself against his rigid length.

Mightily encouraged, he slid his hand down the crease of

her ass. He stopped at the first bit temptation he came to. He circled his fingers, rubbing her through the sexy swath of panties there, then pressed the silk just a little into that forbidden opening.

She shrieked his name, but she didn't sound entirely unhappy, and she didn't stop humping him. If anything, she ground herself more strongly against him and panted like she was about an inch away from a rocking orgasm.

Always willing to help, Will took his less-occupied hand to the bodice of her dress and tugged it aside to bare one breast. She had one of those push-up deals on again that left her nipple uncovered. It called to him as it had the night before and, this time, he answered.

He plucked it between thumb and finger, tweaking and tugging. He bent his head and put his mouth at the juncture of neck and shoulder, grazing with teeth and then sucking hard, leaving his mark. At the same time, he took the middle finger of his right hand, still covered in silk, and probed a little deeper. Then he gave her a swivel.

She cried out, laboring against him, and came hard. It lasted and lasted until finally she finished, collapsing enough that his fingers were forced to cease their business so he could support her in his arms.

Well. Wasn't that a very fine, if unorthodox, way to initiate their sexual relationship?

And he was so not done.

She was moaning weakly and might have said his name. He patted her, friendly and, he hoped, bolstering.

"It's okay, sweetheart. We've just gotten started. Come here."

He walked her over to the bed, high and blessedly king-sized, and did what that dress had been begging for all day. He turned her and pressed her down so she bent at the waist, flattening the top half of her body onto the bed. And there she was, just for him, everything from her tall heels up her long legs to that slit in her dress pointing him directly to heaven.

It was just out of sight, but he knew it was there.

He tugged her panties down just a little—just so they were visible, an enticing hint of black silk at the top of the slit. Then he slid his fingers under, not mussing the dress at all, but reaching up to find gold.

He went properly to her wet heat this time, sliding his middle finger once all the way up inside her. She was wet and slick and very, very tight. He bit back most of a moan himself, imagining the almost painful pleasure it would be to force his way into that hot, tight space.

She moaned right back, and again as he began to stroke her. He worked at her, first with one finger and then two, stirring her interest again, very glad to learn she had some stamina. She was pretty hot, whimpering a bit and chanting out his name—begging him? Directing him?—before he stopped.

He didn't touch her at all as he reached into his coat pocket for a condom—she wasn't the only one who came prepared—but just left her there, panting for him, her needy breath turning a bit frantic. He unzipped his fly and pulled himself out. Freedom from the restriction of his pants was a blessed relief that almost made him groan.

As he covered himself, he started talking to her. How that dress—that fucking dress—had been tormenting him, *goading* him all day. What a turn-on it was to know that all he had to do was slip a finger up under that slit and he'd have her. A turn-on and an out-and-out torture.

His cock, he said, would be the next thing she felt, the only thing she felt. And then he did it, with both of them still fully dressed. He pressed himself up under that slit until he reached her. He sank in just a little, letting her stretch around him, waiting for her body to accommodate him. Making sure she felt the whole breadth of him. Giving her a hint of what she was in for.

She let out a long, slightly panicky, entirely needy groan. Her fingers dug into the bedspread.

He took hold of her hips then, through the sleek fabric of the dress, pushed further into her, and held.

Her breath huffed out hard a few times. Then she arched a little, inviting more.

He gladly complied. He shoved hard, sinking into her all the way.

She screeched just a bit, but then she flexed, moaning, grinding herself against him.

And with that, he was a goner. He pulled out and then

thrust in again, gnashing against her. Again. And again.

Then he was pounding into her, his breath, like hers, huffing out in urgent need. He lifted her and arched back, stroking deep, stimulating her. As he moved into her, he brushed against her panties, yet another exquisite torture.

Finally, she screamed out her orgasm. He followed, every bit as loud as she, pumping into her, spasming as jets of hot fluid surged through him.

He nearly collapsed on her. Just barely, he gathered the wherewithal to slip out of her, drop the spent condom ignominiously to the floor, pull her up onto the bed, and crumple beside her. She lay on her side facing away from him, and he was draped like a wet noodle, half over her. They both struggled to catch their breath.

After many minutes, he collected himself enough to skate a hand along her arm and lightly stroke her.

She stirred just a little. "Will?"

"Hmm?"

"Was that normal?"

He could hear the smile in her voice, the pleased satisfaction—*satiation*—and smiled back. He knew how she felt.

"Do you mean was that in the normal realm of absolutely spectacular mind-blowing sex?"

She lifted a shoulder, like that might have been what she meant or maybe not, but was interested in his answer either way.

"I think, *no*. I think there was something otherworldly about it, something *para*normal. I've heard it rumored that once every few centuries a little known figure from Greek mythology, the god of sex—"

"And goddess of sex."

"Uh-huh. And goddess of sex inhabit the bodies of two mere mortals and—"

"*Voilà.*"

"Exactly. *Voilà.*"

They were both chuckling, but they quieted a little as his hand happened to find that breast he'd left bare.

"On the other hand," he said, as his fingers started a bit of investigative research.

"Yes?"

"If you meant, do I normally bring a woman to two unforgettable, ruinous-for-all-other-men orgasms while we're still fully clothed?" He left a little question at the end of that, daring her to deny it.

She laughed fully outright and rolled over to look at him face to face. She had a hand against his wrist, securing it in place.

Gratifyingly, that added the visual to his exploration of her lovely breast. "Or, if I normally dispense with any semblance of romance and go directly for a, uh, end-run approach—"

Katherine laughed again, but circled her arms around his neck and brought him close.

They both sobered as their gazes met.

He swallowed hard and simply held his hand over her breast, feeling the beat of her heart, seeming one with his.

"Katherine." He touched her lips with his, then lifted again to meet her eyes. "I'm falling in love with you."

It was very close to the truth. Just a matter of tense. Not falling, but *fallen*.

She sighed. Mournfully? Regretfully?

No matter. He'd take Canaan's advice and chase harder.

And he could do romance if she wanted it.

He kissed her—gently, as he should have initially. He touched her full lips softly with his, and took his hand from her breast to stroke her face. With his thumb, he traced the line of her high cheekbone, the soft curve of her neck. Then he lifted to watch as he rubbed her lips. He chafed his thumb over them, separating them just enough to get a glimpse of the moist pink of the inside of her mouth.

Her eyes darkened, and from the edge of his vision, he could see her nipple tighten. He took her mouth again, with more pressure now, more friction. But still he took his time.

He wasn't even using his tongue before she began to show a little restlessness. She grasped his wrist where he held her, pulling him a little closer, and lifted up a bit against him, making more of it where their mouths met. Then she arched, her breasts rising, a little wave of tension riding through her.

He wasn't falling for it. He was going to be a gentleman about it this time. Even if it killed him.

Pulling away a bit, he turned his wrist to grasp her hand and slide it up over her head. That did nice things to the one breast he had bared. The fabric that he'd pulled aside to get to it rode up a little, bringing it a little more to attention. The dress had a couple fastenings at her neck and back—he could admit he'd scoped them out earlier—and he reached behind her to unfasten them. He found the hidden zipper under her arm—he knew where to look now—and inched it down to her hip. Then he put his hand in and rode up the curve of her side, opening the dress as he went.

In just a moment, he was at her other breast and had them both bare now. A little swath of black silk lifted them, offering them for his delectation. The bra crossed somehow in the back, following the jeweled straps of fabric, he guessed, that had held her dress in place against all probability and the laws of physics.

He appreciated the effort the garment was making well enough and so left it to do its job. He kissed Katherine a little more, using his tongue to explore her mouth. He bent one knee to press between her legs and deliberately maneuvered to tease the little folds of his tuxedo shirt over the nipple nearest to him.

She squirmed and arched against him. Soothing, he slid his mouth from hers and ran his lips along her jaw, down her neck. Using his tongue, he left a line of wet kisses down her chest until his head hovered between her breasts. Waiting through a handful of breaths—she had a little catch to them that was very gratifying—he took a moment before turning his head and taking a nipple in his mouth.

Will sucked gently, teasing with tongue and lips. Katherine whimpered a little and brought her hands to stroke fingers through his hair. He held her back, though, and took both her arms up to rest over her head. He kept her two hands in his for a moment, letting her know she was to stay put.

She huffed out a little complaint of frustration but then settled back. He rewarded her acquiescence by giving a due measure of attention to her other nipple. Or maybe even a little more, considering just how enticing it was. Her lithe body was straining against him again before he moved on.

He slid her dress lower and followed down her belly with his tongue. He circled around the stud there—a surprisingly classy square-cut emerald rimmed in white gold—then took it into his mouth to give a little tug. He let it go and put his tongue into her belly button. His face pressed against the smooth, taut skin of her abdomen and he breathed in her scent.

He held there, grasping her hips in each hand, flat out savoring the taste and natural fragrance of her. He reveled in it like an addict, teasing himself with this little prelude, knowing there was much, much more to come.

Finally, he lifted his head to watch her. She shimmied a little to help him as he tugged the dress down over her hips and along her legs. He nearly dropped it to the floor, but he got up off the bed instead. The dress was a work of erotic art and deserved much better than to be tossed aside with nothing but a spent condom for company.

Besides, he liked the view from where he stood. He reverently laid the dress over the same chair he'd used the night before. But he kept his eyes glued to the spectacle on the bed.

Her high-heeled, strappy silver sandals hung from her red-lacquered toes just at the edge of the bed. From there, her long legs seemed to go on forever. Where they joined, finally, there was that coy little triangle of black silk, having found its way up again to nestle her sweet little honey pot. Above, past that glimmering emerald, the other swath of silk cupped her breasts.

His gaze roved from one magnificent sight to another. An embarrassment of riches and he really couldn't choose one over another. So he enjoyed it all while he reached up and slowly worked his tie from around his neck. He was no Lance Duguid, but he was happily aware that Katherine watched him with appreciation in her eyes.

He insinuated himself between her feet, spreading them apart with his hips, even rubbing himself a bit against one of those sandals. She caught on and gave a little resistance back, flexing her toes against his rising hard-on. Still, she kept her gaze on him as he shrugged his coat off—he flung that toward the same chair, but didn't really care or look to see if it made it—and then started on the studs that closed his shirt.

He was sure he could smell her arousal then. With her legs separated, he even saw a little tease of moisture on the black silk. He felt his nostrils flare as he worked his cuffs loose.

"Touch your nipple for me."

Maybe that wasn't so romantic. But she met his eyes, her gaze flashing heat, for just a few moments before she slowly moved one hand and placed it over her breast. He paused in the process of arching back, stripping his shirt off, to watch. He waited through several breaths. Then she slid her hand along her breast, fingers separated, so her nipple popped up in between. A little further, and the swollen bud sat all perky right between two red nails.

Her fingers flexed a little, rubbing little circles over the nipple, her nails abrading slightly. Will shuddered and tore his shirt the rest of the way off. Then he toed off his shoes, unfastened his belt, and dropped his pants and shorts to the floor. As an afterthought, he snagged his socks off.

One more time he covered himself with a condom. They were going to have to negotiate that issue soon. He wanted that intimacy, to be bare inside her, feeling nothing but the sweet clasp of her body surrounding him.

"Don't stop doing that." The words were maybe just short of a growl as he came up onto the bed, his knees between her legs, pushing them apart. He took in the movement of those fingers for another moment, then slid his hands under her hips and brought her to his mouth. Through the silk, he stroked her with his tongue, finding her taste at that bit of moisture, massaging over her swollen nub. While he worked her, he looked up to get another glimpse of that action at her nipple.

She tossed her head to the side, moaning in a very encouraging way. He lapped at her some more.

"Katie. You taste so fucking good." Will slid one hand behind her and twisted it into the string of her thong. He tugged it up, chafing her ass, pulling that little triangle tight against her.

"Will!"

He wrapped his hand once more and pulled further so the triangle of silk slipped down, revealing her little rosebud and digging into the slit at her center.

She cried out again and arched up, bringing herself right to his mouth. He kissed just the little bud that was bare to him, suckling and stroking. She began coming, shuddering, bucking up against him, then rocking back against the hold of his fist in her panties behind her.

Her orgasm was long and vocal. When she began to settle, he crawled up the bed to take her in his arms. She wrapped into him, burying her face into the crook of his shoulder, her body wracked with tremors and her breath rasping.

She was still trembling when he rolled her to her back. He slipped her panties down her legs and away as he did so. Then he rose over her, covering her with his body, and slid himself home, deep, all the way into her.

He'd propped himself just a little off her, his elbows at her shoulders. But he dropped his head alongside her neck, nearly collapsing now, his eyes practically rolling back in his head at the exquisite feeling of her heat surrounding him, clasping him. He groaned out a protest—how could he be expected to tend to her needs when it felt so fucking good? He shuddered through a couple breaths, manfully clutching at control, just barely keeping himself from letting go, from pounding into her like an unleashed beast.

"Will." It was a whisper, a whimper.

He lifted his head and framed her face with his hands. He flexed just once, pushing a little further into her, against her. "Katherine."

"I can't move."

He debated for just an instant. Did she mean he'd laid her low, exhausted her, muscles turned to jelly? Or was she referring back to their earlier conversation, that she couldn't leave her life in Manhattan, even for incredibly hot sex? Both?

It took just that instant to decide it didn't matter. "It's okay, sweetheart. I'll take care of it." He would. Whichever.

He began to move, sliding out of her and plunging back in. He steadied her head between his hands and took her lips, her mouth. Then he shifted his weight to one elbow and freed a hand to cup her breast, to toy with her nipple, to slide down her ribs, past the curve of her waist to grasp her hip, stabilizing her to receive his thrusts, to slip between their bodies to finger her core, stroking, stoking.

After a while, she figured out, apparently, that she could move. Her breathing tautened and her body began to respond. She arched to meet his lunges, dug her heels in to lift herself against him, cradled him between her thighs.

Sweat slicked their skin. The sounds of their rough breaths mixed with the slap of their bodies coming together, with the groans of the bed. Will was fighting off the urgent call of a wracking, gut-wrenching orgasm when, in the very nick of time, Katherine peaked too. They went over together, crying out hoarsely, grasping with bruising intensity, grinding out every last bit of ecstasy.

He poured himself into her, feeling like that jet of semen tore away from his very core. That what left his body for hers was his heart, his soul.

Their bodies still melded, arms clenched around each other, Will wouldn't be surprised if they'd driven a furrow into the bed. He still pushed into her, still vibrated with the force of his climax. His face, burrowed into the crook of her neck, still clenched with the grimace of his release.

But he lifted his head to look at her. Brought one hand, none too gently, to her face. Turned her so she would look back at him.

Their breath, shared now, still clamored. Their gazes held and the brimming moisture that he saw in hers might have been matched in his.

Damned if I'll let you go.

They'd settled just a little when he nudged her. "Come on. Up here."

He helped her slide under the covers and joined her there. Pulled her close so they'd still be together when they fell asleep. And wondered if he'd said those words out loud.

CHAPTER THREE

Katherine stood a long time in the shower. She'd already shampooed and soaped off, having to take gentle care of certain tender parts. She was well done with her ablutions.

And still she stood there.

The warm, almost hot, water was a comfort and always had been. She was the third child of her family, the first daughter, and younger by several years than her brothers. The length of time she spent in the shower had become a family joke—*legendary*, as her brothers would say.

Back in those days, the shower had given her a bit of solitary time. Her mom was a nurse and worked just part-time during the years she was raising children. Her father taught theater tech at the state college. They had enough money, but their house was small and busy, and the bathroom was one of the few places she could be alone.

So she'd showered until the water ran cold and minimized the harassment she took for it by making sure hers was the last shower of the day.

This, in a hotel with apparently endless hot water, was heaven to her.

Feeling in need of it, she let the water soothe her, physically and emotionally, spiritually maybe, as well.

She'd awakened still wrapped in Will's arms. He slept soundly, but nonetheless, there was strength and determination in his hold on her. Not letting go—she thought he'd said something like that in those last moments of lovemaking during the night.

Lovemaking. Her body thrummed a little as she thought of it.

She'd fallen for a man just once before in her life. She'd been home from school for the summer and was helping out at the theater. The college had a summer program and their big production was always a musical. Each year they had a visiting actor. Ninety miles up the Hudson, and you'd have thought Cal Jameson was light years away from Broadway. All full of himself and disdainful of the locals, the amateur actors.

But not too above himself to dally with the technical director's daughter.

Katherine—Katie, back then—had thought it was love. She disregarded her family's exhortations to be cautious. She fell hard.

And when he left without looking back, Katie nearly didn't recover.

Three days into the weeklong volleyball try-outs that preceded the start of the semester, Sadie came and dragged her out of bed. And saved her.

Katherine had not been entirely grateful to her at the time.

But now, she knew she owed her friend her life.

Cal had stirred her young, innocent blood. He looked like a god, all chiseled face and sculpted body. She wanted him. Their few sexual encounters, in his hotel room or backstage in an empty theater, were incredibly hot. For him.

It was all about Cal. Certainly, he made sure that everything he did to her felt good—to him. And, weeks into their affair, when fall approached, she realized he made sure that what he did *looked* good, too. She saw him then, in the theater that was not quite as empty as he'd thought, pumping into, ew, was that Mrs. Gilman, the third grade teacher? Midstroke, he arched back and turned his head to a mirror to follow the lines of his honed body as he worked. Then he lifted a hand to slip his golden curls back from his face. Wouldn't want those lovely features to be obscured.

At least he brought Mrs. Gilman, one of the amateur actors, to orgasm. Or at least, she *acted* like he did. Would he even know the difference?

Katherine's experiences with Cal had not been even that gratifying. And she'd felt burned in such a way that it was years until she'd ventured into another sexual relationship.

It was until *this* year, in fact. This *weekend*.

Well, apparently, she'd saved up. After years of deliberately squelching all hint of sexual desire she felt for any man in her life, she'd let go. And how.

She was stunned and a bit embarrassed at the extent of her passion for Will. The aggression of her body, eagerly taking from him what it wanted, demanded. Of its collusion in accepting what he offered, its rampant participation in a sort of sexual revelry.

That was so not her. Or had not been her.

Apparently, she had something new to learn about herself.

She supposed that was what living was.

Her eyes were closed, the spray of water running over her head, when she felt the draft of cool air. Then warm hands at her waist, hard body snugging up against hers.

She leaned her head back and rested it on his shoulder. He put his lips against her temple for a long moment before he turned her.

His eyes searched her face, watching, she thought, noticing like he did. Taking her in. Concerned for her.

"I'm fine."

He tilted his head, studying her. "I'm glad. You left the bed kind of stealthily. And then you spent so much time in here."

"I just like a long shower." She knew she spoke too quickly and the lift of his eyebrows confirmed it. "I wasn't sure what to do." She raised a hand to his chest, a light touch of fingertips meant to reassure. "I don't have much experience with this, Will."

He put his hand over her fingers, held them there. "Define 'not much.'"

"I had an affair with a man when I was in college."

"Dick."

She shook her head. "No. Cal."

He smiled and skidded his finger along her cheek. "I mean he *was* a dick."

She blushed at her misunderstanding, though he was entirely right. "How so?"

"He had a shot at you." He grasped her hip and pressed a little, emphasizing his point. "You gave him a chance. And he didn't dig in and hold on for all he was worth."

She tiptoed up and kissed his cheek. "You're absolutely

right. He was a dick."

He nodded.

"A big dick."

He grinned then. "Just to be clear, we're not saying he *had* a big dick."

"No. It was a short little pencil-sized dick."

"'Atta girl." He wrapped her in his arms, chuckling.

Katherine laughed too. "Thank you. That's the first time I've ever laughed about him."

His warm hands gently cradled her. "He hurt you. If life is fair, he's bald now too."

He wasn't. Cal had made his way onto the big screen. His hair was still thick and full, alas. "No," she said. And added, with just a bit of an evil grin, "But I'm very happy to tell you that the sun-kissed blond of his always just slightly mussed, wind-swept hair comes from a bottle. And his piercing blue eyes are the result of colored contacts."

Will smiled but read something in her eyes. "Do you still see him?"

She thought for a moment, but then shook her head. "No." The big screen didn't count.

"Good."

Implied in that one blunt word was something like, *so I won't have to kill him.*

"And then?"

She looked up at him again. "Hmm?"

"After the dick?"

"Oh." She shook her head again. "No one."

"Jesus." He grasped her arms and rotated the two of them around so he got the better part of the shower spray. Watching her—inspecting her, it almost felt—he started to soap himself. "No wonder." He said it quietly, but not quietly enough.

She crossed her arms under her breasts, an action he didn't fail to notice. It wasn't just the focus of his gaze that reacted either. "No wonder what?"

"Well, you—"

Katherine tapped a foot, waiting as he seemed to sift through a half-dozen ways to finish that sentence.

One corner of his mouth quirked. "You seemed to have a kind of short fuse."

She waited some more, still tapping. He continued to slide the bar of soap over his skin, but watched her warily now.

"You, uh, demonstrated a lot of enthusiasm."

He laughed as she reached up to scratch a nonexistent itch on her chin with her middle finger. Then he grabbed her up and pulled her close so his slippery, soapy body slithered against hers. His erection pressed eagerly into her belly.

He spoke into her ear, his voice low, husky. "You were fucking hot, Katherine. You nearly killed me. It was like nothing, *nothing*, I've ever experienced."

Taking her mouth, he kissed her then. Sweetly. Lovingly. Hotly.

She slid her arms around him, reveling in his kiss, in the feel of his body against hers. Their lovemaking had been like nothing she'd ever experienced either. There was no surprise in that. But it warmed her heart very, *very* much to hear the same from him. She was afraid her heart was in trouble.

He pulled back a bit from the kiss. She followed—enthusiastically, she had to admit—and arched a little to nestle against his erection.

"That will go away if we just ignore it."

Her lips still weren't done with his. "You're not interested in shower sex?"

"Darlin', I think we can be pretty sure that when I'm around you, I'm interested. Anytime. Anywhere." He accepted her kisses, even lingered a little, but then pulled back again. "I was just thinking I might have already taken too much advantage of your, uh, drought."

That was sort of sweet. He thought she might be...saddle sore. He might be just a little bit right, but not so much that she was going to miss this chance. She was on a roll.

"I said I was okay." She slid her hands in between their bodies and took hold of him, wrapping them around his hard length and stroking him.

"Jesus, Kate." He dug his fingers into her back and didn't hold back a shudder. "Are you sure?"

She rocked into him, opening her hands so she could rub him against her belly. "I want you, Will."

He pulled her forward so they were both under the spray. With one arm, he held their bodies close. He put his other hand on her breast, covering her, massaging, teasing the nipple. She moaned in response and found his mouth with hers again.

After a long minute, he broke the kiss and rested his forehead against hers. They were both breathing hard. "I noticed this, finally." He ran his fingers over the little adhesive patch that was low on her back, toward her hip. "You're on birth control."

She nodded, distracted, and arched to press her breast more fully into his hand.

"I get tested with my physical every year, Kate, and I haven't been with anyone since my last check-up. I haven't had sex without a condom since I was nineteen. I want to be bare inside you. I want to feel all of you, Katherine, nothing but you."

His words sent an erotic quake through her. In answer, she leaned her back against the warmed tile of the shower wall. Then she lifted one leg, taking her knee up to his hip, wrapped it around him, and brought him close.

A feral groan grated from his throat. Blazing, his gaze captured hers. He reached behind her, hooking both her thighs with his forearms, and lifted her other leg. Then she was open to him, completely vulnerable. To steady herself, she grasped his shoulders, digging into the bulky muscles there, and clenched her legs behind him.

Keeping her gaze locked with his, he arched just enough for the head of his erection to find her entrance. He held there, his breath jerking, and then pressed in. He breached her a slow inch at a time. It took a long time.

When his full length was buried inside her, he groaned again, a long, rasping exhalation. He let go of her gaze and pressed his forehead into the tile beside her. Every muscle in his body strained.

"Kate. Katie." He flexed just a little, arching against her. "You can't imagine how good this feels."

Katherine huffed out a breath. She didn't have to imagine. She was filled with him, stretched with exquisite tension. Not just connected to him, but bonded, mated, as one. Something new to learn yet again, she thought briefly. Sex was not only incredibly pleasurable, but stirring, heartrending, as well. Expressing, conveying love.

Almost overwhelmed, she slid her fingers into the wet hair at his nape. On a moan, she tilted her pelvis, making the most of his penetration.

"No. Don't move."

But it was too late. With a guttural curse, Will began to plunge into her. He wrapped one arm behind her back, protecting her from being pounded against the tile. All other consideration was gone then as he took her, lancing into her, each thrust long and full, each time faster.

They were both lost to it, bodies clenched, cleaved to each other. They breathed as one, rough, fierce gasps that tore from their throats.

She began coming before he did, overstimulated by the unbearable pressure of his body against hers, inside hers. Letting out a long wail, she spasmed, bucking, jerking hard against him.

In short moments, she took him with her. He clutched at her, growling out his release, filling her, shaking with the relief of it.

It went on an immeasurably long time, a prolonged ecstasy that held them in its grip. Their arms still clenched around each other even as the tremors of climax began to fade.

To Katherine, it was an unknown amount of time before she became aware of anything but that remarkable fulfillment.

He was moving, and she couldn't understand why. He was speaking, she knew, but she couldn't process the words.

Then she heard, and felt.

"Cold," he said. "Hot water's gone."

Shivering now, she stayed wrapped around him. He'd turned off the faucet and got the shower door open. He slipped out of her as he moved. "Shrinkage," he complained. "Think nothing of it."

She had little energy to giggle, but appreciated that he managed to get one of the inn's luxurious robes somewhat around them. Then he got them to the bed and dropped them down on it. No longer physically together, but still wrapped around each other.

Still one.

Will thought they'd dozed just a little, though he considered that he might have fucked them both unconscious. Either way, she stirred as he stroked his thumb along her cheek. She opened her eyes to his, just inches away, and lifted her fingers to rest them along his jaw.

For several minutes, they stayed just like that, touching, breathing together, taking each other in.

Finally, Will cleared his throat and spoke. "Can you stay for a while?"

"Yes. If I leave by four or five, I'll have time to get back, to turn the car in and get home."

His lips quirked. "That won't leave you much shopping time."

She smiled and spoke loftily. "On rare occasion, I've been known to drive by an outlet mall without stopping."

He grinned back at her. "If the enticement is great enough?"

"Um-hmm."

Will gave her bottom a little squeeze and crawled off the bed. "I'll see what I can do."

He went to the bathroom and came back, toweling off a few still damp spots. She'd wrapped herself rather carelessly in the robe. Her long legs were bare, all smooth white skin over toned muscles. And one breast peeked out, the pink nipple soft now. Maybe it hadn't been so careless. He had to stop moving to finish looking. "You are so fucking beautiful."

A siren's smile and she stretched a little. More of that breast now, and the nipple began to pucker. Her eyes flashed a little heat as they met his, then lowered to where his penis stirred, filled.

"Guess you got over that shrinkage problem."

He laughed, purely happy in a way he'd never felt before. "They might tack a little extra onto your room bill for emptying their hot water tank." He nudged her foot with his knee. "Let me know if they do. I'll pay it. Worth every last penny."

That smile again. She was proud of herself. As she damn well should be.

Disciplining himself to show some restraint, he bent over to rummage in the clothing on the floor and came up with yesterday's boxers. She sat up, taking no care about bringing the robe with her. One leg through his shorts, he paused to watch. And swallowed hard. He wasn't a fucking saint. "We could ask for a late checkout."

Clearly pleased with the outcome of her tease, Katherine relented and covered herself a bit. "What do you normally do on a Sunday morning?"

"If I'm not working, I usually pick up some things and go have breakfast with my mom."

"Is that something I could do with you?"

Hell. Was she *trying* to make him love her? "Yes. I'll have to call her, but, yes."

"Good." Bare-ass naked, she stood up and strode like a queen toward the bathroom. She paused in the doorway, a natural pose that could knock the legs out from under a marine. "Then what?"

"You have any real shoes?"

"You don't like my heels?"

"I fucking love your heels. Can you hike in them?"

"I'll find something."

And she did. He guessed that when you packed three suitcases for a long weekend, you could pretty much be ready for anything. By the time she'd done her thing in the bathroom and had her stuff packed up—both taking significantly less time than he'd anticipated—she was dressed perfectly appropriately in a cropped knit top, cargo shorts that looked much cuter on her than on most, and truly decent hiking boots.

He was impressed and let it show. She walked to him, went a little on tiptoe—had to, no heels—and kissed him lightly.

"I like to be prepared."

"I like your thinking."

She went flat-footed and eyed him. "Are you perhaps referring to certain items you saw when you searched my purse the other night?"

"I didn't search your purse." If he had, he'd know that she'd had four twenties, a five, and three ones, instead of just guessing it, and he'd know the number on her credit card. "But, yeah, when I took your purse because your drunken ass couldn't find your own damn key"—she sniffed at that—"I did notice certain items." He crossed his arms over his chest, enjoying himself immensely. "That seems like a lot of preparedness for a near nun."

"Um-hmm." She picked up one suitcase and headed out the door. He took the other two—as she correctly judged he would—and followed. She headed toward the elevator, but he herded her around to the stairs.

"'Um-hmm?'"

She grinned over her shoulder at him. "I won those."

"Won them?"

"At the Easy Rider Friday night. Joss brought them. We took a vote on who was most likely to need them." As they stepped outside from the lobby, she made sure to look back at him. "I won."

He let that settle with a mental shudder.

"I voted for myself."

He managed a quick kiss despite the two suitcases. Then considered as he loaded luggage into her rental. "They usually come in packages of five. What happened to the other two?"

"She gave one to Seffie, just in case."

"Huh. In case of what?"

"In case Canaan did more than look at her."

"Canaan and Seffie? No way. She's not even legal." But Canaan had been looking back at her. That was good to know. "She's like, sixteen."

"She's twenty-one."

"Huh. And the other one?"

Katherine smiled. "Joss kept it for herself, just in case the old guy at the bar got past you."

He wasn't even going to try to comprehend that.

"And the patch—your birth control?"

She shrugged. "I get bad cramps. The patch helps."

He had to suppress a shudder at that, too, and covered it by opening the driver's side door for her. "Follow me to my place?"

"Not going to your mom's house in yesterday's tux?"

He kept his gaze on her face as she seated herself—*well*, maybe just a glimpse at those long legs. "Nope, I'm not. Plus, I have a dog to feed."

"A dog! Cool."

He closed her door, but kept his hands resting on it until she put the window down.

When he didn't speak right away, she lifted a brow.

He rolled a shoulder. "So, just for future reference, that story about the condoms, winning that contest?"

"Yeah?"

"And the, uh—"

"Cramps?"

He winced, couldn't help it. "That might be the kind of thing you don't have to tell me."

"So you're saying you don't want full disclosure."

Yeah, he was struggling with that. "Maybe not quite—but *almost*."

She seemed to understand his issue. "I imagine we're both good at keeping secrets given our lines of work."

"Yeah. But personally—"

"You'd expect it to be close to zero."

He gave her a long look, appreciating her perception. "Yeah. Or even all the way to zero."

She nodded, serious. Then he saw a twinkle in her eye as she started the car. "So, like, if Sadie told me that Leet squeals like a pig when they make love—"

He laughed out loud and softly chucked her chin. "If you knew a thing like that and didn't tell me, I'd have to kill you."

A beautiful, big blond waited politely for him at the gate of the wrought iron fence that surrounded his home. It was a dog of some sort. Living in the city, Katherine was used to dogs that sat on one's lap and got carried around in purses. The size here was a little intimidating.

But any caution she might have felt was gone the minute Will called out his pet's name and opened the gate. Here was mutual, true love. The dog—Wolf?—barked with joy and leaped, resting his paws on Will's shoulders. With the equivalent of hugs and kisses, they greeted each other, celebrated coming together as though they'd been apart forever.

She wasn't forgotten, though. Will maneuvered his dog around so he could catch Katherine's eye. He nodded her close. "Come in. This is Beowulf. Beowulf, be polite. Meet

Katherine."

With one last lap at Will, Beowulf went down on all fours and waited for Katherine to approach. When she got near, the dog very charmingly offered a paw. With a laugh, Katherine took it and then acquiesced as he sniffed and licked her hand.

"Good boy," Will said. "Friends."

Beowulf happily turned and leaped up the front steps, barking for them to follow.

Katherine stood where she was, taking in the gorgeous property. The house was a grand old Victorian, all sharp angles and interesting details. It was a light pink, trimmed in pristine white. A wide porch wrapped around two sides. An octagonal extension pushed out at its corner, constructed on top so the upper floor had a small, walk-out porch. It was classically finished in dark wood and made homey with cushioned wicker and hanging pots trailing colorful blooms.

The house had a double front door with leaded glass panes. Pots of ferns set on thick balusters along the wide steps made a welcome entrance. There was a second door around the corner at the far end of the porch. The dog door there signaled Will's ownership.

"How beautiful," Katherine murmured.

Will took her arm and walked her closer. There was a flagstone walk with a separate path curving around to Will's entrance. A smaller set of stairs gave porch access there. The grounds were meticulously landscaped and maintained. Summer flowers bloomed in bright batches—roses, peonies, daisies. Shrubs blossomed now, distracting attention from the wilting leaves of spring tulips and daffs. She could see there would be fall interest, too, with coneflowers and rudbeckia coming and arching Japanese maples that would grow crimson.

"Remarkable. Really, Will, it's gorgeous."

"Yeah. I rent the upstairs from the owner, Mrs. Dern. We're trying to work out a deal so I can buy it from her. Her children don't really have an appreciation for it, except for its value in cash. She's approaching ninety, though she won't admit it. She doesn't get out much anymore. So I help out with the upkeep and take care of the yard."

"The yard? You mean these lovely gardens?"

"Well, Mrs. Dern is the expert. She gets things started under grow lights in the basement and winters over a lot. She tells me what to do. I'm just the grunt."

She wasn't buying it. "But you're learning, aren't you?"

He shrugged. "I know some stuff, I guess. My grandparents were basically gardeners."

He motioned her to his door and she smirked when he opened it for her—no key involved. He'd checked her room for security, even reached in to lock her car door as they left the lot at the inn, but he left his own door unlocked. He caught her look and shrugged again. "Small town. Big dog."

She laughed and went up the stairs ahead of him.

She stopped there, taking it in. She was in his space and very interested to look around.

Will watched her. "Go ahead and snoop. I know you want to. Consider the place yours."

She looked him over. "No secrets?"

He touched her lips with his. "None. Start in the bedroom if you want to. I have to feed the mutt. Then I'm going to change clothes."

Fair warning. If she didn't want to see him naked, she'd better get moving.

Not that there was anything wrong with seeing him naked.

The main room was large and open, separated from the kitchen and dining alcove by a long, granite-topped island. There was a river-stone fireplace along one wall and the inevitable entertainment center—large flat screen television, at least one gaming system—along another.

Two rooms came off the main area. One door was open and clearly led to his bedroom. Morning light shone there and she knew that was where the porch was. The other door was closed—maybe a second bedroom or office.

The space was neat and orderly, the furnishings large and aimed at comfort but still stylish. A huge, exotically populated aquarium added an interesting, attractive focus. And there were a lot of very well maintained houseplants.

She was doing exactly what he expected her to—learning about him by studying his home.

What she saw pleased and impressed her, but didn't surprise her. He was a caretaker. He took care of his dog, his plants, his place. He took care of Mrs. Dern. And at a guess, he did it subtly, slyly. So the old woman would hardly know it was happening.

She took a deep breath. The man was just too attractive.

She grabbed a peek into the spare room. Unlike the main room, it had an unfinished appearance, not quite making up its mind whether to be second bedroom or office. An oak desk and file cabinet fought for space with a large bed and bureau.

Will caught her eye as she came back out. "It's supposed to be my office. Leet bought the bed—he needed a place to crash for a while."

Katherine remembered. There had been some dark days for Sadie when Leet's first wife had seemed to come back from the dead.

He stood behind her, looking at the room over her shoulder. "I use it sometimes now when I sleep days." He gestured toward the heavy shades. "I can darken it. My room has a lot of light."

She nodded, brushing by him. He went to chat with Beowulf over the dog's breakfast while she checked out his bedroom. The room was large and also open. And he was right about the light. It was a corner room with large dormer windows on two sides. The sharply slanting ceiling rose to a square cupola at its center. Light from there angled into the room, bouncing off the polished wood floor. Access to the porch was at the far corner. The double doors there were filled with glass panes. They were set at angle, with a Palladian arch of etched glass above.

It would have been impossible—to say nothing of criminal—to mute the light with shades and curtains. He'd left it all open, a place to welcome—and glory in—morning sunlight.

The bed was big as a lake and looked like one, made up as it was with shades of blue and green woven into a gorgeous light covering. A ceiling fan hung over it, promising a cool breeze for summer. The furnishings—bed, dressers, armchair—were dark wood with the patina of age. She liked that there was no second television in sight.

The door to the bathroom was open and she took a look. More blue here—deep, shimmering blue in the tile. Lines of flat, smooth stone were worked in, adding to the sense of a lake scene. Dark, polished wood in the vanity and cupboards, and then a soft blue on the walls. All neat and clean. He lived alone, so had a fair excuse for leaving the toilet seat up.

Will walked into the room and went to the closet. He shrugged out of his tux and slipped it onto a hanger. But he watched her as he did it.

Katherine resisted the temptation to watch back. She went to the doors that led out to the porch. She opened one side and stepped through.

It was a great spot. Mrs. Dern had a corner lot at the top of a rise. The two-storied house rose above its neighbors. The porch, with its ornate white rail, almost felt like the bow of a ship, looking out over its own little world. Will's world.

Church steeples—three of them in this small village—were the only structures that reached so high. He had a view of the business area of the village—the grocery, a gas station, small shops, and offices. Looking away to the east, she could catch a glimpse of the Connecticut River and, a bit north, there was a glimmer of lake.

A teak recliner was placed to face the view. She put her hand on it—the back was upright, she understood, so he could watch his town through the rail. Very clearly, she knew he sat here often, in the dark, looking over his world. Taking care.

Will came up behind her and turned her into his arms. He was dressed neatly in chino shorts, belted, with a light blue polo tucked in. The shirt seemed built to draw attention to his broad shoulders, his muscular build. The sleeves pulled tight where his arms flexed to hold her. She sighed. How could a woman resist this?

He caught her gaze. "Learn everything you need?"

She bit at her lower lip as she looked at him. "Like you wouldn't do the same thing? Come to my place, look around, learn what you could about me?"

He watched what she was doing with her mouth. "I'd do exactly that. I will do exactly that." He kissed her, tugging that lip free. "Say when."

Hmm. They'd have to go there, but this wasn't the moment for it. She turned away, but kept her arm around him. She gestured out to the view, his town. "You love it here, don't you?"

She could hear his sigh, but he relented, letting her

change the subject. "Yeah, I do."

"Your town. And here, this very spot, where you can watch over it."

"Yes."

"They're lucky to have you."

He was quiet for a minute. "It works both ways. Come on. We'll take my truck."

And his dog, as it turned out. But Beowulf was very well behaved, keeping to the half cab in the back and resting his head on Will's left shoulder when he needed to see where they were going. They stopped at a bakery and the small grocery. At both places, packages were ready for him. Croissants, apparently, at the bakery, and fresh orange juice and strawberries and bars of gourmet chocolate at the grocery. Katherine learned that Will and his mother had developed their Sunday breakfast tradition under the influence of his French paternal grandmother.

He was clearly expected at each shop. Mrs. Janisch at the grocery remarked that he was late. He told her he'd been running a little behind, and didn't squawk when Katherine crunched her heel down on his toes. As he shouldn't, since he'd been squeezing her ass when he spoke. *Little, huh*.

Both Mrs. Janisch and Mrs. Vincenzo at the bakery gave her a friendly greeting and a good looking-over when Will introduced her. And both gave him news of someone needing a hand. Luke Tyler had gotten called down to Pennsylvania to run a baseball camp, Mrs. Janisch said, and so hadn't been around to mow his grandmother's yard in more than a week now. And that foolish old Clinton Shepherd had fallen off a ladder and broken a hip while taking his storm windows down, and that job was only half done.

In both cases, Will had simply nodded and said okay.

It seemed that was all it took to have Deputy Hunter taking care of things.

Beowulf waited patiently outside each shop, a behavior that was well rewarded with the apparently anticipated and appreciated treats from each woman.

Back in the truck, Will drove with extreme competence

while he told her about his family. His grandparents, he said, had owned most of Fergus Mountain. They'd been early hippies, bought up the land before "outastaters" had driven the prices so high, and then farmed it in old, simple ways. In fact, they'd laid some of the groundwork for organic farming. Their use of the land had been a model cited frequently in the early development of organic agriculture science.

Back in the day, they'd had sheep. They'd carded wool, spun it, and made their own cloth. These days, his mother, Elyse, leased the land out to a local sheep farmer. Their arrangement involved supplying Elyse with wool for her weaving.

"Wait," Katherine said, as they turned onto a gravel road climbing up what she assumed to be Fergus Mountain. "Fergus Weaves? Is that your mother?"

Will nodded, the moron, as if it were nothing.

"Holy cow," she said. "I want one of her pieces. I mean, *want*. I love her work. You might have noticed that I'm willing to spend a fair part of my income on clothing—" She punched him for his snort, as she was sure he expected. "There's this Fergus shawl in a little gallery in SoHo—well, it's on my before-thirty bucket list."

He grinned at her. "Your before-thirty bucket list?"

"Yeah, you know, the things I want to do or own before life gets all crazy with—"

"With?"

With a husband, kids, maybe...a dog. She lifted a shoulder. "You know, just more busy."

That dodge didn't work. He gave her a look that very clearly said he knew exactly what she meant. And wasn't afraid of it.

"Well, it's just possible I can get you a discount. Knowing, as I do, the artist." He smiled, but in a quiet way, and took hold of her hand.

Katherine worked to jiggle that piece of information into the puzzle that was Will Hunter. A famous artisan mother. Whom she was about to meet. Suddenly, she was a little nervous. Will glanced at her, seeming by the squeeze of his hand on hers and the reassuring smile to follow her mental processes.

But he came to alert a minute later—a very abrupt transformation into Deputy Hunter. He let go of her to take the wheel with his right hand and put down the window with his left. He pulled the truck to the side of the narrow road—she thought to let an oncoming car pass. Instead, the two vehicles stopped side by side. Will moved the gearshift to park, then passed a hand over his belt where carried his cell phone.

He waited while the man in the other car—a sheriff's unit, Katherine saw now—put his window down.

"You looking for me, Sheriff?"

Katherine peeked around Will's wide shoulders. She took this to be Will's boss. He wasn't in uniform, though he might as well have been. He wore a pale blue dress shirt that had neat creases pressed into it. She imagined the creases in his trousers would be sharp enough to slice bread. A light suit jacket was folded with military precision on the seat next to him. His gray hair was buzz-cut trim, his face thin and craggy. His eyes were a sharp, piercing blue, gentled just a little by crinkle lines at their outside edges. There was a chance those were laugh lines.

His gaze went past Will's shoulder to take a good long look at Katherine.

He spoke in a drawl that should have seemed out of place but didn't. "Nope. I could have found you if I needed you, Hunter. I know your truck was outside the Easy Rider most of Friday night. And I know where it was parked all of last night."

That might have set Will back a bit, but it was clear he had a greater concern. "Is my mother okay?"

"She's fine, Will." The words, and the eyes, were softer now—aware of Will's concern and reassuring.

Will was apparently having none of it and held the man's gaze. "Then what were you doing up the mountain, Sheriff?"

To Katherine's amazement, the man's cheeks reddened a little. He cleared his throat. "I drive up once in a while to check on Elyse." He seemed about to say more, but then hardened his gaze and stared back at Will.

Will seemed to expect more, too, and waited. He couldn't outwait the sheriff, though. After a long moment, he spoke quietly. "I didn't know that."

"You mean to be impressing me with your detective skills?"

Will took a breath, looked off up the mountain, and then leaned back, letting the sheriff get more of a look into the cab. "This is Katherine Noble. Katherine, Sheriff Jeff Anderson."

The sheriff nodded and lifted his hand as though touching the hat that wasn't there. Leaning forward some more, Katherine could see it sitting all neat and tidy next to the suit coat.

"Katherine. Pleased to meet you." His gaze went back to Will. "I was there when you called. Your mother said you were bringing a woman."

There was another long silence between the two men that strongly piqued Katherine's interest.

Beowulf had apparently had enough of all the waiting and poked his head out over Will's shoulder with a polite bark.

Anderson eased again. "Yes, Wulf. I see you there. Hello to you, too."

He nodded once more—to all three of them, it appeared. "I'll see you tomorrow, Hunter. You two enjoy your day."

Silently, Will re-engaged the transmission and started back up the hill.

"So—" Reading his body language, Katherine thought perhaps she was supposed to remain quiet. But she'd seldom known silence to accomplish anything. "The sheriff is surprised that you're taking a woman to meet your mother. And you're surprised that he's seeing your mother."

"He said he was checking on her, not seeing her."

Okay. Apparently that was a difference that meant something to him. "And?"

He glanced over at her, a muscle working in his jaw. "And?"

She was made of sterner stuff than to be intimidated by that. "I heard your call to your mother. I heard you say, 'Yes, she is.' What had she asked you?"

He studied the road ahead as though he didn't know where he was going. "She hadn't asked me anything."

Okay, again. She could do semantics. "What had she *said*?"

That muscle flexed a little more. They must be close to the farm now—in the back seat, Beowulf was definitely getting excited. Will stopped the truck and opened the door. "Go," he said. Beowulf, at least, took that to be directed at him, and leaped out. Katherine was grateful for that bit of clarification. It kept her from jumping out her own door.

Keeping his foot on the brake, Will turned to face her more and took a slow breath.

She beat him to the punch. "I can be irritating."

"I see that." He looked away, up over the small rise ahead, and let out a heavy sigh. "I've never brought a woman to meet my mother before. She said you must be important. You heard my answer."

Well. That made her feel a bit guilty for pushing him. And also warm and glowy inside.

He wasn't done. "The rest of it is complicated. I would be very grateful if you would come and share a meal with us, and let me answer your questions later."

There was pain here and she regretted adding to it. Doing the best she could, she reached across the seat to touch his lips with hers and then kept a hand against his cheek. "All right."

Opportunistically, he put his hand over hers and kissed her back. He was longer at it and more thorough. "Thank you."

Beowulf was back, barking at them from the top of the rise.

Will took the truck there, where the road widened to a small farmyard. A tiny cabin was at its center, set amidst bloom-filled gardens that looked like more of Will's work. It had a little covered porch that held a bench swing of aged wood. The main outbuilding had clearly been a small barn now converted to workspace, Katherine assumed. It had a lot of glass—large windows cut into each wall and skylights in the roof. It was filled enough with light that she could see a number of looms set inside.

Beowulf had found his canine friends—family by the look at it—and was happily cavorting. As Will shut down the truck, a woman strode out from the barn.

With a squeeze of Katherine's hand, Will climbed out. In a couple steps, he had the woman in his arms.

Some of Will's height might have come from her, but his breadth must have come from his father. Elyse was a tall woman, but slight and with an air of fragility about her. But she hugged her son heartily. The pair held each other for a good long embrace.

Elyse's hair was a rich brown threaded with silver and

woven into a loose braid that fell past her waist. Her eyes were the same blue as the lake Katherine had seen from Will's porch. They were warm as she'd greeted Will, but shadowed now as she looked around her son's shoulder to see his passenger.

Beowulf had brought his buddies to meet her, so she stepped out of the truck to greet all three dogs. Will walked closer, keeping his arm around his mother. "That's Wulf's mother Lucy, and his brother, Spinner."

Katherine looked up from their enthusiastic greeting.

"Mama." Will said it with a French inflection that sounded entirely natural. "This is Katherine."

Appearing shy as a deer, Elyse looked at her for a moment from the safety of Will's arm. Then she stepped forward, grasped Katherine's shoulders, and brought her into a hug. Katherine gently wrapped her arms around the woman, instantly aware that the apparent frailty was a mistaken assumption. She had strength, despite her slimness and timid appearance.

A bit surprised at the warm greeting from such a wary woman, Katherine looked into Will's eyes from the hug. Something moved there, deep, as Will's dark gaze met hers.

With arms still circling, the two women leaned back to study each other's face. Elyse must have been young when she became Will's mother, Katherine thought. Her skin was still fresh and smooth, with just little lines of laughter or worry bracketing her eyes and her mouth. Her blue eyes seemed a contradictory mixture of innocence and knowledge, guardedness and perception.

Katherine spent just a moment wondering what experiences underlay that appearance, but squelched her natural urge to analyze. She didn't want to risk offending this woman who seemed almost fearful. Nothing like the self-possessed, highly confident and, likely, flamboyant successful artist Katherine had anticipated.

Besides, Will had promised to answer her questions later.

"I'm so glad to meet you, Mrs. Hunter. I have to say, I'm a huge fan of Fergus Weaves. Will just told me. I've admired—and coveted—your work for years."

There was just the slightest pause. "Thank you. Call me Elyse, please. You're very welcome here, Katherine. Come inside." She turned around to look at her son. "Did you go by the bakery, Will?"

Will spent another moment taking in the two of them with his eyes. Then he nodded to his mother—a communication Katherine thought indicated more than just the availability of croissants—and turned to the truck for the supplies.

Katherine followed Elyse through the cabin—she caught a quick impression of an L-shaped kitchen and living area with a dining table and a cozy cluster of armchairs surrounding a stone fireplace. A small television sat on a console off to one side, opposite a well-worn sofa obviously chosen with comfort in mind.

She assumed that the closed room that filled in the L was a bedroom. Above, an open loft ran the length of the cabin. The far side of the kitchen opened to a good-sized deck.

They went there, where bright sunshine warmed the space, setting aglow the Fergus cloth that covered the small table with its fresh flowers and three place settings. Two chairs matched the table, and one had clearly been brought out from the kitchen. Delicate lace stirred at the open doors to the bedroom. The backdrop was a lovely panoramic view of blue-green mountains.

Elyse still held Katherine's hand, and she gave it a small squeeze. "Make yourself at home. I'll just help Will bring things out."

"Thank you. It's wonderful here."

Elyse paused to look around just as Katherine was doing. "Yes, it is, isn't it?"

The deck's railing was a pretty affair of glossy white wood with copper details. The top rail was a wide deck board that provided casual seating. Katherine took a perch there and enjoyed the view while Will and his mother worked in the kitchen.

They came out together, both carrying trays. Will's contained the croissants and chocolate, with the strawberries neatly sliced in a ceramic bowl and the orange juice that had been transferred to a graceful pitcher. Elyse brought a sleek glass teapot filled with dark, rich tea swirling through the central infuser.

They all took a seat. Will filled juice glasses while Elyse poured tea. Following their lead, Katherine layered a croissant with chocolate and strawberries and discovered her new favorite breakfast. Will ate heartily as well, though she noticed he drank the tea grudgingly. She figured that explained the cups of coffee he'd gotten them at the bakery.

Conversation was a little awkward at first, focused on the lovely weather and setting. Then Elyse asked about the wedding and that settled into a long, comfortable conversation.

Will gave his mother extensive details, describing the setting and the ceremony, and updating her—even gossiping—about the guests. She seemed to know, or know of, many of them, and eagerly questioned him about those she didn't know. He faltered, though, when she started asking about Sadie's wedding dress.

"Kind of white," he said.

Elyse rolled her eyes and looked to Katherine.

"Pearl," she said. "Sleeveless, satin fit and flare, with a little flange for a train. Strapless sweetheart bodice of shirred tulle. No veil, but a little satin bridal cap with flowers and a bit of netting."

Elyse looked back at Will with a raised brow.

"What she said."

The women laughed and Katherine gave more details of flowers and bouquets. Then Elyse asked about the bridesmaid dress and that led to another lengthy description. Pencil-thin skirt to the knee. Slit in the back.

"Of course," Elyse breathed, caught up in the romance of it. "For dancing."

"Yes," Katherine replied, very careful not to look at Will, who suddenly found more interest in his tea than he'd shown before. "For dancing."

There was a short pause that had Katherine imagining Elyse had magical powers of discernment. Then she spoke casually, as though there were no suspect undercurrents. "Will looks good in a tux, doesn't he?"

Maybe it wasn't so casual after all. Katherine looked over the table at Will, who peeked up from his tea with an evil twinkle in his eye. "He does," she said. "All the women thought so. Some of the men, too."

That earned her a little nudge under the table from Will's foot, and a chuckle from his mother. Elyse seemed to enjoy a little mischief making. "Did he dance with you?"

"He did. He was very—" Sexy. Hot. Provocative. "Sweet."

"Uh, Mom." Will seemed to think it was time for a change of subject. "We passed Jeff Anderson on the way up here. He said he comes to...see you sometimes."

Elyse began to stack dishes, not meeting Will's gaze. "Oh, he just likes to check on me. Usually he comes when he knows you've been busy with work." There weren't so many dishes that she could keep busy for long. She looked at Will. "His wife Karen and I met each other when, um—when we were all much younger. She used to come visit me now and then. She died." Elyse turned to Katherine now. "Of breast cancer, three years ago. When she took ill, Jeff would bring her up to see me. It became a habit, I suppose. He comes and we chat a little. He still misses her. We both do."

Will watched his mother carefully for a moment before he spoke. "Are you comfortable that he comes here?"

Elyse looked surprised. "Of course. He's very kind."

Will nodded, though he still watched. "Good. I'm glad, then."

Elyse stood, put her hand on her son's shoulder, and leaned down to kiss his temple. She ran her fingers through his hair. "It would be okay for you to worry less about me, you know."

Will put his hand over hers, where it still rested on his shoulder, and looked up at her. "I'm not sure that's something I know how to do."

With a look of regret, Elyse rested her head against his.

Katherine watched them, touched by this moment of intimacy, feeling very honored that she wasn't excluded from it. She spoke when Elyse's gaze came to hers. "He can't help it. He's a caretaker."

Elyse held her gaze a long moment. "You mean if you love him, you just have to accept that's who he is."

Yes, Katherine thought, and then said it. "Yes."

"I can't believe you do all this yourself."

Just like a mother, Elyse had assigned kitchen clean-up to Will and brought Katherine to the barn. That was what she called it, but it was a studio, worthy of the name as much as that of any artist.

Katherine slowly turned around, taking in the dozen looms of varying sizes, racks filled with spools of yarn of every color, bundles of raw wool, spinning machines, and even an old fashioned spinning wheel. Beams of clear light ignited the space, making the gold and red hues blaze, the blues and greens glow, the whites and pale pinks shimmer.

Elyse shrugged with absurd yet apparently honest modesty. "It's what I do. You know I don't...I don't leave the mountain."

That drew Katherine's attention. "No. I didn't know that."

The older woman shrugged again, this time with chagrin. "It's where I feel safe." She gestured around, giving a small, embarrassed laugh. "And I love to weave."

Katherine took care not to push. "You do beautiful work. Amazing. Really. You have a gift."

Shyly, Elyse looked away. Her gaze went to a window, where Will was visible now, entertaining the family of dogs. She straightened. "I've been given a lot of gifts. I'm very fortunate."

Katherine suspected the woman had experienced some significant misfortune, too. She was reminded of the most satisfying aspect of her own work—observing the remarkable strength of the human spirit. And here, the drive to find, to make beauty. "Who does your photography?"

Because of the extensive windows, there was little wall space. All of it was devoted to gorgeous photographs that were obviously the inspiration for Elyse's work. There were glossy scenes of mountains, rivers, forests, lakes, and ponds. They were drawn from all seasons, all conditions of light and weather. They were beauty in their own right, captured on film and then translated, and forever held, in Elyse's work.

"Well, until three years ago, it was Jeff's wife Karen. She was an amateur photographer, but an incredible artist, as you can see. She'd have been madly successful in the art world if she'd wanted, but she never pursued it. She loved taking care of Jeff and their two girls. She kept her art as a hobby."

Elyse touched a photograph on a wall near one of the smaller looms. It was a spectacular maple in brilliant fall color. The cloth that was emerging from the loom mirrored that color. The touch told Katherine how much Elyse missed her friend.

But that spirit—Elyse took a breath and moved to another photo. "Now I use a young man who just completed an MFA at BU. Leet introduced him to me. Trace takes photos of trees that Leet uses in his work, and then also of Leet's finished sculptures."

"Cool. Leet's work is amazing, too, isn't it?"

"Yes. I've—seen photos."

Right. She didn't leave the mountain.

"And, look—"

Elyse took her to a far window, to where the land ended on a small bluff. There was one of Leet's trees, a tall willow with branches weeping down nearly to the ground. In the light, it sparkled with its glittery leaves and scattered crystals.

Katherine shook her head. "It really *is* amazing, isn't it?"

Elyse nodded. "He has a show this summer. I know he'll be a huge success. I suspect what he gave me as a gift would be worth a fortune."

"Um-hmm." She put her arm lightly around Elyse's shoulders. "This little town has more than its share of remarkable artists, doesn't it?"

"Thank you." Elyse slipped her arm around Katherine's waist. "Come here. I have something for you."

They walked over to a bank of shallow wooden drawers. Elyse pulled one open and took out a long shawl. It was of fall colors, fringed in a dark, earthy brown. She held it out for Katherine.

"No. I can't accept that." It was very nearly the one she'd seen in SoHo and been coveting ever since. Only better— richer, deeper in color, more intricate in design.

Elyse smiled, tucking it around her. "Of course you can. It's perfect for you." She turned them toward a full-length mirror at the end of the set of drawers. "Look. It's just your color."

Katherine looked—longingly—and then shook her head. "I love it. But it's too much. I can't take it."

Elyse showed some of that subtle strength. "It's mine to give. It's always been one of my favorites, and I could never bring myself to sell it." She touched Katherine's cheek. "I must have been saving it for you."

Katherine nodded her head, almost a bow. "I do love it. Thank you."

"That's better." Elyse held her arms, rubbing over the shawl. "You make my son happy."

Katherine wasn't sure whether that was an observation or a directive.

"Now, come. Let's get you back with Will before the dogs wear him out and he's of no use to you this afternoon."

Katherine looked up sharply. "Uh, yeah. He has a hike planned."

Elyse almost seemed to humph. "Right."

In fact, the hike Will led her along was a vigorous tramp. Katherine stayed in shape through frequent participation in court sports—squash mostly, through the winter, and tennis when she could—and so didn't embarrass herself, but it was a close thing. They started at that lake she'd seen—Lake Fairlee, he told her—and followed from there a stream that rose up to a very pretty glen with a series of small waterfalls. Then the serious climbing began and they scrambled up a trail that ended on a high bluff over the river.

Beowulf had tracked along with them—not following the trail, but scampering over rocks and fallen trees, ducking under brush. He was nearly always in sight, but she'd only spot him if she really searched.

The woods were thick and lush. The fresh green leaves of the hardwood trees contrasted prettily against the darker pines. The earth was a rich brown, softened by many years of falling leaves and pine needles. In places, the spines of the once-rugged mountain jabbed through so that sometimes they were scrambling over rough granite. Squirrels chattered as they chased each other from tree to tree, and a doe nudged her still spotted fawns along a deer trail.

The hike ended with a remarkable surprise. A music major at Bennington College, Will said, had built the wind harp. It was a huge, weathered wooden structure, nearly as tall as Will's house, built with a triangular body and strung with long lengths of wire. It generated a quiet, deep hum continuously, with spurts of increased volume and resonance with any gust of wind. Its placement on this craggy mountain's edge assured a magical, never-ending concert with nature as the conductor.

He'd pulled her to the top—she hadn't objected to the bit of help—then held her, back pressed against him, as they looked out over the river, serenaded by the harp. She leaned against him, covered his arms with hers, and closed her eyes.

They'd been mostly quiet during the hike, Katherine feeling comfortable to wait for Will to speak.

He'd stopped his play with the dogs the moment Elyse and she had walked out of the barn. He'd looked at them both quietly, then taken hold of the shawl that Katherine wore and drew her close. He dipped his head and kissed her, softly, but for a very long time. Then he turned to his mother, held her gaze for a moment, and wrapped her in a hug.

They'd walked to the truck all together. Will made a plan for seeing Elyse later in the week and explained that Katherine was leaving for Manhattan in a few hours. Katherine saw the look the other two exchanged over that—concern from Elyse and a kind of unhappy acceptance from Will. Support from her and maybe a bit of determined reassurance from him.

Now, facing the view of river and New Hampshire mountains, he unrolled the blanket that he'd carried along and shook it out. It was a Fergus weave.

"Oh, no. You're not putting that on the ground."

Will smiled as he settled the blanket onto the soft earth. "It's a blanket," he said.

"Heathen."

With a smile, he lay down on his side, bending at the elbow to support his head on his hand. He reached up with his other hand to tug her along. Gingerly, she stepped forward and lay close beside him, her head tucked against his arm, propped by the thick mass of his bicep. He pulled her closer with a hand at her waist. With a kiss to her cheek, he looked out over the river when he spoke.

"My mother survived an experience of unspeakable horror."

Katherine placed her hand over his at her waist and turned to look at him, even while he kept his gaze focused—

or not focused—on the horizon.

"She was young, just eighteen, when...my father came here. He was an FBI agent. He'd been wounded in the line and spent the summer up here recovering. I suspect Mom was very naive, very innocent. My grandparents kept her on the farm—they home-schooled her, protected her from out-siders. Somehow, Truman Hunter got by them. He met my mother and they spent that summer together. He married her, and then left. He was supposedly going back to D.C. to resign his job, to clear his desk."

Katherine turned more toward Will and lifted her hand to his face. She'd heard the hesitation when he used the word "father" and read significance into the way he used the man's name.

"A few days after he left, Mom disappeared. My grandfa-ther used a telephone for the first and only time in his life, and called Truman back. Apparently, he really had done what he'd said he would. He'd gone to his office, closed out some files, and packed up his desk. He'd planned to spend a couple days with his mother. Grandmère owned—owns—a gallery in Georgetown. She'd been an art history student in Paris, but her studies were interrupted by the war. She immigrated to D.C. when she met my grandfather, and eventually opened the gallery. Truman had seen Elyse's work and knew Grandmère could sell it. He'd taken boxes full down to show her. He was there with her when my grandfather reached him."

Will lay back, looking up at the sky. He kept his arm around Katherine and she rolled over to him, propping her-self now to watch him as he spoke.

"He came back and searched for her. Jeff Anderson was here then, new on the job, and remembers it. He says the FBI agent was driven, mad with worry and despair. The local force might have suspected him initially—he was an outsider, an outastater. But his urgency, his anguish, rang true.

"All suspicion was put to rest when they found his body, a few days after he'd disappeared, too. They found my mother at almost exactly the same time. A hunter was out in the woods, hauling some lumber to build a tree blind. He actually stepped on her. She was naked, wrapped in a bed sheet. Hypothermic and comatose. They thought she'd been there for three or four days. It had rained every day, and fallen below freezing at night. Reading the tracks was almost impossible. But they believed that Truman had found her. He'd been captured himself—they both had torn skin on their wrists and ankles from rope bindings. Hers were scarred, older, but his were worse. The skin was torn and, underneath, bones were broken. They figured he'd pounded his hands against cement, shredding skin and breaking bones, to free himself. To free them.

"Apparently, he escaped with her, carrying her away and then stashing her there in the woods. With his broken hands, he dug out a shallow hole, put her in it, and covered her with leaves. Then he went back—either to confront their captor, or to draw him away from Elyse. He saved Mom, but died doing it. Whoever had taken them hunted him down, killed him with multiple shots from a high-powered rifle. The kill shot came last. The others were just to toy with him."

He paused again and Katherine rubbed her hands over his chest, wanting to warm him, that impossible cold deep down in him.

There was more, and it was as unspeakable as he'd said.

Elyse had been raped, multiple times. And tortured. They found the same scarring on her skin—bruises and burns, lacerations and abrasions—that they found as fresh injuries on Truman Hunter's body. And deeper wounds—broken bones, internal hemorrhages.

She'd remained comatose—or something like it—for more than a month. Her parents took her back to the mountain when she regained just minimal awareness. She stayed in her loft there for weeks more. It was months before she spoke again. She gave birth to her son there, assisted only by her mother and a midwife who'd trained on The Farm in Tennessee.

She'd never spoken of her experience. Will believed she didn't remember it. Certainly, his grandparents had felt that they'd learned their lesson—visitors from off mountain brought only danger. Elyse never saw a doctor again, never a psychologist or therapist.

Jeff Anderson had told Will he'd gone up the mountain to see her every couple months for years after. He'd been one of the men from the sheriff's office to bring Elyse out of the woods; he'd been the one sent up the mountain to take the news to her parents that they'd found her, to transport the Ferguses to the hospital. He'd been one of few allowed up the mountain once Elyse came home. After the first couple trips, while Elyse was still not speaking, he'd started taking his wife Karen. He'd tried to make his visits feel more like social calls than part of an investigation. When Elyse started talking, it was clear she felt more comfortable with Karen than with him.

But she never spoke of her experience, of her horror. And she never talked about Truman, until years later when she shared stories of him with Will.

Jeff had given up after a while. They'd followed every bit of evidence to its end, fruitlessly. Without Elyse's statement, the investigation died. Karen was convinced, and convinced him, that Elyse's memories of her days of captivity were locked deeply away. And to force her to confront them, even if she were able, would be to inflict the horror all over again.

It was a cold case.

"She has a happy life, in her limited way."

Will spoke again after a quiet that had lasted several minutes. Katherine had long since dropped her head to his chest, seeking and, she hoped, giving comfort just by listening to the beat of his heart. And to the lonely-sounding moans from the harp.

She found his hand with hers, twined fingers. "And you feel that's all you can do. Help support her limited happiness, protect it as best you can."

"Yes."

"You believe that the risk would be too great to do otherwise." She lifted her head to look at him. "You know that there are techniques to help her recall those moments in her life. And that I'd know how to employ those techniques. You suspect that I'd be inclined to believe, professionally, that she could have a richer, fuller, *happier* life if she were helped to remember and process those moments. But you believe that the suffering would be too great. You're afraid there's a chance that she would never recover from it. Just as she almost didn't recover before. You think what saved her then, what gave her purpose and *necessitated* her coming back, the only thing that did so, was the child she carried. You believe all that, even though it's obvious that she's a woman of remarkable strength."

He'd watched her eyes as she spoke, his own dark and fierce. "Yes," he said. "Yes, to all of it."

This, she thought, would be the deal breaker. He would live with their geographical separation. He wouldn't like it, but he would find a way to deal and, she knew, to get his way about it eventually. It was abundantly clear to her now why he would never consider leaving the Basin. He'd said he couldn't relocate in order to be closer to her, and that was the right word after all. He couldn't leave Elyse unprotected, uncared for.

So she would go back to Manhattan and they would, indeed, travel back and forth until either their relationship ran its course or she was compelled to move up here. He would be willing to compromise, to the extent that he could, about that.

But she could see he would not compromise in this, would not tolerate her, rightly or wrongly, deciding that her expertise in psychology counted for more than his decades-deep knowledge of his mother.

Wrongly. It would be wrong of her to think such a thing. If he didn't know it, she did. It would also be unprofessional. Even a freshman psych major would know about family-centered care, would know that one didn't treat a patient in a vacuum, but within her family and community systems. And that presuming to know better than her loved ones was a gross misconduct of practice.

If there came a time for such an intervention, her loved ones would know it, too.

Katherine took a moment to stifle her disappointment that he didn't think better of her, or more accurately, of her profession. There were so many misconceptions about her work. *Ah, well*. That was another day's battle.

His gaze, tougher even than the one he'd used at the Easy Rider, met hers bluntly.

"You're right in thinking that I believe your mother could have a happier life. She was obviously deeply wounded. She mastered her injury, allowing it to scar rather than heal. And rightly so, given that she had to go about the business of raising a child. That took incredible strength and it would require nothing less—more, even—to poke around under the scarring in order to heal now." She paused for a moment. "Based on my training and my fundamental beliefs about human nature, I believe it would be worth it."

His eyes flared then and she quite firmly put her fingers over his lips, shushing him.

"But I would never think to know before you do that the time has come for it. And you should never think to know it before she does."

She watched him for a long minute, waiting until his gaze gentled, before she lifted her hand.

"Thank you."

"You're welcome," she said, accepting the apology she knew he meant.

But she kept watching him, running her thumb now along his temple, his cheek, until he grew suspicious about her attention.

"What?"

"You're afraid, aren't you?" She was amused but not at all surprised that he lifted an indignant brow at those words. "You're worried that he could be your father, that man who...that monster."

Will's body stiffened and he abruptly turned his face away.

Katherine followed, crawling over to his other side to put her face to his, keeping her hand on his cheek. Looking directly into his eyes, she spoke. "You're afraid of that, aren't you?"

He huffed out a hard breath and started to pull away. But she kept her hand firmly against his face, kept her eyes fixed on his.

They both knew she didn't have the physical strength to keep him still. But he relented, gradually softening his breathing and relaxing the muscles that flexed at his jaw. It was, she knew, a thing he did for her. She took it as an acknowledgement of his feelings for her, more significant than any words he'd spoken, more meaningful than the tenderest moments of their lovemaking.

He spoke quietly, almost a whisper. "Yes, I'm afraid of that."

She smiled gently, stroking his face. "It doesn't matter, you know."

He closed his eyes through a long exhalation. "Oh, yes, Kate. It matters."

She just held him and shook her head.

"I won't want to father children, Kate."

"Oh, Will." She lifted up and curled around him, cradling his head against her breast. She pinched her fingers into his hair and tugged a little. "You haven't done anything about that, have you?"

"You mean, like get—snipped?"

"Yeah."

"No."

She knew he held back a shudder, just as she had to hold back a chuckle. Here was a case where men's extreme protectiveness about their ever-so-important manliness was a blessing.

Arms wrapped around him, she squeezed tightly. "Your genes don't make you who you are, Will. You choose who you are. Your mother who raised you, the family that helped shape you, everyone in your life who's had influence—all those things count. But you choose who you are."

"Genes count, too. You know they do."

He was right, but also wrong.

He sat up to face her, leaning in close. "My mother didn't have a choice. But I do. I'd like a family. I want children. But they won't be mine biologically."

Katherine rested her head on her knee and studied him. "What a loss that would be. You're a good man, Will. Your mother is a good, strong woman. And if your father was Truman—he was loving and brave and loyal. How sad for all those qualities to end with you."

Will shook his head. "I can't take the chance."

She nodded, accepting, for the moment, his reasoning.

He looked away, into the woods behind them, though she suspected he didn't really see what was there.

"Anyway, you don't know everything about me. You can't claim to."

"No." She didn't touch him, didn't pull his focus back. "Do you feel a little darkness in you, Will? We all do. We are all humans, biological organisms like any other, with basic drives to survive, to reproduce, to protect our tribe. We all have it in us to do awful things in order to satisfy those basic drives. We all feel darkness in us. But you are a good man. We would all know it, even if you didn't work so hard to prove it."

That was what he did. He worked to be the perfect son for his mother. He took care of the people in his life, both through his job and the helpful chores that were his good deeds. He watched over them all.

His gaze, his awareness, came back to her. "How can you be certain?"

That was easy. She smiled and touched him again. "I'm a professional shrink, dude. Plus, your dog loves you."

He didn't smile back, but looked hard into her eyes for a long time. Then he pushed forward, taking her mouth, taking her down onto the blanket. He covered her, a deep groan rumbling through his chest.

"Come back with me," he urged, his mouth still on hers. "My place. Please. It's not private enough here for what I want to do to you."

It was a near thing, in fact.

His tongue had swept into her mouth, his body—hard everywhere—pressed her into the earth like he would have her right there. With another groan, he'd reined himself in, pulled her to her feet as he nearly tugged the blanket out from under her, and whistled for Beowulf.

She was getting a bum's rush down the trail when they passed not one but two parties of hikers just minutes from the summit. Will had greeted them—some of them by name—assessed them in his automatic, official way, told the group of probably slightly underage boys not to leave their beer cans up there, and moved her quickly past them. In his pickup, they'd sped back to the village. She'd wryly asked him if he didn't want to put his lights on. And siren. The look he gave her back made her know he'd already considered it.

Then he had her on that lake of a bed in his home. Really. Had. Her.

He'd lost some of his urgency by the time they got there. He'd smiled indulgently when she stopped him from laying her down on top of that Fergus bed covering, compliantly assisting as she'd reverently folded it and laid it aside. Then he started sweetly, holding her face and kissing her gently. Breathing her name and letting her know that he was silently saying more. Not just Katherine, but *Katherine, I love you.*

She heard it and felt it. In the gentleness that came first, and then in the passion that rocked them, left them, breath heaving and spent, tangled in one another.

And finally, in the quiet that held them after, when the movement of light through the room marked the passing of the day, signifying the time that she would have to go.

He held her head against his chest, repeatedly pressing his lips into her hair.

"What's your work schedule like?"

He spoke softly, quietly. This was the conversation they'd been avoiding, and it was a hard one. She stroked her thumb over his side, feeling the lean muscle along his ribs.

"I have weekends off, and every other Monday."

"Every other, or like, first and third?"

"I work first and third, have second and fourth off."

"And fifth, if there is one?"

"Yes, off."

"Okay. My schedule is different all the time. I rotate through nights and weekends. I can request off some of your long weekends, but not right away. Our schedule is made out a couple months ahead."

Against his chest, she nodded her understanding.

"Sometimes I can negotiate a change with another deputy in a schedule that's already set. But I doubt if I can manage it by this weekend."

"I can't come here either. My parents are coming down for a theater weekend. My sisters-in-law are joining us. We have tickets for three shows."

He lifted her head so they could see each other. "It's a five hour drive—and that's if traffic doesn't suck, which it always does. I don't want you to have to make it."

She smiled to herself. He was caretaking again. "It's not a problem, Will."

He slid his fingers along her shoulders, a soothing touch. But his voice was stern. "Do you even drive, really? Are you one of those New Yorkers who gets behind the wheel once or twice a decade, putting themselves and everybody else at risk?"

She chuckled, delighted by his Deputy Hunter attitude and tone. "Yes, I drive, *really*. I didn't grow up in the city. I even used to drive the truck we borrowed for the theater—hauling sets up from Broadway and back."

"But you don't own a car."

Katherine sobered. "I rent one when I need it, Will. It's what I do when I go home to visit, when I don't take the train." She grasped his wrist with one hand, securing his hold. "It's what I'll do to come here."

He lifted up to touch their lips together. "We'll see. I'll try to clear my schedule for three weeks from now. I'll come there."

She pushed up over him to make more of the kiss. Then she lifted her head and for a long, sad moment they looked at each other. Will's eyes darkened and, as one, their breathing hastened. Gazes still locked, not moving otherwise, he grasped her hips and slid her down onto his erection, making their bodies one. She shuddered once as he filled her and then they held like that, almost not moving at all, just the barest straining, flexing. Until their breaths became groans, the straining became writhing, and the flexing became thrusting. Still their eyes held until that last second when their bodies wracked into orgasm.

They stood for long minutes beside her car, arms wrapped tightly around each other, exchanging long kisses.

Will saw the first-floor curtains flutter often enough to know Mrs. Dern was getting a good look at Katherine. He figured she had the right to peek. Surely, she wasn't so deaf that she hadn't known he'd been upstairs finding exquisite, loud pleasure in a woman's body. He just hoped they hadn't knocked any plaster off the old woman's ceiling.

He'd anticipated that it would be impossibly hard to let Katherine go. It was worse than that. It felt all kinds of wrong. He'd found her. He'd made her his. He wanted to keep her.

There was some gratification in seeing that Katherine was struggling with it, too. She hadn't admitted her feelings for him as much as he'd wished. She might be trying to cling to a measured, reasoned, and reasonable approach to their re-lationship. She might even think she could wriggle a little longer. But he was sure he had her hooked.

Mrs. Dern had apparently seen her fill by the time he loosened his hold on Katherine long enough to let her get behind the wheel and fasten her belt. He engaged the door locks—not missing her indulgent smile—then leaned in to kiss her one more time. "Call me when you get there."

"I will."

"I'll see you in three weeks. Don't forget."

She smiled again, but it wobbled a bit. "I won't forget, Will."

He let her start the car, but he wasn't done. "I love you, Katherine."

She leaned back against the seat and took a breath, not looking at him. "Forty-eight hours, Will. We haven't even known each other forty-eight hours."

"Doesn't mean it's not true."

She chewed at her lower lip for a second before she looked up at him. "*Maybe*. Maybe it just means you're crazy."

She smiled just a little and he did the same. Then they spoke together. "Or both."

He stood back and let her go.

CHAPTER FOUR

Will walked into the sheriff's office earlier than necessary for his shift on Monday morning. As usual, Beowulf was at his side—he was an accepted member of the team in the office and patrol cars. Both of them were satisfied with their stop at the bakery. Mrs. Vincenzo made great breakfast sandwiches and the best coffee in town. Will carried his second cup with him. Beowulf didn't care for the coffee, but he'd had half a sandwich.

In an effort to distract himself, Will had spent the rest of Sunday doing chores. It worked out pretty well for Mrs. Tyler, who not only got her yard mowed, but also the deer fence around her vegetable garden repaired. And for the Shepherds, whose storm windows were brought down and clean screens put up.

But it hadn't been particularly effective for him. He'd worried more than a little about the drive for Katherine, constantly aware of the hours passing until he could expect to hear from her. That issue was settled soon after dark when she called to say she was home. The trip had been uneventful, she said. And then there wasn't much more to say. It was lame to say he missed her, but he said it anyway. It was too damn true.

So he spent the rest of the evening feeling what he'd felt since she'd left—lonely. It was a sense that he knew would not be appeased by a trip to the Tap with Canaan—the man had called to offer, demonstrating an insight into Will that was both touching and a bit scary—or by a good tussle with Beowulf, though that helped. So by moonrise, he was on his deck, nursing a single beer, watching his town. And missing his woman.

He'd slept eventually, embarrassingly comforted by the scent of her still in his bed. He accepted that he was a man in love and dealt with it. He woke with the sunrise—early these days—and brought himself to the office.

The sheriff's building was new—just on the outskirts of the village, along the river. Decades ago, they'd outgrown the little clapboard in the village they'd used previously and finally, the county had raised the bond money for construction.

The modern building had a processing area and deputy cubicles on the first floor—generally referred to as the pit. In the back were the holding area and a couple cells. Above, on what was only a half second floor, were the dispatch and admin offices, and the sheriff's office. A glass wall to the front gave the man a full view into the pit.

Will took an early briefing from the off-going shift. Then he sat with his coffee at his computer, reviewing reports from the night and weekend and working at clearing his desk. He nodded a greeting when Jeff Anderson strode through the pit and up to his office. And waited the forty-five minutes it took for the man to come stand at the glass wall and beckon him up.

Jeff was finishing a cup of Mrs. Vincenzo's coffee, too. He motioned Will to a chair and then waited.

Will waited longer.

Finally, the sheriff broke. "All right. What do you want to say to me?"

The list was endless.

Will started easy. "I'm going to be requesting some long weekends off."

"So you can see Katherine?"

Will nodded.

"Is she going to come up here?"

"Maybe some. I'll be going down there."

"You don't like it in the city."

Will took a breath and tried to relax his jaw. Anderson knew his men—and women—well, and was an astute man. He'd always seemed particularly aware of and watchful about Will. Will figured it had to do with Anderson's early history with the Fergus family and tried not to be paranoid about it. And had to try hard now not to resent it.

"I can go there."

"You don't *do* well in the city, Will."

"I'll manage, Sheriff."

"This is one of those conversations where you should call me Jeff."

Will gave an assenting nod. He was pretty sure he was more comfortable with the other kind of conversation.

"When are you going to move her up here?"

Move her. Like that was a thing he could do. And like he hadn't already thought of it. He gave the man a hard look. "As soon as I can convince her."

Jeff nodded, completely unruffled. "I'll do what I can with the schedule, but make it happen, soon."

Will grimaced. "She seems to have a mind of her own."

That brought a grin from the older man. "I'm glad to hear it. You know, Karen always had hopes for you for our girl Jennie."

Will had been between the two Anderson girls in school. Jennie was the younger. He couldn't say he hadn't looked. Jennie might have looked back some. And that was as far down memory lane as he was going with the woman's father looking at him from across his desk. Her father and his boss.

The sheriff continued, seeming to follow Will's thoughts. "It wouldn't have worked. Jennie's very sweet and eager to please. You'd have run roughshod over her." Jeff waved him off before he could object. "All I'm saying is that it wasn't a good fit. Jennie is very happy with her...*chiropractor*."

Will could hear the effort not to put any inflection into the word and stifled a grin.

Jeff shot him a look for it anyway before he went on. "Dave's a fine man and they have a good marriage. It's just that you need someone with—"

"A mind of her own."

"Yep." He paused for a minute. "Your mother likes her."

Will wasn't completely lacking in detective skills. "You called her?"

Jeff's gaze was on his, steady. "She called me."

Ah. That got them through the easy—*easier*—part of the conversation. They were both quiet for a long moment.

Finally, Will spoke, picking his way carefully. "Karen was a good friend to my mother, one of very few. You made that happen. I'm grateful for it. I always was."

They watched each other for a bit.

Jeff spoke next. "It went both ways. Karen loved Elyse. It meant a lot to her that Elyse used Karen's photographs for her weaving." He looked around at the walls of his office, scattered with Karen's photographs—of the lovely Vermont countryside, of the loving Anderson family. "It gave her a sense of pride that she didn't get from just taking care of the girls and me.

"When Karen took ill, she didn't ask for much. But she did ask me to take her up the mountain when I could. I went again after she died—I believe it was a comfort to both of us, your mother and me." He was silent, meeting Will's eyes before he carefully went on. "I believe Elyse is comfortable with me going up to see her."

"I believe she is, too."

"I mean to take it further, if she's willing."

Will took a long breath. "You wouldn't push her."

"I would not."

They both found interest elsewhere—Will on Jeff's desk, Jeff out the glass wall.

Jeff stirred first. "I know children, even grown children, are uncomfortable thinking of their parents as sexual—"

Will lifted a hand. "Yeah. Enough said."

Jeff's eyes sparked in laughter for a second, then he sobered. "I plan to get her to marry me."

Wow. That took a couple breaths. And then it settled, feeling surprisingly good. He'd liked and respected Jeff since he'd come to work for him. He did believe he could trust the man to safeguard Elyse's wounded self. He believed Jeff could possibly make Elyse happy. And he didn't have to think about having the sheriff as a stepfather if he didn't want to.

He grinned just a little. "She has a mind of her own."

"So she does." Jeff caught the irony. "She doesn't look it, but she has remarkable strength."

"Katherine said that, too. And that Mom could be happier."

They looked at each other a long moment.

"I want to take a look at the files from Mom's case." That was the last, and perhaps the hardest, of the things Will had to say to his boss.

Jeff rocked back in his chair, gazing out through the glass

again. Kept looking there, even as he spoke. "I expect you'll want to take the files home? Read through them on your own time?"

"Yeah."

"No."

Will pushed to his feet, biting back bitter anger.

At the same time, Jeff rocked forward. "If we're going to do this—" He pointed Will back into his chair.

Will settled, heartened in the extreme by Jeff's use of the word "we."

"If we're going to do this, I want it done here. Treat it as a real investigation. Find a space, set up a board. I'll meet you there and we'll look at it every few days. And I want a weekly formal report."

Will considered the significance of those instructions. Professionally, Jeff would be thinking about having new eyes, fresh eyes, on the case. It was the thing that sometimes gave cold cases new life. He'd be thinking about looking again into a case that had left him frustrated as a young officer. Personally, he'd be looking to finally find justice, if not vengeance, for Elyse. Will knew it had mattered to him always, but it meant more now that Jeff's feelings for Elyse were involved.

And, perhaps most importantly, Will knew, Jeff was making sure that Will wasn't alone in it, spending long nights reading the accounts, studying the photographs that documented the horrific torture of his mother and the murder of his father. They'd be in it together. And they'd bring it into the light.

Grateful to his toes, Will nodded. "Thank you. I'll get started today."

Jeff nodded, too. And had one more thing to say. "We all could be happier, Will. But it's always up to us, our own selves. We can't make it happen for anyone else."

In the end, Will chose the utility room in the basement as his workspace. The files related to the case took up three boxes—more than he could keep in his cubicle. And he couldn't stomach the idea of putting his board in the pit. It wasn't that he didn't want others in the department to look at it. They all came by that first week as he was organizing and setting up. They all looked it over, chatted with him about the case. It was their case, the department's. They would all own it.

But he felt it needed some respectful privacy. There were photos of his mother, battered and torn. There were photos of the father he'd never met. Somehow, it was better there, with the storage shelves, with the furnace and water heater. With the quiet and solitude.

Along one wall of the room was a large, locked evidence freezer. It held blood and tissue samples. In it, he knew, could be found vials of blood from Elyse and Truman Hunter. Somehow, that made this place seem right, too

He'd moved a desk down there and often sat, feet propped, studying the board. He read through the files, scanning at first, then going back for details. Initially, he used his own time, working before or after his shift, and coming in on his day off. But over the course of a couple weeks, he started to work it into his on-duty hours. In an unspoken show of support, his fellow officers began to clear a little time for him—taking a call out of turn, volunteering to make his rounds.

He spoke with Katherine every day—sometimes even from here, with his eyes on the board. Sometimes from his bed, where the conversation would take a distinctly differ-ent—and interesting—turn.

She told him more about her family and animatedly de-scribed the Broadway shows they'd seen together. She be-gan to talk a little about her work experiences—the sad cases she ran into at the women's shelter, the very bleeding-heart approach she had to the women in prison. His concern was all about her safety and not the women she treated. They both seemed able to accept that difference.

Will shared his life in much the same way. He told her stories of his extended family, especially the locals that she'd met. He related some of the cases he handled—those with a little humor in them, or poignancy.

But he didn't talk about having re-opened Elyse's case, not even as he sat gazing at the board.

He told her he'd cleared that third weekend and would

drive down after work on Friday. He didn't tell her that the sweet anticipation of seeing her was significantly marred by the dread that grew stronger as the day grew closer. Jeff was right. He didn't do well in the city.

But he did his best to suppress that particular thought and immensely enjoyed the closeness—limited and frustrating as it was—that they found on the phone. She hadn't forgotten, he could tell.

She'd smiled a little as he'd said it—"Don't forget." He knew she'd thought he meant something simple, something concrete. Like, don't forget him. Don't forget that he'd be coming in three weeks.

He'd meant something complicated, something less than tangible. Don't forget what they'd been feeling for each other. Don't let that rational brain of hers override the convictions of her heart. Don't forget they'd been experiencing love.

So far, she'd complied with his directive.

He was grateful to his soul. He knew she was someone who wouldn't follow directions just on his say-so. Or anyone else's.

Each call, he ended with, "I love you, Katherine."

Each call, she ended with a little indulgent pause before she said goodbye or goodnight. He read a lot into that pause.

"He was looking for unsolved cases of missing or murdered young women. He'd worked his way down here from Montpelier. He'd gone northwest first, up toward Burlington."

It was late evening and they were both working on a longneck. Will had his feet up on his desk. Jeff did too, from the side corner, in the chair he'd long since brought to the utility room himself. They were both studying the board, specifically the FBI ID photo of Truman Hunter.

They'd spent a couple late evenings this way—Jeff didn't have a lot to go home to either. It would be different for Will the next day—he'd be driving to Manhattan.

Will had raised the issue in his first written report and Jeff had followed up on it. He'd gone to see the chief investigator from when the case first opened, a man now long retired and just recently back from his winter in Florida. From that source, he'd gotten the names of old timers in Montpelier, then Waterbury and Burlington. And then in the other direction—Northfield and Randolph.

Jeff had confirmed it. Truman Hunter wasn't just recovering from his injury. He hadn't just happened upon the case of the missing Melissa Hancock, a case three years cold. He'd been looking for it.

"Why?"

Jeff shook his head. There was nothing unusual in an investigator revealing as little as possible about his case. But it was decidedly unhelpful now. "If he ever said, it wasn't to anyone I've found to ask."

He took a long pull on his beer before he spoke again. "He was dogged, though. I'll give him that. He'd been at it for three weeks before he got here. And a few weeks later, he was marrying your mom. He didn't make that happen by a casual little knock on the door at the Fergus cabin. Your grandparents weren't quite the isolationists then that they became after Elyse was taken. But they weren't exactly friendly to strangers even so. He had to woo her in more ways than one."

His eyes went to one of the photos of Elyse—it was taken on her wedding day, the only one they had of her from before her capture.

"She was such a pretty little thing, though skittish as a deer. To be honest, we all thought she was a bit tetched, in fact. It was just her incredible innocence and her wariness of strangers. Truman saw it better than any of us. That was just like him. He was a big guy, tough. Not hard, though. And perceptive as hell, sharp. But not in a way you caught onto right away. More subtle." Jeff gestured to Will with his bottle. "You're just like him."

Will knew he was being watched as his own gaze went to the image of Truman Hunter. The man who might have been his father.

"It's not true, you know, what you're thinking," Jeff said, still watching. "There's no question you're Truman's son."

Will rolled his shoulders, trying to shrug off that monkey constantly on his back. He stood and walked to the board, looking hard at the brown eyes that were indeed very like his own. "There's no way you can know that for sure, not without seeing the perpetrator as well. They likely had many of the same characteristics. The man who took my mother was also likely a big guy—he took them both captive, held them both. He was also probably sharp and perceptive. He's presumably still at large, right? You can't know. No one can."

"I do know. And your mother does, too." Jeff came and stood beside him. "You could test it. Check the DNA. Why haven't you?"

Will didn't answer.

"Because of Elyse, right? You're protecting her. You always do." Jeff didn't have any problem in the face of the glare Will sent him. "I'm not saying you're wrong to do it. I do the same. But you know, I suspect we both don't give her enough credit." He put a hand on Will's shoulder for a moment, then walked over and dropped his empty bottle into the recycling bin. "I think I'm done with underestimating her, Will. Goodnight."

Will was on the road earlier than expected on Friday. It had been a quiet day, so nobody objected to his taking a late lunch and checking out a little before two. He'd arranged for one of Mrs. Vincenzo's grandsons—Tony, he thought it was—to feed and walk Beowulf. He'd been early up the mountain to say goodbye to his mother for the weekend.

And so he had nothing to do but head his pickup south and try not to think too hard about it. Manhattan. Population over one million. More than seventy thousand residents per square mile. Buildings seventy stories tall and more.

People living there, stacked one on top of another. Buzzing around like bees in a hive.

Upper West Side, Katherine had said. A doorman midrise, a mere sixteen stories. He kept working at not thinking about it, which was harder as he got closer. Traffic thickened and slowed, so that vehicles were bumper to bumper, boxing each other in. Will practiced taking deep, slow breaths, consciously loosened the muscles in his neck and shoulders, relaxed his grip on the steering wheel. And focused a lot on his purpose in making this drive. The very significant reward at the end of it.

He began to feel the weight of the noise as he got into the city. He turned on the radio as a countermeasure and had to search for quite a while before he found a country station. Lyrics he could understand, tunes he could sing along with, and some humor to lighten the mood. Maybe someone would shoot a jukebox or meet another wife in a traffic jam.

It was still light when he found the parking garage Katherine had directed him to use. He walked the three blocks to her building, using his deep breathing and trying to move with the flow of pedestrian New Yorkers—pacing along quickly, even on this summer Friday evening. A lovely moment, if one could see the sunset, feel the soft earth underfoot, enjoy the breeze with the scent of trees and summer flowers on it. He used imagery to connect his senses with those comforting memories.

He paused outside Katherine's building and looked up, unable to see the architecture of its roofline. He turned all around, standing at the bottom of this manmade canyon, the sky with its pinks and blues of sunset visible as just a narrow strip above his head. Some of the buildings had little urban gardens visible a few stories above the street. They didn't help. It was nothing like the earth as he knew it. He felt like he was two hundred feet under water, struggling for breath.

Recalling with effort his purpose here, Will walked through the door of the building.

"Katherine Noble," he said to the doorman. The man had obviously been on the job, so Will showed him his star and they exchanged a nod. There was an acknowledgement in it of the work the man had done, and an understanding of the reasons for choosing this boring-ass position over it.

"1506. She gave me your name. Elevator's over there."

Will followed his gesture, but looked beyond to the door just past the elevator. "Stairs?"

The man, D. Braiman by his name badge, shook his head. "The doors to each floor are locked. You can get out by the stairwell, but not in."

Will nodded, unsurprised. It was perfectly reasonable security. So he bit the bullet and walked over to press the up button.

Matters got significantly worse when the front door opened and a group of twenty-somethings who'd obviously taken advantage of a couple of happy hours greeted Braiman and then joined Will just as the elevator arrived.

He took a back corner, crowded there by the six happy partiers. He cursed when they pressed the button for the fourteenth floor. Really, was there any reason that whichever of them lived in the building couldn't have taken a second floor apartment?

Will's breath was shuddering out by the time the car had emptied and then moved on to the fifteenth floor, and he felt cold sweat run down his back. 1506 was the last apartment on the left down the hall. He considered taking a few minutes to collect himself, but he figured Braiman would have already announced him. So he lifted his hand and gave a short push of the buzzer.

He was very much anticipating seeing Katherine. He'd spent the last three weeks anticipating it and, acutely, the last four and a half hours. He *expected* to see Katherine. And so he was very much surprised when a man opened the door.

Blond hair. Sun-kissed and wind-swept, some might say. Piercing blue eyes. When Katherine had described her first lover, she'd failed to mention a long, lean body with sculpted muscles—kind of a neo-Viking build. Against his better judgment, Will looked. Didn't seem like all that much of a pencil-dick. All of which he could see because the man wore only cut-off sweats and a slightly damp sleeveless T-shirt.

Just the kind of thing you'd pull on quick if someone buzzed your doorbell unexpectedly early, interrupting some hot, sweaty—activity.

Will couldn't help but reconsider that pause in Katherine's response when he'd asked her if she ever saw the guy anymore. Nor could he help the way his fingers curled to make fists of each hand.

Pencil-dick had sported a look of kind of amused challenge as he opened the door—he'd held it just partly open and blocked the entrance with his body while he looked Will over. But amusement faded to caution as he watched Will form fists. He stepped back, to the side. "Uh, Katie?"

Katherine came from another room. She wore slim-fitting shorts and a little cotton blouse—which she was still buttoning. "Will!" She sounded nothing but pleased. "You're early!" *And surprised*?

She put her hand on Thor's arm, as though to move him aside to get to Will. Her smile and the anticipation in her eyes faded when she got a good look at him.

"Will? Are you okay?"

No. He so wasn't okay. He felt the muscles in his jaw clench, grinding his teeth. He glanced over at Thor once more and stepped back, out of reach of the hand that Katherine extended.

"Will, what is it?" She searched his face, and suddenly, he knew he was seeing her shrink look.

That, among all the things in this bizarre scenario that he couldn't take, was the very final thing he couldn't take.

He turned abruptly and hightailed it for the stairs. He pushed the door open, letting it swing wide, and tore down the stairs.

He knew Katherine had followed him, but he was already a flight and a half down when he heard her huff as she caught the door on the back swing. "Will, stop!"

He kept going as she called out to Kyle—Kyle, not Thor?—to hold the door open for her. She took the stairs, fast too, even as she yelled again for him to stop. But he was well ahead of her and she knew it. About three fights down, she halted. But she didn't stop yelling at him.

"Damn you, Will Hunter. You're an idiot!"

There was more, but it got harder to hear. He was pretty sure there was something about him having to grovel before she ever spoke to him again. And that idiot thing once more, with colorful descriptors attached now.

It didn't matter. He was down to the ground floor, through the lobby and out of the building without even a glance at D. Braiman. Then he ran three blocks—heedless, this time, of polite pedestrian behavior, and was in his truck. North. Going north.

Katherine stood outside the idiot's door a week later. Friday patients be damned, she cancelled all but two so she could be here.

Briefly, she'd considered not coming. Will hadn't answered her calls—not in the minutes after he'd fled from her apartment, not an hour later when one might think he'd had some time to see reason. Not that night, when it would have been at least polite for him to let her know he'd gotten home safely. Not the next day, or the next, or the next.

It wasn't exactly true to say she'd considered it. It was more the case that she thought she *should* consider it.

From an entirely rational point of view, she might just decide that he'd done her a favor, tearing out of her building like that—tearing out of her life, if she were to judge by his refusal to take her calls.

Because it hadn't seemed entirely rational, as she'd contemplated it in the three weeks after Sadie's wedding, to have fallen in love with a man she'd known for two days. Or, at least, for him to have fallen in love with her. She was attempting to maintain a healthy state of denial about that first part. But that second part, well, he was very convincing about it. And he didn't seem the sort to claim such a thing lightly.

Apparently, he was just the sort to leap to an astoundingly wrong conclusion based on very little data—*well, okay*, Kyle wasn't so *little*—and go off in a huff.

All in all, it was some crazy behavior. She really ought to weigh whether it wouldn't be best to let it go. To accept the favor that had been given.

But, in fact, she'd seen crazy, and Will wasn't it.

In the two days she'd spent with him, and the weeks of phone calls after, he'd demonstrated remarkably good mental health. He was warm and caring and took responsibility for his life and those around him. He had a sense of humor and was respected and even loved by his community. He had friendships. Sadie and his dog liked him. He had strength, character. He was gentle.

Well, he wasn't gentle *all* the time. There were times, very fine times—well, that wasn't really the point. He was hot and sexy, a gorgeous hunk—but that was just icing on the cake. The beefcake, so to speak.

The point was, Will's behavior when Kyle had gone to the door hadn't suggested a man of short and violent temper, of suspicion and distrust.

It had taken her a while to see it. She had to replay her memory of it a bit, to think of Will's appearance as well as his behavior.

He was wet with sweat—even more so than Kyle, who'd just come from the gym, entertaining her with stories of his most recent failed audition while she dressed for Will. He was trembling, despite the way he'd clenched his hands against it. He was hyperventilating.

Will was in a panic. It wasn't a reaction that had just occurred when he came face to face with a man in her condo.

She was sure he'd been fighting it before Kyle went to the door.

So his reaction to Kyle was a result of the panic rather than the other way around.

She was certain that Will had suffered for it. She knew that the loss of control associated with a panic attack would be a difficult thing for Will to cope with, even to admit to. He would be embarrassed, even ashamed. It would be enough to keep him from answering her calls, from seeing her.

Katherine maintained a pretty fluid definition of mental health. She accepted as truth that the human psyche developed over time as the basic, biological nature of a person was influenced and shaped by one's experience of life. By love or rejection, by nurturance or neglect, generosity of spirit or miserliness.

She accepted that all humans were imperfect and, therefore, all parents were. She believed that what truly defined mental health, even the human spirit, was the ability, the determination, to overcome the limitations of nature and nurture, to make the most of what one was.

She believed Will had more to overcome than most. He had fears that a monster sired him. His young mother had struggled her way back from an overwhelming psychological trauma in order to give birth to him, to raise him.

He had made quite a remarkable man of himself.

And yet, clearly, he was suffering.

It just wasn't in her to let it go.

So she greeted Beowulf, who'd been dozing on Will's front porch. And when Will didn't answer her first knock, she raised her fist and pounded again.

Will rolled over in bed and debated about whether to get up. He'd heard the first knock—he never slept that soundly during the day. Not even when he'd worked the day shift through the night and then half of the next day, too. An old boy down outside of the Junction had finally gone over the edge of alcoholism, unemployment, and my-woman-done-left-me. He'd taken his kids hostage—never a way to get one's wife back. Didn't these guys watch television? Anyway, it had gone on through the day and the night until it finally ended peacefully just before noon when the guy had finally drunk himself to sleep and the older son crept out the back door with his little sisters in tow.

So he needed sleep, wanted sleep, and was pretty sure he didn't want to see who was at the door.

It was someone he knew, since Beowulf hadn't run him off. And it wasn't a local, because everyone local had followed the hostage story and knew he'd be sleeping now, finally.

Someone he knew, but not a local, and someone with a certain amount of determination, given the pounding on the door that came next. That pretty much left Katherine.

Did he want to see her?

Kind of like he wanted to bite into his wrist and tear at the flesh until he geysered blood.

He couldn't say he hadn't been expecting her. He'd never known a woman who could see the writing on the wall and still didn't have to talk it to death. For a trained shrink, it was probably legally mandated.

But he'd hoped she'd gotten the message when he hadn't answered her seven calls. *Don't. Want. To. Talk.*

Ever.

That turncoat Beowulf was outside his door now whining at him. It was no small transgression—the dog knew that when he slept here, in his spare room that he could dark down for daytime sleep, he was not to be disturbed. The damn woman had just countermanded years of good dog-training.

Having a little mad on about that felt better. Way better than the seven days and nights he'd spent feeling depressed and frustrated, embarrassed and ashamed.

It had taken two hours of the lunatic drive away from Manhattan for him to begin thinking rationally again. It took him that long to remember that he'd fallen in love with Katherine and that he knew enough to not fall in love with a skank. She hadn't lied to him about not having a lover for years. She hadn't lied about her feelings for him, the ones she hadn't admitted yet. Which was not the same thing as lying about them. She just very much was not the sort to spend the weekend she had with him, follow it through with the many sweet phone conversations they'd had, and then hook up with pencil-dick a couple hours before Will was due to arrive.

She just wasn't the sort.

So in the last seven days, minus two hours, he'd had to accept that he was monumentally stupid. That this difficulty he had—with crowds, with closed-in spaces—was not just a minor nuisance, a small character flaw that he could reasonably expect those who knew and loved him to accommodate. A little thing that he could work around. It was full-blown insanity. It didn't just cloud his judgment, but made him blind. He lost all powers of observation, all trust in the truths he knew.

It made him crazy, unreliable.

It made him question whether he could count on safely doing his job.

It made him know he shouldn't be with Katherine. With any woman who had any sense. But especially not with Katherine.

Because he loved her. And would never want to hurt her. And wouldn't want to saddle her with a crazy man.

So he dug for the mad, clung to the thin strands of it, and pushed himself off the bed.

He'd dropped the uniform he'd spent more than thirty hours in alongside the bed when he'd finally made his way there. He left the smelly mess where it was and went to his own room to find something clean to pull on. It had nothing to do with the fact that it was a woman he was about to see. Katherine.

He reached first for a pair of sweats, but thought better of it after a glance at his dick, which appeared to have the mistaken impression that the presence of Katherine at his door signified time for fun and games. Instead, he pulled on a pair of tight-fitting jeans and tucked his wayward self in.

He very deliberately did not brush his hair or teeth. He barely opened his eyes.

But he went down the stairs and opened the door.

She fucking made his heart hurt.

She had a little yellow summer top on, cropped high enough to show off the emerald at her navel. Her cut-offs were so short the pockets peeped out at the tops of those long, smooth thighs. *Fucking bitch*.

It didn't help that he already knew what she wore under a get-up like that.

His dick remembered and gave him a little twitch of reminder.

And his own dog, henceforth to be known as Beowulf-the-traitor, sidled up against her, shamelessly basking in the stroke of her fingers over his head.

All that helped with the mad. So he kept his hand on the door, blocking it. And kept his gaze on the floor, where he could get some more irritation from her painted toes and sexy little sandals. Rather than on her eyes, which had been all calm and tender when he'd skimmed his gaze by.

He scrubbed his hand over his face. "You probably want to talk. It's not a good time."

Her eyebrow arched. He knew it, even though he wasn't looking at it. "Not a good time?"

"No. I'm sleeping."

She stretched the silence out, and stretched her body along the damn doorjamb.

"When do you think you'll be done sleeping?"

"I don't know. I guess it depends on whether Beowulf does his job and keeps the next a—the next *person* from pounding on my door."

"You were going to say asshole."

"No, I wasn't." Her brow was lifting again. He just knew it. And couldn't outlast it. "Wipe. I was going to say asswipe."

If he thought that would send her off in a huff, he guessed he really didn't know Katherine. Even looking at her feet—*okay*, her legs—he could see the little roll of her abdominals that signified a laugh held back. Mostly held back.

Laughter was in her voice, too. "*God*, Will. No wonder I love you."

That stopped his breath and forced his gaze to hers

whether he willed it or not. He nearly cringed, seeing her amused but still calm and steady regard of him. Seeing, indeed, love in her eyes. He fought the dampness that threatened in his own eyes and a groan that wanted to shudder through his body. He didn't entirely win on either count. "Katherine."

She lifted a shoulder. "It's not like you're forgiven."

He nodded once, gaze falling back to the floor.

She took one step—into his home, into him—and then touched her lips to his. Just a touch, so he didn't have to feel too bad about not brushing his teeth. "Sleep, Will. I'll go to Sadie and Leet's. Come get me there when you're ready."

She stepped back and pulled at the door. She had to give it a good tug to get his hand to release it. Because his hand didn't let go willingly.

Once she got it shut, she looked at him through the beveled glass pane. After a minute, she gave him a little nudge with her head—*go, go sleep*.

Then she turned around and strode along the porch and down his steps. The dog accompanied her to the gate, snug at her side, stupidly missing the golden opportunity to watch how her ass moved, just barely covered by those damn cutoffs. Beowulf-the-oblivious.

She said she loved him. Love, present tense.

He was going to have to give her a chance to take it back.

He was going to have to insist, because it was still true that he was too crazy for her to love. She was crazy to even think it. And two crazies didn't make a right.

He went back up the stairs and plopped down on the bed. After a couple minutes, he rolled over, unzipped, and slid out of his jeans. His dick insisted on blind, stupid hope. He cussed once, thinking he'd never fall back asleep now. And then he did, and slept, really slept, for the first time in a week.

It was nearly evening when he woke, maybe three hours from sunset on this long summer day. A storm system was moving down south and held a tense mixture of heat and humidity over Sussex County. It would break by dark, making a busy night shift for his partners who were working. He'd been scheduled off, in comp time for the extra shifts he'd worked through while on site at the hostage situation.

Will couldn't help the bit of anxiety that crept over him before he rolled out of bed. He considered it an unbelievable stroke of luck that Katherine had come, but he couldn't quite trust that she hadn't had the good sense to just turn around and go back home. Somewhat sheepish, he grabbed his phone and dialed Leet.

"Hey," he said when Leet grumbled what might have been a greeting on the fifth ring. "Katherine said she was going over there. Did she show?"

"Yeah," Leet said, sounding distracted. "She came."

"Is she still there?"

He sounded cranky now. "I don't know. What are we, girls?"

Cottoning to the situation, Will huffed out a breath. "Get your tongue out of Sadie's mouth, Hayes, and whatever from wherever, and tell me whether Katherine's still there or not."

"She's out at the pond. She's got two itty bitty scraps of something on she probably paid a lot for and thinks is a swimsuit. Are we done here?"

"Hey, keep your eyes off my woman. You've got your own."

"Oh, yeah. I do."

Will closed his eyes against the image Leet's words put in his head. It didn't help. "Jeez, Louise. You're just back from your honeymoon. Can't you leave Sadie alone for one day?"

"Sadie doesn't like it when I leave her alone. Do ya, babe?"

Will took a breath for a pithy comeback and then, words failing, just hung up. He got up, showered, and made a quick run into the village, stopping at the liquor store and Power's grocery so he'd have something to offer Katherine. Though he did all that without thinking her name, very deliberately without making any plan, without imagining that he'd have her here in his house again. Ever.

He called Elyse and told her he was going to miss Friday dinner.

Then he bit the bullet and drove out to Leet's.

He parked in the drive and followed Beowulf, who'd clearly sniffed out the activity out back. Leet, apparently done tending his woman—the one he'd gotten to marry him, the one he had with him every damn day—was on the stone terrace outside his studio, working on one of his sculptures. He shot Will a hard look, but the effect was muted by the happy afterglow aura of a well-satisfied man.

Will rolled his eyes. The man should be embarrassed.

Jace and Tino were at the pond—Jace swimming driven, efficient laps, Tino poking around the edge, looking for frogs, at a guess. Beowulf was there in a minute, enthusiastically barking away Tino's chances of amphibian success. Luckily, a playful, water-happy dog was a fine substitute.

The long, lovely, sun-tanning redhead laid out on the wooden float in mid-pond lifted up onto her elbows to watch the play. The skimpy little bikini she wore was barely enough to keep Will from having to arrest her. She shot a quick glance over to where he stood next to Leet. Apparently, being nearly naked in front of the law didn't worry her. In a none-too-subtle snub, she lay back down, all about letting the last of the sun worship her some more.

Leet, good buddy that he was, snorted. "Looks like you got trouble."

"I helped you put that float in."

"Yeah. You weren't anticipating this situation, were you?"

"Who would have?"

"I suspect she's going to make you go in there and get her. What did you do anyway?"

Leet and Sadie had just gotten back from some island a teammate of his owned. Apparently, it was all white sand, warm blue water, and a romantic boat ride away from fine restaurants and lively nightlife.

So Leet didn't know about Will's disastrous trip to Manhattan, and Will didn't know if he'd have told him about it if Leet had been around. He'd been all right not having to make that decision.

It had been tough enough having to talk with Jeff Anderson about it. That, he'd felt he had to do. Will had gone to Jeff's home, heart like a stone in his chest, with the plan to turn in his star along with his gun. Jeff had tossed him out, told him to show up for work on Tuesday as scheduled or face disciplinary action, and said they'd talk again in a month.

"It's complicated."

"It always is, man."

"I'd do better to let her go."

Leet looked at him with his full attention for a long moment, then turned and walked into his studio. He came back with a couple bottles of beer. He handed one to Will and propped himself along the stone wall of the terrace.

Will took him up on the implied invitation. He took a good slug of Belgian and sat next to Leet.

"I went to see her in Manhattan."

"That was a bad idea, wasn't it?"

"Oh, yeah." Leet had been a friend for a long time—one of those he could count on to accommodate his particular craziness.

"I don't know Katherine well. But Sadie loves her. And you fell for her, didn't you? Those are pretty good recommendations, yeah? I think she'd be able to understand your..."

"My limitations?" He said it with finger quotation marks.

"Your issues. We all have them. You think she could only love you if you're perfect? Then, yeah, give her the boot. I don't even like her."

Will snorted and took another long swallow. "I feel like it's not right to burden her with my crap."

"Bullshit. You're a good man, Will. She's got crap, too, or she's not human. Give her some credit. I'm sure she can deal."

Will's gaze went back to the float. His heart longed for the woman there. So much so that he wanted to rub his hand over his chest, like it was a pain he could soothe. "She's a freaking shrink. I'm not going to be able to slip anything past her."

It was Leet's turn to snort. "She's a *woman*. We never slip anything past them."

Will slid a look over. "You got Sadie to marry you."

Leet's grin was yet another picture of male satisfaction. "Yeah. She's got a blind spot."

"Have a good honeymoon or something?"

"Oh, yeah."

"Shut up."

"You know where Sadie is right now?" He didn't bother waiting for an answer. "She's in the kitchen. She's making potato salad."

"*Really*. Shut the fuck up."

Leet laughed. He killed his beer and then spoke more seriously. "I'm grilling in a bit. The moms are coming, and that definitely suggests there's gonna be pie. You're welcome to stay. The virago, too."

Will set his empty down. "Thanks. But the virago and I have unfinished business."

"Good luck, man."

"Yeah."

Katherine smiled as Tino paddled over and took hold, causing a small dip of the float. "Will's looking at you. He drank Papa's beer and now he's looking at you. Now he's coming over here." He whispered next. "Now he's here."

No need to discreetly spy on Will out of the corner of her eye when she had Tino as scout. Maintaining her dignity was well worth the dollar it had cost her. She lifted a little, then propped on her elbows, looking across to the pond's edge where Will stood.

He looked very appealing, rested, and substantially cleaned up from when she'd seen him at noon. He still had a rough shadow of beard, but his hair was freshly washed and he was dressed in a black tee and jeans that were inordinately sexy. She spent quite a bit of time admiring him before he spoke.

"You going to make me come in there and get you?"

She glanced over at Tino, who vigorously nodded his head.

It was very tempting.

"Are you asking me to come out?"

"Yes, please. If you would."

"I think Tino would like to see you jump in, clothes and all." She'd kind of enjoy it, too, matter of fact.

He slanted a look at the boy. "Thanks, dude." Then he unfastened his phone from his belt and started emptying his pockets.

"I'm coming." Katherine laughed and stood up, much to Tino's audible disappointment.

She dove in, surfaced just at the dock, and extended a hand. Will was there and pulled her up, face to face with him, in one long, muscled swoop. He seemed to be interested in the way water sluiced down her body, but he carefully kept their hands locked in between them, enforcing a safe, dry space. He let her go after a minute, then turned back to the pond.

"Come on, Tino. You're out, too, until there's someone here to watch you."

"Aw. Jace is here."

"Yeah, but he's busy. Out you go."

Tino paddled over and caught a bigger, swinging ride onto the dock that made him squeal. He was off then to pester Leet.

Katherine stayed where she was, arms crossed over her chest. She could feel the reluctance as Will, having watched Tino scamper off, brought his attention back to her.

"Think you might be willing to have a conversation now, big guy?"

"I'm sorry about that. It had been quite a long time since I'd slept."

She nodded a scant acknowledgement. What with one thing and another, he'd caused a bit of pain. She really wasn't entirely ready to forgive.

"Katherine. I wish you hadn't come."

"Because you think we're done? Because you think it's okay to say you love me, then run away at the first thing you don't like? You think you can call it over then and not have to talk to me about it?"

"Would you please come with me to my house? You can bust my chops all you want—I deserve it and more. But I'd rather not do it here with Sadie looking daggers at me out the window."

"Sadie loves me. She says it, and I can trust it. She won't take it back just because it gets hard sometimes."

She was interested in the way his jaw flexed. After a moment, he stepped back and gestured her ahead of him with his hand. "Please."

She made him wait another minute and then swept by him. "I'll go in and change. I'll meet you in the drive." She wasn't going into this conversation wearing a bikini. Besides, it had already done its work. His eyes were glued to her backside as she strode away; she was entirely sure of it.

Katherine remained a little prickly. Will offered her a ride, but she insisted on taking her rental car. He nodded and said he'd lead her over to his place, but she said she could find it. He said he'd follow her then, and she said she didn't need that either. Okay, he said, he'd go out of his way to take a different route.

Fine, she said.

Apparently, taking a reasonable and rational approach to their predicament was optional. For her, at least.

At his house, Will bade Beowulf to stay outside and dry off. With mild trepidation, he opened the door to his apartment for Katherine, and politely stood back to let her pass. She generously consented to that one, and went ahead with a regal lift of her head.

She'd changed into a clingy bronze top with skimpy little straps that crossed in back and a long, swishy skirt. He glimpsed just a bit of lithe ankle and calf as she took the stairs ahead of him.

At the top of the stairs, she waited. With fair grace, she accepted a glass of wine and his suggestion that they sit out on the porch off his bedroom. She paused and looked back at him as she passed through his room. Obviously, she'd seen her pair of heels that he'd retrieved from the Easy Rider. He'd left them on the floor beside his bed, in a way that had comforted him at the time, but now he suspected was just pitiful. Still, she'd have to ask for them back, or leave them where they fucking were.

He was glad he hadn't had to go so far emptying his pockets at the pond that she'd see him pull her earring out. He'd carried it with him for four weeks now, but she didn't have to know every damn thing.

She stood out on the porch, the wind lifting her hair and billowing out her skirt. Clouds had formed now as the storm gathered. The sun, just setting, shone through in golden, heaven-sent rays that lit up the village church steeples, the tops of the trees on the last ridge down to the river, and her.

He stayed in the doorway, watching her set aglow like a woman in a Vermeer painting. She lifted her face into the wind, taking obvious delight in the approaching weather. After a few minutes, she slipped out of her sandals—a different pair than she'd worn with the cutoffs, of course. He knew now how she packed. She gracefully swung up onto the wide porch rail and turned around sideways. Knees bent, bare feet flat on the rail, she tucked her skirt around her legs and then looked back at him.

Will wished he had a tumbler full of whiskey in his hand instead of the prissy white wine. He downed it anyway, little help that it would be, and set the glass aside.

The roof of the first floor porch extended a good two feet further out than his rail. Nonetheless, he moved close enough that he could grab her if she lost her balance, sending her a look that said he didn't care how she felt about it.

She watched him with those knowing eyes, but let it pass. She gathered her hair, taking possession of it from the wind, and secured it in some kind of knot at the back of her neck.

Through it all, her eyes kept that steady focus on his. "So, Will. You have a phobia."

He crossed his arms over his chest and looked out over the village. With just a little corner of his gaze kept on her for safety. "This isn't going to happen. You're not my shrink, Kate."

"No. I'm not your shrink. I'm considering whether I'm going to be your—" She waved a hand. "*Whatever*. Girlfriend."

Shit. He didn't say it out loud, but he knew she read it in the glance he shot her. He didn't speak. He couldn't.

"So. Will. You have a phobia." Slow, like she was talking to a moron.

Now that just pissed him off. He put his hands on his hips and faced her squarely. "I don't have a damn phobia."

She didn't seem the least intimidated. A lift of her brow was the only response.

He turned his back and strode to the far end of the porch. But he couldn't get himself to stay away, not with her sitting right there on the ledge like that. He walked back to her. "All right. Maybe spiders. Don't think if we ever live together that I'm going to get all the spiders just 'cause I'm the guy."

She continued to look at him calmly, moving just a little. He couldn't even tell what it was, just a little arching movement that shouldn't even have been noticeable. But it called—fucking *screamed*—his attention to her breasts. He knew they were bare under there. Not even she could find a bra that would be concealed under that little excuse for a top.

He cursed richly in his mind. He wanted to stomp his feet, to pull his hair out. He thanked God his friends weren't there watching, because he knew the phrase they'd use for what just happened. "All right, Goddammit! I'll get the spiders."

Katherine stood, chuckling just a little—and *yes*, he watched what that did to her breasts—aware of her siren's power, willing him to know what she mostly held back. She stepped close and wrapped her arms around him. And held him.

He huffed some breaths out, trying to convince himself he was just relieved that she'd moved away from the ledge. But sinking, sinking into the comfort of her, with her arms holding him, her strength there, her warmth.

Suddenly, for the first time in a week, he felt okay. He dropped his head into the crook of her neck and breathed her in. He closed his arms around her tight, tight. A shudder tore through him and some kind of groan let loose from deep in his chest.

He clutched her to him, not seeming able to get close enough. More harsh breaths and he turned her head and took her mouth in one rough kiss. Then he held her head in his hands, letting loose the knot of her hair, watching the wind take it, watching her eyes.

Behind her, storm dark had fallen. The distant light and sounds of the weather had moved closer. Thunder was overhead now and lightning flashed close.

She was unafraid. Of the storm, of him. And she loved him. He could see it there, in her eyes.

She smiled at him, then stretched her arms up. She turned away, stepping back to the porch's edge, facing the storm. She lifted her head and turned her face into the wind, into the large drops of rain that began to splat down.

Enthralled, Will watched her glory. Strands of her hair whipped around her head, lit like flames in the flashes of lightning. The wind lashed at her skirt, billowing it out then bringing it in to hug the curves of her bottom, her legs. He heard her laughter torn away by the storm.

Will was nearly brought to his knees by the intensity of his want of her. He stepped close behind her, fitting his body against hers. He set his hands at her waist and waited. With gratifying, blessed haste, she arched back, pressing her head into his shoulder, curling one arm back behind his neck.

The arch of her spine had very accommodatingly left his raging hard-on nestled against her ass. And lifted her breasts, thrust them out in invitation.

She didn't have to ask twice.

Following the instinctive craving that had been driving him for the last hour and more, Will thrust his hands up under her top and covered her breasts. They were slightly chilled from the rain, the nipples already hardened peaks. He rubbed his palms roughly over them, chafing.

She breathed out a low moan, twisting fingers into the hair at the back of his neck and gripping hard. A sinuous tremor coursed through her, bringing her head harder against his shoulder, treating his eager dick to an erotic, gyrating thrill.

Will arched his head back, wanting to howl into the storm. She was his, fucking *his*, and he wasn't going to hold back the urge, primal and unrestrained as it was, to have her. To take her.

He took her nipples between thumbs and forefingers, squeezing and tugging hard. He turned his face into her, scraping teeth along her neck, sucking bruises into her skin.

Katherine cried out, moans and his name mixed together in an incoherent chant.

He was nearly bent double by the force of his erection, the force of his need for her. With one hand, he tore at his jeans until he was free, shoving them barely halfway down his ass. Then he lifted the back of her skirt and tore aside the little swath of silk he knew would be coyly covering her.

He sank to his knees then, wholly unable to remain upright. He brought Katherine with him, one hand still working her nipple, the other directing her pelvis so she came down right onto him.

Her legs were spread wide, straddling his. She shuddered, rasping out a hoarse groan as he penetrated her. She fell forward, clutching the rail in front of her.

Will rested his head on her back, wallowing in the unimaginable pleasure of just being inside her.

Katherine's breath keened out of her, catching as her weight settled her more deeply onto him. Will started skimming his lips, his teeth, over the smooth, rain-soaked flesh of her back. He brought the full attention of one hand back to her breast and, with the other, he found and ruthlessly stimulated that hot spot of stretched, sensitive nerves at her core.

In just a minute, she was coming, writhing, crying out. And he hadn't even moved inside her.

And then he did, even before she was done riding out her orgasm. He lifted up, tilting her forward so he could withdraw and then plunge in, sinking to the hilt and then holding there, filling her deep, all the way. He ran a hand around and squeezed her ass, holding back a rousing climax that threatened with just that one thrust.

It was a hopeless effort. In another second, he splayed his fingers over her center again and began humping helplessly into her. He rubbed her hard as he took her, driving into her deeply, scraping his teeth over her back, pitilessly pinching her nipple.

They convulsed together, loud and prolonged, bodies spasming together again and again. He wrapped his arms around her with his last thrust. With his face pressed into her back, he groaned away the last of his ecstasy.

It took him several breaths. Finally, he disengaged and lifted back. He turned her around to nestle her against his chest. They stayed there, wrapped in each other's arms, as the storm passed and the rain fell away to nothing.

CHAPTER FIVE

Katherine had felt Will roll out of bed a few minutes before, but had left him to it, whatever he was about. She was entirely too comfortable where she was.

Which was in his bed, snuggled warm, where he tucked her after he'd carried her in from the porch. He'd stripped them both of their rain-soaked clothes and then toweled her off. He'd burrowed in there with her after he'd done something responsible, no doubt, with the wet pile of clothing.

Then he'd held her and they'd both dozed until he left her with a kiss.

He came back to her the same way, nuzzling his lips into her neck. "Come on. I intend to feed you."

"Not hungry." He nuzzled a bit more, then slurped wetly against her skin until she swatted him away. "Okay. I'm up."

He was all sexy bare chest and feet, with a snug-fitting pair of old jeans that were torn and faded nearly to white his only clothing. With an indulgent smile, he held a robe for her—her own robe, the silk kimono that was one of two she'd brought with her. She searched his room and noted that he'd brought in her luggage from the car. And also that a small table and a pair of chairs were situated at the open doors to the porch. The table was set with blue-rimmed stoneware and cloth—Fergus Weaves—napkins. A trio of white candles was lit, flames sheltered from the dwindling storm by glass chimneys. And there was food.

Maybe she was hungry.

She ignored his smirk and slipped into the robe. She went into his bathroom then, not surprised to see her makeup and toiletry cases already there, and not deigning to warn him that she would be a while. She suspected he already knew.

In front of his big mirror, well lit, she dropped the robe. Her hair was a wild mess, doused by rain and tossed by the wind and Will's greedy hands. Along her neck, sucking bruises stood out slightly darker against the burn from his whiskers. Her nipples were still reddened, faintly throbbing yet from his brutal use of them. At the crest of one hip, there were finger-shaped smudges where he'd held her as he'd come into her.

There were more, she was sure, on her back. Signs of his taking of her, imprints of his possession.

He'd made her body his, staked his claim, marked it like a wolf securing his territory. She would swear, like that wolf, he'd nearly howled out his ownership, his feral triumph.

She hadn't resisted it. And wouldn't, despite the fact that it struck her as a pretty primitive way of mating, of establishing a pair bond. Perhaps it was just that basic, that primal a process.

In the complexity of the man that was Will, there was that possessive wolf. A loved one became his, to guard and to protect. To care for and to please. To defend with snarls or combat against enemies and threats. To lay down his life for. It was not the least inconceivable that it could come to that.

For her, it would be a balance of giving over to that fundamental urge, that need that she was certain was of his essence, without giving up her own sense of self. She knew he wouldn't expect that, demand it or even want it. She was sure, in fact, that he'd be surprised that she'd even see it as an issue. He would see his desire to protect, to take care of her, as a show of his love and support.

He wouldn't see that a woman could lose herself in it if she weren't careful.

Katherine would be careful. She had learned in her first meager foray into love that she could too easily lose her sense of self. She'd spent many years building it back up, being sure of a firm foundation, to risk it now.

Lucky for him. Otherwise, she'd have to turn tail and run.

Katherine showered, dried her hair, and applied a touch of makeup. She didn't exactly dawdle, but she didn't hurry either. It was good to have a little time to gird up a bit before facing the man on the other side of the door. At least long enough for that sizzle his touch had left on her body to cool.

His eyes were on hers as she opened the bathroom door. He was perched casually on one of the chairs he'd set out, his feet propped on the other. He held a book in his lap, lit by a reading lamp over his shoulder. He closed the book, dropped it to the floor, and reached up to flick off the lamp, all without moving his gaze from hers.

Light shone in his eyes as he watched her walk to him. Lithely, he stood. When she got close enough, he took her hand and squeezed it gently before settling her into the second chair. He poured wine for both of them and then he sat with her.

"Mrs. Janisch's seafood salad," he pointed out. "It's Friday."

There were also small bowls filled with olive tapenade, roasted red peppers, and crumbles of Asiago cheese. A delicious crisp-crusted loaf of Italian bread complemented all of it. Katherine ate with enthusiasm, aware of Will's careful gaze on her even as he took his own meal.

Outside, the storm settled into distant rumbles of thunder. As Will finished eating, the only thing that distracted his gaze from hers was the occasional breeze that played with the edges of her robe.

Katherine took a last swallow of wine and sat back, mirroring his posture.

He watched her another minute, eyes glimmering in candlelight. "Well, Katherine. It appears I have a sort of phobia."

She let one corner of her mouth lift in just the smallest way. "Yes, Will. Do you want to talk about it?"

He smiled grimly and came forward, resting his forearms on the table. "Not really." He looked at her and she saw the urge to touch. "But I guess I have to, don't I?"

She didn't speak, but leaned forward too. He watched the way the silk of her robe caressed her breasts for only a minute or so before he met her gaze again. Then he spoke slowly. Reluctantly, she knew.

"Until I was five, when Elyse walked me down the mountain to get on the school bus, the only four people in the world I'd known were my mother, her parents, and Grandmère, my father's mother."

"Known?"

"Seen."

"That must have been some first day of school."

He huffed out a kind of laugh, then looked away at the candlelight swirling through his wine. "I adjusted."

"You spoke in class?"

"After a while."

"When?"

"By third grade."

"You made friends?"

"Yeah."

"Who was your first friend?"

"Leet."

"That was high school."

He shrugged a shoulder and took a swallow of wine. He didn't look at her when he spoke. "Adjusting took a while."

Katherine's heart ached. She stood up and reached out her hand for his. When he took it, she tugged. "Come here."

She led him into the living room, to his big recliner that was placed for viewing his spectacular aquarium as well as his big screen TV.

"Sit."

He complied and she curled up on his lap, facing the aquarium. He kicked up the footrest and tucked her in against the warmth of his chest.

"This isn't some new form of psychoanalysis, is it? Some updated version of the couch thing?"

"No," she said as she slipped her arms around him. "I never sit in my clients' laps."

"Good to know. For more reasons than one."

"Pretty much this is me giving comfort."

He touched his lips to her forehead. "Good. Thanks."

She leaned back to watch his face. "So, you have a social anxiety—get stressed in the presence of too many people?"

"Yeah."

"You can go to something like a wedding, especially if it's mostly people you know. But you feel more comfortable at the fringe—at the edge of the crowd."

"Yeah, I guess."

"And the people who know and love you come visit with you there. They take care of you, just as you take care of them."

"I'm more comfortable with the one than the other."

"Of course you are, my big, strong man." She gave a squeeze to the bulge of his bicep.

"And you're pretty observant."

"You're remarkably strong, Will."

He flexed his jaw. "Things help. Leet got me into football. He was a star quarterback from the first, joining up with the Basin's little Podunk team that had barely ever seen a winning season. He walked up to me during lunch on the last day of freshman year."

"You were sitting by yourself, in the cafeteria?"

"Outside—we were allowed to go out at lunchtime after middle school."

"Hmm."

"I was a big guy already—like Leet. But I knew nothing about football—nothing more than you can learn in a couple games of flag ball during gym class. Leet said he needed me. He did. He needed a few seconds of protection, so he could set up a play or get a pass off. He spent the summer teaching me the game, then introduced me to Coach Morgan. By fall, Leet and I were friends, and I was on the team. That first year, we went eight and six. Senior year, we took state."

"So having a role, a structure like the game, helps."

"Yeah. I did okay being on the field, but wouldn't have been able to tolerate being in the crowded stands."

"Have you ever seen Leet play professionally?"

He paused, looking at her. She knew he was feeling exposed and not at all comfortable with it.

"You know too easily what matters most to me, don't you? I see him play once in a while, when he can get me down on the field." He lifted a finger toward the screen. "Otherwise, I watch on TV."

She was quiet for a minute, listening to him breathe, thinking about his life. "And at work, your badge—your star—helps."

"It's hard to explain, but yeah. Things don't bother me so much then. Like that night at the Easy Rider. I could be there, watching you and the other women. But I wouldn't normally go there for fun."

"It helps if you have a task, a—quest, that takes you outside of yourself."

"*A quest.*" He huffed out a little laugh, then owned it. "I guess."

"Some people medicate, like with drugs or alcohol."

He pressed his arms around her. "Nothing wrong with a shot of Mark's."

"Do you have trouble with closed-in spaces?"

He eased out a breath. "You mean like being boxed into traffic, driving into New York? Walking down streets jammed with people through a concrete canyon like Manhattan? Riding a crowded elevator to the freaking fifteenth floor?"

She sat up and looked at him, holding his face to hers with her palm. "Yeah, like that."

He shrugged with a wry grin. "Nah, doesn't bother me."

He turned his head away, but she forced him back, both hands holding him now. It took a moment for him to lift his gaze to hers. "I'm so sorry, Kate. I'm so sorry for what I thought of you. As soon as I got away, I knew I was crazy. But when I stood there looking at Thor—"

"Thor?"

"Blond and blue, all hot, sweaty muscle?"

Katherine looked, just kept from rolling her eyes, but couldn't help the burst of laughter. "Kyle. Downstairs neighbor, old friend from college, sometime actor, all-time waiter, and entirely *gay* Kyle."

"He is not gay, sister."

"*Oh yes*, he is."

Will watched her for a moment, obviously speculating. She arched a brow.

"All those years you've known him, and he's never made a pass at you?"

She shook her head. "Not once."

"Hell. He's gay then."

His line of reasoning made her chuckle.

Plopping his head against the soft chair back, Will heaved a sigh. "I was ready to kill him."

"Flight or fight. You fled. Good choice."

"You're saying I was in a panic."

"Um-hmm."

"Shit, Katie." He turned back to her, stroked his fingers through her hair. "I'm a freaking nutcase. How could you ever trust me to love you? To love and care for our children, if we have them? How could Jeff trust me to do my job?"

Katherine touched her lips to his then clambered over him, straddling his lap, and leaned back to bring the chair more upright. As an afterthought, she tucked her robe discreetly around herself—his eyes wanted to wander. This was serious.

"Have you ever hurt anyone, Will? Put anyone in danger?"

"I was completely irrational, Kate. I thought horrible, impossible things of you. And I honest to God wanted to strangle Kyle."

She clutched at his shoulders and gave him a little shake—very little, given the solid mass of him. "Have you ever hurt anyone? Put anyone in danger?"

He held her wrists, thumbs stroking. "I hurt you, didn't I?"

"Mostly you made me mad. That's just love, Will. That's going to happen—and it will go both ways. You know that's not what I mean. The answer is no, isn't it?"

"You said yourself I'm phobic. That's certifiably crazy, isn't it?"

Katherine stood and paced a bit, stopping a minute to watch the fish swim while she gathered her thoughts. This was her favorite lecture from Psych 101. She moved in front of him.

"In humans, as in all animals, Will, there are extremes of behavior. We're not all the same, not *meant* to be. It's advantageous to our survival, it's *adaptive*, to have variation.

"Think of a field full of rabbits. Some rabbits are homebodies—they stay close to the nest, they keep the young nurtured and safe. Others are more adventuresome. They wander farther, take risks. It's good to have both. Without the adventurers, they might miss the best feeding grounds or good sources of water. On the other hand, if they were all adventurers, they might all be eaten by predators, their nests abandoned.

"Most people, most organisms, cluster around the middle. But it's good to have the extremes. They make things happen."

He watched her, serious now. "You're saying I'm an extreme. That's who I am, a thing I should just accept? I expected you to recommend therapy or something."

She turned her hand out in an ambiguous gesture. "It's often not comfortable at the extremes, Will. Just like the rabbit that gets eaten, humans often suffer for it. You suffer for it sometimes, don't you?"

He gave a small nod.

She shrugged. "You have remarkable strength. You've compensated extremely successfully, built yourself an admirable life, an effective one that works for you. You seem happy. I'm not sure anyone can tell you that you should do something different. Maybe, sometime, the suffering will be too great, the limitations you feel too restrictive. You can get help for it if that happens. There are techniques, even meds that might help you. But yes, you are who you are. You have a phenotype—your genetic makeup—and years of conditioning. You won't overcome that. You don't need to. You're a good man, Will. There's nothing wrong with you."

Will let go of a breath he felt like he'd been holding all of his life. He looked at Katherine—so beautiful it hurt, so crucial to his heart, his soul. He got up and stood facing her.

He knew it wasn't as simple as she'd made it out to be. He blessed her for it, thankful to his toes that she could understand it, accept it. But his—whatever, *condition*—was more than a little nuisance that they could work around. He couldn't expect her to just deal with it. It was too much to ask.

"It kept me from getting to you, Kate. What if it was an emergency? What if you needed me there, in Manhattan?"

"I think you could do what you had to do, Will. You always have, haven't you?"

He looked at her, unable to touch. "It seems like too big a risk. You, our children." Stopping himself there, he swallowed hard against impossible images—Katherine pregnant with his child, their baby at her breast, their toddler swinging along between them, clasping hands. *His* child. She would make that happen. He'd sworn he'd never father a child, but he was dead sure it was an argument he wouldn't win.

Not against Kate. Not against her good heart and calm confidence. He was seduced by the thought and terrified by it at the same time. He shook his head. "If something happened and I couldn't deal with it—"

She took a step closer and tangled her fingers in his. "You already have techniques you use, Will. I've seen you. Deep breathing. Focused relaxation. There are things you can practice—mindfulness, being in the moment. You can study tai chi, or yoga, meditation. You've dealt, Will, ever since that first day on the school bus."

She took a last step so there was just a whisper of air between them. "This," she said, "between us? It's not going to be that hard."

"It's more important, Katherine. It matters. More than anything else in my life."

"As it should, yes? I'm not saying it will always be easy. We'd be foolish to think it. But I can trust you to always do your best by me, can't I?"

Anchored by the touch of her fingers in his, he swallowed hard. And swore it as truth. "Yes."

She nodded gravely, acknowledging it as oath. "You'd give up your life for me, Will, wouldn't you?"

Simple. "Yes."

She smiled. "That wasn't even hard for you. God's truth, and not even hard. Love from you is a very strong thing. Everyone who has it is very fortunate."

"You have it. I love you, Katherine."

"Yes."

He touched his lips to hers, just a touch. He'd taken her so roughly out on the porch, in the storm. His need had been so great he'd barely been able to leash it. His need was just as great now, but it was for something different.

And so he touched for just a moment, just the slightest friction of his lips against hers before he lifted his head and looked into her eyes. And waited.

And knew it was a solemn oath when she spoke, too.

"I love you, Will."

He knew she could see his eyes blaze with feral victory before it settled in his heart. She didn't seem to be afraid of it. Though she might be if she could see the way his dick responded, straining to get to her even through his jeans.

He took her in his arms and carried her into his room. He laid her across the bed, pressing one knee between her legs while he loosened her robe and slipped her out of it. Then he stood up and stripped his jeans away.

When he came back to her, he was between her legs. He used his hip to bring her one knee up so she was open to him. Lifted on an elbow, he had his full view of her—her bare breasts, firm and tipped with the coral pink of her nipples that furled as he watched. The slim, toned and tanned belly, the flare of her hips. Her mons, with just the littlest swath of clipped velvet that led to her core.

And her face—lips parted, waiting for his. Eyes gleaming heat.

His erection stood up between them like a damn flagpole. He needed it buried deep inside her like he'd never needed anything before.

Watching her eyes, he took his fingers to his mouth. He collected some spit, then moved to slide it into her opening. He took the head of his dick and pressed it into her.

She was tight, just barely moist enough. Unable to hold back, he groaned out his need and shoved all the way into her.

He clutched his hand into her hip, holding her against his penetration. Vaguely, he heard a small cry from her. But it was all he could do to hold still inside her, surrounded with heat, clasped by her, and press his face into the mattress beside her shoulder, struggling to master the urgent need to just let go and pound into her.

His breath was harsh, painful in his throat. He dug in with his knees to press further into her. And held there, having all of her, trying to ease his breath. Grasping harder at her hip, he rubbed his forehead into her arm and then slid his mouth over her, skimming with his teeth.

Finally, he lifted up again so he could see her. She raised a hand to his face and he burrowed into it, catching her fingers in his mouth, biting into the fleshy part of her thumb, relishing the taste of her.

Meeting her gaze, he slowed his attack. Her fingers grazed along his cheek before tangling in his hair.

He let go of her hip and brushed his hand up along her side, up her arm, to hold her face. He rubbed his thumb along her cheek and slid his fingers into her hair.

His breath was slower now, calmer. He had what he needed.

Katherine knew what he'd done, what he'd needed. He'd made them one. With his body deeply penetrating hers, their fingers clutched in each other's hair.

It had almost carried him away, the ecstasy of it, the fulminant power of their joining. That was what had taken them when he'd had her out there in the storm. This was something different.

He moved now, to touch her lips again, a soft kiss that brought love, tenderness. Their breath was shared as his mouth moved over hers, a gentle abrasion that set her lips tingling. He took a long time at it, gradually deepening it, taking her lower lip with his teeth, tugging, nipping. Then he slid in with his tongue, tasted, penetrated. At times, he'd lift above her, hold her, stroke her face, make love to her with his gaze.

And Katherine learned he could brand her just as easily with gentleness as with power.

Still, he was inside her, huge and hard, hot. She was stretched around him, exquisitely, impossibly so. He wasn't thrusting into her, though she knew that would come— hard—later. Even so, she felt every small movement he made, every pulse of his heart, there in that most sensitive of places.

He leaned further into her to take her mouth more deeply and she felt that, too, where he penetrated her, distended her. She moaned with the stimulation of it, almost painful. She arched just a little under the weight of him, her body responding beyond her control, seeking more.

He lifted then, easing back, soothing with his hand along her face. Propped up on his elbow, he watched her, waiting as she settled, as her breath eased.

When he'd waited long enough, he moved his hand and palmed her breast. Circling a little, rubbing, he chafed over her nipple. Need shuddered through her and she arched, pressing herself further into his hand.

"Will." It was a plea, a direction, and said on a moan.

His hand left her then and she thrashed her head once, huffing out a breath. She stopped to look at him, almost a glare.

With endless calm, he looked back. He gave her a few moments, watching her settle. Then his hand went back to her breast. He grasped her nipple and tugged, squeezing, milking her.

She flattened herself against the bed, a long, low moan vibrating through her, and then arched up. Her hips rocked, tilting herself more deeply onto him, seeking more. Her knees rose up, legs splaying out, opening herself. A spasm of need rolled through her body.

"Will. Will!"

He dropped his head over her and sucked her other nipple into the heat of his mouth. He pulled hard on her, tonguing the very tip of her, rubbing her against the edge of his teeth. He kept at it even as he took his hand away, clutched her hip again, and helped while she plunged against him, onto him. Impaling herself, pleasuring herself on his body.

It was so much, too much. She filled herself with him, stretching and burning, until she screamed. Her body bucked, taking him to her depths as waves of throbbing, aching pleasure streamed through her. Again. Again. At the end, she called his name hoarsely, riding the last shudders of orgasm, until she lay still, replete, wracked.

In murmurs, his name slipped through her lips. She felt him move, her breath catching a little as he adjusted himself over her, her tissues still overly sensitive. Then whispers of touch—his lips over her face, his fingers stroking over her hip, her side, soothing her throbbing nipple.

"Katherine." His lips touched hers, nudging. "Katherine. Open your eyes."

She meant to lift a hand to touch, to hold, but it was beyond her.

He nudged again. "Look at me, sweetheart."

She whimpered a little objection, and complied only when his kiss nudged her again.

He lay over her, his weight on his elbows, his hands gently holding her head. His chest brushed against her breasts. His knees were bent, spreading her legs wide.

He was still hard, still piercing her.

He kept his hands gentle on her as he flexed a little, into her.

"Oh." She gave a small shake of her head and closed her eyes. Her nerves were still raw, too tender. "No."

"Open your eyes."

She looked at him, at the beguiling heat in his eyes.

He flexed again, a little roll that soothed and stimulated at the same time. "Yes."

His thumbs stroked over her temples, keeping her gaze held in his. He took her mouth in a swift, hard kiss, but kept his eyes on hers.

She keened out a little breath as he withdrew a bit from her, and again when he slid back in.

His eyes darkened. Tension coursed through his body. She lifted her hands to grip the hard muscle of his biceps, squeezing down as he moved inside her again.

He clutched one hand hard into her hair, tilting her head back. That brought her breasts up more, a rougher contact against his chest. He slid the other hand down her hip, her thigh, and brought her leg up around him.

He stroked into her one more time, and waited while she wrapped her other leg around him, too. Then he placed that hand over her breast, cupping her.

"Keep your eyes open. Keep looking at me."

The next movement, out and in, was a hard thrust. Will's breath was harsh now, his eyes fierce. As he watched her, he dragged his thumb over her nipple.

Katherine moaned, arching against him.

He started a slow rhythm, each thrust a complete breach, a complete taking. He squeezed her nipple at the peak of each stroke.

He brought his face close over hers, their gazes locked, their breaths—sawing now in ragged groans—matched, their air shared.

Will stroked harder, faster.

Unable to resist, Katherine gave over. She flexed for his thrusts, opening to him, taking him to her depths.

The tug against her nipple came stronger, faster, as his hips pistoned into her. Her nails dug into the muscles of his arms, clutching him close.

It went on and on, until they were slippery with sweat, until their breathing became jagged panting.

"Now," he commanded her in an urgent groan. "Now, Kate. Come."

He flailed into her and she did as he bade, fracturing, flying. She cried out, spasming, her body wrenching.

He gripped her head, keeping her turned to him as he joined her, rugged growling torn from deep in his chest, his final thrusts grinding into her.

She felt the spurts of his semen, endless and hot, deep within her.

At last he broke eye contact, pressing his forehead into the bed beside her, struggling for air. He kept his hand on her head and shuddered into her a couple more times.

Katherine's own moaning breaths eased to whimpers and then quieted, just as his did. He turned his head to her again and searched her eyes. Then he kissed her, gently, achingly sweet.

He lifted up and looked around, then pulled the light covers up over them. He tucked her into his side, stroked his fingers through her hair, and told her he loved her.

Katherine knew that in that time, he'd checked to make sure the storm had safely passed, the candles had guttered out, and that Beowulf was holding sleepy sentinel at the bedroom door.

When she woke, she was already filled with him. Will was behind her, pressing her into the bed. His lips skimmed over her shoulder and one hand stroked her hip. With gentle, lazy thrusts, he pushed further into her.

He spoke casually, as though he might have been sitting across a table from her. "I was thinking breakfast is on you."

She smiled and suppressed the urge to stretch, arching her body to open herself more to his taking. The storm had left bright, clear sunlight that shot through the room, falling in soft reflected puddles on the bed. It was an effort to match his tone. "I can pour a bowl of cereal."

He squeezed her hip and sank a little deeper. "Come on. Eggs, at least?"

It sounded like he had to work a bit harder, too, to keep that indifferent tone in his voice.

His touch at her breast almost did her in. "I might manage."

He slid his other hand underneath her, finding her with his fingers. Then he rolled them so he was lying fully on top of her. Another slow thrust brought her rubbing against his fingers. He did it a couple more times before he spoke again. "It's Saturday morning b-ball. You got game?"

A good grab at her nipple delayed her answer. That shudder she'd suppressed earlier fought its way to the surface. She pressed her forehead into the mattress, arching up now to receive his thrusts. They were more determined now, more—pointed. "You mean, can I hold my own—" She had to pause here to haul in a couple breaths. "Against a bunch of aging jocks? No problem."

"Good to know. Good." He was having his own trouble keeping up the conversation. "Katherine, that's good. So good."

Apparently, he was done talking then, except for blunt single-syllable descriptions of what parts he loved about her, what he wanted to do to them, and what he wanted her to do back.

He was full of good ideas.

Her first orgasm was a lazy, gentle buzz still muted by sleep. The second was brutal, muscled, tearing through her like last night's storm. He let her come down just a little before finishing himself. She loved that, too—being the vessel for his powerful body, the inspiration for his forceful passion, the fulfillment of his incredible need. He used her, worshipped her, loved her. *Hard.*

And so she was fully content, if still a little tender, showering and then making herself at home in his kitchen while he took Beowulf for a run.

She made Hollywood eggs, the soft yolks blending perfectly with the Worcestershire-spiced toast. Will was duly impressed, enough so that she had to defend her own share with the sharp tines of her fork. And a foot against Beowulf's broad chest.

Will took care of her in bed, he said, and made her admit the truth of it. At the table, he claimed, it was each man for himself. Or woman. Or dog.

Will almost came to regret inviting Katherine to join the basketball game. They seldom had a woman play. Sadie came on rare occasion—she had adequate skill, but not the cutthroat mentality to really engage in a game that was part serious competition and part razz your buddies.

Katherine had the mentality and the physicality. Once they got through the inevitable taunts about whether she played shirts or skins, she ended up on Canaan's team— shirts. Though she might as well have been playing in just her sports bra the way her skimpy shirt swung loose about her and revealed every damn thing. He hoped the other guys didn't think he didn't notice the way they paid attention.

The league maintained friendly games that weren't very physical except during a particularly critical shot. Or block. Point. Game.

Canaan did a good job protecting Katherine from the worst of it. And Katherine did a good job not taking advantage of the guys' moderate caution around her.

Except for when she faced off against Will. She was shameless then, forcing him to check himself rather than run through her when she mustered a late block, or to give way rather than take her down during her own drive.

She took to the air for what was to be the game winning or losing shot in a blatant foul that had him forced to capture her in his arms. Not caring whether the shot was good or not—the shirts seemed to think so—he tossed her over his shoulder and carried her off the court. She beat weakly at his back—not so much having run out of strength, but made weak by her own laughter.

He kissed her hard as he set her down—that quelled the laughter a bit. Then he started it up again by taking a good shot at her with a squeeze of his water bottle. She refrained from retaliating. Much.

Leet and Jace had come late to the game. They sat with them and Canaan and rested on the bleachers for a while. Leet had joined the shirts and so had a good time taunting Will and Jace. Despite that obviously invalid final basket.

Katherine talked comfortably with Canaan about his work on the farm, his study of Tai Chi, and the history behind his prosthetic leg and its effect on his life. Will eavesdropped just a bit and heard more about Canaan than he'd learned in all the years Canaan had lived in the Basin.

Katherine was easy to talk to. Will figured she'd learned some stuff getting her doctorate in psychology, but really, it seemed natural to her. She was interested in people and their lives, and open and supportive.

And she looked back at him, connecting with her eyes, letting him know she was there, with him, at just the right time.

They shared plans for the day as the group broke up. Leet was going to do some work in his studio while Sadie and the boys went berry picking at the farm. Will had to work a night shift and wanted the afternoon with Katherine, so he turned down the invitation to join them. But Katherine agreed to show up for pizza and movie night at the Benjamin-Hayes house.

Lake Fairlee was crowded with families on summer Saturday afternoons, but the climb to the pool and falls above it was tough enough that the area was often deserted. Will drove by his house so they could pack a lunch basket and pick up the dog, then took Katherine there.

They rinsed off the sweat of the game in the chilly water then had lunch on a blanket in the sun. Beowulf hung around long enough to finish their scraps and then went off exploring. Will lay back with Katherine in his arms, replete. Happy to just enjoy the moment, trying to let his concerns about the future rest for a bit.

He knew he'd have to let her go again. This would be a short weekend with his Saturday night shift and her work on Monday.

He didn't have a solution to the problem they had with their jobs and homes being two hundred and fifty miles apart. He knew that Katherine would have to make the move in order for them to be together, and he hated having to wonder if she'd find him worth it. Worthy of it.

She slept in his arms while he kept wondering.

Katherine slept harder than she'd thought she would—she'd known Will was awake, had felt the little drift of his thumb along her arm. She'd known he was troubled, thinking about her going back to Manhattan on Sunday, and unhappy about it. She knew he wanted to ask her to stay—to come back anyway. To tie up her life down there and move up here.

It was what he wanted, but more than he felt he could ask.

She could only help him so much. She suspected his was the more romantic soul, where she was of a practical nature.

She lifted her head to look at him, subtly running her hand over his chest to make sure she hadn't drooled. Or not so subtly, given the glint in his eyes.

He took hold of her hand and tugged a little to bring her close. Then she followed his unspoken command and kissed him.

A kiss was all it would be. They were in a secluded spot, but not so secluded that they could count on not being interrupted.

Still, the man knew how to make the most of a kiss. He pulled her close against him and held her head while he took her lips. He was gentle, enticing. For a long time it was just that—romance, compelling in its own way but not demanding. He lifted her away to meet her gaze then brought her back for more.

Then it was more—hungrier, needier, demanding. Their breathing roughened, their open mouths separating to gasp in air.

But still it was just the kiss. She knew if he pulled her over him, she would find him hard beneath her. He could be stroking her, stimulating her, even bringing her to orgasm with nothing more than his touch.

Almost nothing more than his kiss.

He brought it to a stop then, holding her face above his with his hands, capturing her with his eyes, roughly breathing into the shared space between them.

"Katherine," he bade her. "*Please*. Move here. Come live with me."

She twined fingers along his hair, stroked his cheek, and

tried to master her own breathing. "I will."

His eyes flared. "Now?"

She shook her head just a little, limited by the tension of his hands on her. "No."

He closed his eyes and heaved a breath. Then he sat up, bringing her up, too, so they faced each other. He rested his arm on his knee and leaned into her. "When?" It was just short of a demand. She could see he heard it and tried to gentle it. He brought his other hand to tangle in her fingers. "Katherine, when?"

"First of the year."

He looked at her and ran his fingers along her hair, her cheek. "You'll give up your practice?"

She nodded, very aware of how carefully he watched her.

"And you'll come up here on weekends until then, when you can?"

"Yes."

He stood and walked away from her, standing at the water's edge, his back to her. He looked pretty forlorn for someone she'd just offered her life to.

Katherine got up and went to stand beside him. When she slipped her arm around his waist, he grabbed her shoulder and tucked her in close to him. Then he pressed his lips into her hair.

"You unman me, Katie. I want us to be together. I'd do anything to make it happen, to be with you. But all I can do is ask you to come here, to make the drive on weekends so we can see each other, to give up the life you've built so we can be together."

She leaned a little more into him. This wasn't comfortable to him, she knew. He'd be much happier being the one to make any sacrifice that was needed.

"It's okay. I have a plan."

"Hmm. Now, why does that scare me?"

She chuckled. He had good intuition. "I'll come up here every other long weekend like we'd planned. When it's your turn to travel, I'll take the train up the Hudson. The Metro North goes right from Manhattan to Poughkeepsie. I'll go there and you can meet me. There are lots of things we can do from there—hiking, canoeing. The Mid-Hudson Valley, the Catskills—it's a great area."

He turned and pulled her to face him. "And?"

"My family's there. You can meet them."

His hands locked behind her, but he leaned back to get a good look at her. "I remember that you have a father."

She nodded, a kind of fake enthusiasm she knew he could see through. "I do."

"And you're his baby girl. His only daughter."

"Ay-yuh. I have two brothers, too."

"Yeah." He brought her in close. "You're enjoying this. That worries me."

"They'll love you."

"Because you'll convince them we have a nice, platonic relationship? Otherwise, I don't think so."

She lifted up to touch his lips with hers. "I'm a big girl. They know it."

"That won't keep them from wanting to kick my ass."

"Mom will love you. She'll keep them under control."

"Great. I can count on hiding behind your mom."

"Hey, she's tough. They're all scared of her."

"Oh, good. That makes me feel better."

It was three weeks before Will would have to face a Noble family ass-whupping. He spent the next weekend traveling to a run-down old fishing cabin in West Bumfuck, Maine.

It was an arrangement he'd made during the week he was certain he'd never see Katherine again. It was one he didn't want to unmake, despite the chance that Katherine was giving him.

He'd determined to consider it only a chance.

She'd tried to make nothing of it—the plan she'd developed that still involved them living apart, seeing each other only on some weekends for another handful of months. She'd reassured him, on that Sunday morning when he'd gotten off work, before she drove back to the city while he slept off his night shift, that it was simply a practical approach to the problem. That it implied no uncertainty in her commitment to him, no hesitation on her part.

He'd bit back every urge to push her. *Make it now then,* he'd wanted to say. *Take a damn leap of faith and come be with me.*

He wanted to grab her while he had her. In the best caveman way, he wanted to toss her over his shoulder and cart her off to his den.

She'd said she could live with his social anxiety-issue-thingy, whatever she wanted to call it. She said it. She couldn't expect him to give her endless chances to take it back. Apparently, that wasn't the problem.

Essentially, he trusted her honesty on that one. Naïve or not, deluded or not, she seemed willing to accept his flaws. She was perceptive, bright, and trained to see crazy. If his particular brand of it didn't send her running for the hills, well, he wasn't going to point the direction.

He determined that her reluctance to throw her life over for a chance at true love based on one month's acquaint-ance—which to his mind would have been perfectly reasona-ble decision-making—was typical and pure female wiliness. Just as Canaan had said. He'd chase. She'd run. He'd chase harder.

For some reason, it just seemed important to the female of the species.

Someday, he'd ask for her scholarly-ass explanation of the survival advantage of that particular bit of female tor-ment. He was every bit sure she'd have some rational justifi-cation for it.

Anyway, he could do it. Nothing like a little hot pursuit to get the blood flowing. He wouldn't assume the outcome was certain. There was always a chance she could come to her senses.

But it wouldn't be for lack of his trying.

Just not this weekend.

He was on his way to see Eli Benson. In West Bumfuck.

Eli and Will's father, Truman Hunter, had been members of the same FBI Academy class, graduating together from Quantico. Before the tenth anniversary of their graduation, Truman Hunter was dead and Eli Benson had left the Bureau.

Will had called a dozen of the agents from that class be-fore he learned that, if he wanted to have a chat with some-one who remembered his father, he should find Eli.

Which was a job easier said than done. He'd finally caught the man at the bait and tackle shop, which apparently had the only telephone in a twenty-mile radius. Eli told him he was welcome to come drop a line off his old plywood fishing boat with him. If he didn't mind peeing off the deck into the lake, or otherwise using the outhouse. Morning shower, he said, was drop your shorts and jump bare-assed in the lake. "Plan on eating a lot of fish," he advised. "And bring a sleeping bag."

And so Will sat on the deck—kept in much finer shape than the rest of the ramshackle cabin—that hung out over the pure, clear water of Deep Creek Lake, watching the sun go down behind the mountains. Hoping that he was sitting on the right deck. And that Eli Benson was in one of the boats still making their way back to the scattering of cabins along the serpentine lake.

He'd have liked to have been with Katherine, even if that meant making the acquaintance of the rest of the Noble clan. But he propped his boots up on the rail of the deck, breathed fresh, cool August air, listened to stillness, and thought it wasn't at all a bad second.

Eli was, indeed, it appeared, in one of the boats. Will got up to grab the line as he gently motored in, and took the man's measure. In much the same way as was happening back at him.

Eli's face led with his nose, there was no doubt about that. But his eyes were bright behind the black, plastic frames of his glasses, twenty years out of fashion, at least. Bright enough to belie the scraggle of beard and hair that suggested something more like a slow-witted, slow-moving recluse.

He offered up a firm, lingering handshake that took no umbrage for the embedded grime on skin and around nails that no doubt involved bait and fish guts.

"So you're Tru's boy. Glad to meet you, Will."

The voice was also a jarring contrast to the rough exterior. It reminded Will of a college English professor who had the best reading voice he'd ever heard.

Will and Eli worked easily together so that by the time an hour had passed, they had the boat cleaned out, beer cooled, and a meal set out on the deck that consisted of grilled fish, vegetable kabobs, and corn on the cob. Eli had a barter deal going with a local farmer—fresh fish for fresh produce.

The beer was a pale ale—not Will's first choice, but it

went fine with the meal and a quiet night falling on Deep Creek Lake. Resting back on the Adirondack chairs, feet propped and beers at hand, both men watched stars come peeping out of a deep sky.

"So, nine months before you were born, Will, a federal agent was murdered, and his wife was raped and tortured. I expect you'd like to know why the Bureau ever terminated the investigation of a case like that."

Yeah, in fact. It was a question that had left Will and Jeff Anderson baffled. Every investigative agency, every arm of the law, had to ration its resources. Every case was investigated, but some cases were *investigated*. And no case had resources dedicated—committed and sworn—to it more than one involving the loss of an officer. But he and Jeff had confirmed it—the Bureau's interest in the case of Truman and Elyse Hunter had ended swiftly and finally very soon after it had opened.

The reason behind that surely was something he'd like to know.

He had a lot more interest in that than in the discussion of upcountry Maine lake fishing they'd had over their meal. Bass fishing was never bad, Eli opined. But what he loved was going for landlocked salmon, like Will should know there was such a thing. Great fighters they were, in early summer, when the lake was cool and a strong arm and good fly rod could pull them out. And now, in late summer, when they sought the cold depths of the glacier-carved lakes, and you had to go after them with wobblers on lead core lines. Or something like that.

Will knew plenty about all that now, for the good it would do him.

But this was the conversation he'd been waiting for.

"Do you know what my father was working on?"

"You figure that's the key, don't you? That the explanation for the Bureau's failure to close the case of an agent killed on the job had to have its source in the case Tru was working on. I figured the same. I did then, and still do. And thirty-odd years ago, raising a stink about it was what got me assigned to a single-agent FBI outpost in northern North Dakota. After a year there, I had to choose between my job and my wife."

That had been the other half—the non-fish half—of the conversation over dinner. Eli had left the Bureau. He and his wife took teaching jobs in a community college in western New York. Summers, she traveled with her girlfriends—hiking in Italy, biking tours in Ireland—while Eli fished. His son usually spent a week or two with him, and now his grandson, too. It seemed the Benson family had found a way to live their lives that pleased them. Without the Bureau.

They both watched the stars some more before Eli went on.

"Your dad was working on a case that involved the deaths of young women. It was a serial killer, and he saw the pieces of it that no one else did. He was a bulldog in that way."

Will knew that about his father. He'd heard it in the way Truman had courted Elyse—first as a witness, a source, then as a woman.

"As we graduated from the Academy, back in the seventies, forensic psychology was just developing as a discipline. The Behavioral Analysis Unit was brand new. Tru was all into it. It didn't matter to me what a pattern of killings might represent, what went on inside the head of a killer. To me, if you kill someone you're bad—it doesn't matter what your motivation"—finger quotes here—"is. I'll hunt you down and kill you or arrest you, whichever causes me less grief. I don't want to talk to you about why you did it.

"But Tru loved nothing more than getting into the head of some psycho—it sent shivers down my spine at times. Anyway, he was all hot about this case that came out of New York. He was looking for what he called the birth of a serial killer."

Truman had been hurt during a chase, Eli said. They'd been tracking an escaped convict, making his way from Attica to his home deep in the West Virginia hills. The man had left a trail of bodies in his wake. And he didn't just kill them. He hurt them first. The case had earned Truman's interest—it appeared the killer in the man had been born in prison. He'd killed another inmate—and that was his first violent crime, at least to the knowledge of the law. And then the path of death that led to an isolated cabin in the mountains.

They'd thought they had him surrounded there, but the guy had dug an escape route from his cellar into an old mine adit. Truman went after him.

"He and I kept in pretty good shape. That was back in the day before TV got everyone thinking that lawmen were all hot and buff. The two of us used to go up to the roof of the Justice Building and work out. Back before Quantico, what they used to call the Police Training Academy did their physical training up there."

Will knew some of the history. FBI training had once been housed in the Justice Department Building in D.C. When an agent had been killed in a shootout with Pretty Boy Floyd, the Bureau began firearms training. They built a shooting range on the Marine training base in Quantico. Over the years, they added buildings and the FBI Academy was born.

"There was still some equipment left up there. We liked the history of it, the feel of it. Up there on the rooftop, surrounded by the buildings and monuments that made up the heart of this country. Well, it meant something to us. So when this old country boy took off through that mine shaft, Tru gave chase. Your dad was strong and in good shape, fast. I'd have put my money on him.

"Tru went into the mine at dusk. It was noon the next day before we found him. Both he and the fugitive were at the bottom of a mineshaft. Truman was unconscious from a head injury, had a broken tibia, and a torn up shoulder. The other guy was dead.

"Something ugly happened in there. I was with him during the debrief. He told the facts, but we all knew there was more he wasn't saying. He wasn't himself then. And didn't begin to sound like himself until he'd spent some time with Elyse." Eli took a long pause to go through the ritual of lighting a cigar. He offered one to Will and grinned when he turned it down. "Is that the kind of limit you have on how far you'll go to work a source?"

Will sighed and hoped it was good-natured ribbing. "Do I have to smoke a cigar to keep you talking?"

"Nah. But you do have to get me another beer."

That he could do. Will suspected this was just the sort of interplay that Eli had when his son came up to the fishing cabin. He got up, fetched the beer, and tossed it to the older man, then went with the ambiance and peed off the deck.

He was enjoying himself.

When he settled back in his chair, Eli continued his story.

"As soon as he could hobble, he went up to Vermont. There'd been a series of girls gone missing up there. There were no bodies, so it wasn't certain whether the girls were dead or had just taken off. Truman was treating it as a serial killing case. He was all interested in what he called first kill—what it is about the kill or the killer that turns it from a single experience to the start of a series."

"He was looking for the first kill," Will said.

He thought he'd found it, he'd told Eli. Truman would call every week or two and talk with Eli about his progress. Eli heard about Melissa, the fifteen-year-old girl gone missing from her parents' summer cabin, and about the young girl, Elyse, who'd become her friend.

Truman had worked his rehab out on Elyse's family farm—he'd strengthened his leg and got his shoulder operational by pitching hay and then clearing fields. And he'd gotten Elyse—skittish as a deer—talking to him.

And doing all that, he'd fallen in love.

"I could hear it happening," Eli said. "I think I knew it before Truman did. Your father had the connections to succeed in the Bureau. I don't mean just as an agent. He had the political sense to make it to the top. He was born and bred in D.C. His father was very well respected, a true government man in what used to be fine tradition—the kind of man that kept the country running competently and honorably.

"The FBI was probably not quite the right choice for Tru. He was drawn to it, no doubt. He liked the issues that came up—the discussion of right and wrong, the nuances associated with law and the use of it. But I think he liked it theoretically better than in real life. He should have been teaching at the Academy, and would have been, no doubt, in a few years' time.

"The summer ended and Tru showed up in the office. He'd married Elyse and set up a job teaching college sociology. He came to clean out his desk. He closed up his case file on the missing girls and handed it in to our chief. He and I had a couple beers and made a plan for my wife and me to go up and meet Elyse in the fall. He didn't figure he'd ever get Elyse to come down to D.C.

"Then he got the call that she'd been taken, and he was

gone. And then he was dead."

Eli got up and walked to the rail. Will watched the arc of orange glow as Eli's cigar went flying out over the water and heard the hiss as it splashed down.

"The field office out of Albany took the case and worked with the locals. I asked to be assigned, too, and got permission to join the staff from the field office. Three days after I got there, I was called back. Within the week, the field agents got pulled back to Albany. I went to the chief and put up a fuss. I was lucky not to get my ass handed to me right then. Two weeks later, I was shipped out to North Dakota. Minot is fucking cold and dark. When I couldn't take it anymore—well, when my wife couldn't—I quit." Eli turned around then, leaning his ass against the deck rail. "It was politics, power, or money, and in that town, they tend to be one and the same."

Will met Eli's gaze, just visible in the starlight. "Somebody in D.C. was protecting a killer."

"That's how I figured it. Still do."

"Somebody—fairly high up—in the Bureau caved in to whatever kind of pressure was brought to bear."

Eli was silent.

"What kind of pressure would have managed that?"

There was a shrug in the next words. "Budget, probably. It could have been something personal. You know, somebody had something on somebody else. But the chances of that—"

Will understood the point. Someone might have information on someone else—enough to blackmail, enough to strong arm. But it would be unlikely in the extreme that a person trying to cover up murder would just happen to have something to hold over someone in a position of power in the FBI.

But money was power. Especially in D.C.

"So who controls the budget?"

Eli came back to his chair. His voice was tired when he spoke again. "Eight Senate and House Committees oversee FBI funding and operations. Judiciary and Intelligence are important to operations. But the money would come through Appropriations."

"So, what, a senator—"

"Or congressman—the House and Senate have the same committees."

"Okay. So a senator or congressman was a serial killer?"

"Or protected one—a brother, a son."

"A son." Will sat back and pondered. "A boy or young man. Living—or spending a summer—at the lake in Vermont. Someone who would be appealing to a girl of fifteen, someone a girl might flirt with." He looked up at the sky. "Maybe they flirt. Maybe he wants to take it further. She rejects him, maybe laughs at him."

"There's your dad in you."

That stopped Will. He looked over at Eli, wishing he had more light.

"Honest to God, you're just like him. The way your brain works. I mean, you look a lot like him, sound a lot like him, but you freaking think *just* like him. You take me back thirty years." He took a long swig from his beer, killed it. "You make me miss him, Will. He was a good friend. A good man. I'm so sorry you never knew him. That he never knew you."

They were quiet for a while and then spoke a bit longer. They talked more about what Truman might have discovered that led, indirectly or directly, to his death. And then to what was essentially a cover-up of his death.

Eli asked about Elyse. He'd never met her. She hadn't been at Truman's funeral—she was still in the hospital then. And a few months later, when Eli had gone to Vermont, she still wasn't speaking. And no one on Fergus Mountain was talking with a lawman.

But Eli had met Truman's mother—he'd eaten more than one Thanksgiving meal at Tru's family home, had drunk a few beers in front of the TV on occasional fall Sunday afternoons. In the years since Tru's death, he stopped in for a visit on the rare trips he made to D.C. So he'd kept up a bit about Elyse, and heard a little about Will.

Isabela Hunter—now that was a woman. He was a little bit afraid of her, and so was anyone else with sense in D.C. Not, he said, that everyone in D.C. had sense. In fact, some might think it was a small minority. Clearly, Truman had gotten at least some of his smarts and his toughness from his mother. And Will had gotten them from his dad.

His dad. Will went to bed—well, to the hammock slung across the deck—that night thinking for the first time of someone as his dad. Someone good.

CHAPTER SIX

It was a theme that played in the back of Will's mind two weeks later as he drove south to Poughkeepsie. The meeting of Katherine was a lovely, enticing thing, a thing he'd been looking forward to for three weeks now.

The meeting of Katherine's dad—well, that was something else.

The feeling of family had been in his head since he returned from Maine. He'd spoken at length with Elyse, more than once. They'd sat out on her deck—in the dark, much as he had with Eli—and talked of Truman Hunter.

To some extent, Will had been thinking about the case. He'd had conversations with Jeff, too, in that regard. They'd looked at the board and thought about the houses that circled the lake. In particular, the houses that had been there thirty years ago.

Today, there were still a handful of small cabins that were just a bit of lake front property used as a staging area for family play in the summer. Some of those were owned by outastaters who came for a few weekends in season. Most were owned by locals who lived even just a few miles away, the cabin smaller but not much different in style or market level than their own homes. At the far end of the lake, where the road dwindled to not much more than a trail, there remained a small cluster of tiny rental cabins.

But many of the old cabins had disappeared when land values had risen so high about the time Truman had come to Vermont. Suddenly, little lakefront cabins were sitting on small fortunes in land. They were bought up—mostly by wealthy outastaters—and replaced with high-end vacation homes.

The profile of property and owners had changed signifi-cantly since Truman had run his investigation. Will spent hours at the county clerk's office, looking at the trail of prop-erty ownership.

But with Elyse, the conversation was all about Truman. Eli's words had settled in Will's heart. For the first time, he thought of Truman Hunter without having to wonder if he was no more relation to him than any man he happened to walk by. For the first time, when Elyse talked about him, Will felt included in the love she described.

Elyse seemed to be aware of the change in Will's feelings, and was clearly grateful that Truman's good friend Eli had helped bring the change about. She held Will's hand when she talked of the children that Truman had wanted. She had teased him, she said, about having a daughter, that he'd have to learn to tie hair ribbons, that he'd pace a furrow in their floor waiting for her to come back from a first date. But he'd wanted a son, she knew, though he never said it. He'd be so proud, she said, to have Will.

She spoke just a bit of it, but she made sure Will knew that he was what had made her come back. After the trauma of her captivity—when she was taken, was how she referred to it—when she had known, *known* that Tru was dead, the comprehension that she carried his son was the thing that made her come back.

On their last night together, just before the weekend when Will would see Katherine again, Jeff had joined them on the deck. Though it was dark, Will knew that it was Jeff's hand Elyse was holding. And when he left, Jeff's car was still in the drive.

He had felt it then, in the company of his mother and the man who, as much as anybody in his life, stood as his father. He had felt family.

And he thought about it now, as he waited for the train and anticipated seeing Katherine in the setting of her family. But mostly, he was anticipating seeing Katherine.

It was a tired bunch offloading from the train. Many, Katherine had said, were midweek commuters—folks who squeezed five days of work into three or four so they could spend a few short days with their families. Some, she swore, commuted daily. To Will's mind, it was no way to live.

And then he forgot about them, could not even see them, for his universe narrowed to the vision that was Katherine.

He realized he was seeing her in her professional clothes for the first time. No surprise, really, that she was a hot shrink. She wore a sleek suit in some color between red and pink that sizzled. The narrow skirt went to her knees, and he was pretty sure there was going to be one of those damn slits in the back of it or she wouldn't be walking in that long, sexy stride of hers. As it was, the skirt clung enough that he could see the outline of her thighs and just a little, fleeting hint of a vee–shaped fold of fabric that formed and unformed with each step. The jacket fit closely to her waist then flared out with a little flounce. It was closed with just a couple buttons over— well, if there was anything but skin, he couldn't see it.

It was fucking worth the wait. He'd have just stood there and enjoyed the show as she came to him if she hadn't been lugging three cases—her weekend's worth of clothing and accoutrement, the ridiculousness of which he could now merely humbly appreciate. As it was, the only gentlemanly thing to do was to go give her a hand.

And that worked out okay, as it had her in his arms all the sooner.

It was a lovely thing, the way her face lit when she spotted him, the way her arms lifted to wrap around him, the way her mouth opened to accept his tongue. The way she arched against him when he put his hands on her ass and pulled her close, and closer.

He slid one hand under her jacket and found the skin he expected. "You look fucking hot."

He'd mumbled it into her mouth, but she seemed to catch on.

"I came straight from the office."

"I'd pay ninety-five dollars an hour just to look at you. You wouldn't even have to talk."

"One-seventy-five." There was a pause as she found her way around his tongue. "Fifty minutes. And you'd be the one talking."

"I don't think so."

Then they were laughing and pulling back a bit to sink into each other's eyes. After a long moment of that, they were serious again.

"Hello, Katherine," he said. "I love you."

"Hello, Will. I love you, too."

Then he kissed her again, holding her tight against him, using his mouth to forge the closeness, the attachment he'd been craving for nearly three weeks. He didn't stop until the third time a perfect stranger gave entirely unsolicited advice about getting a room.

When it happened, he grunted at the back of the nosybody. "Motel 6 got you on their payroll or something?"

At that, Katherine gave him a swat. He straightened himself as best he could and, in a manly fashion, gathered the woman's luggage while still keeping an arm around her. He walked her to the parking lot and loaded her into his truck. He celebrated the little bit of help she needed climbing in, and the view he got of the way her skirt caressed her ass as he gave it. And the tease of the slit he'd known would be there.

She directed as he drove them across the river and a few miles north. It was farm country, rougher than one would guess, and beautiful. It was the stuff of Sleepy Hollow and Rip Van Winkle, settled by Huguenots and the Dutch. Rivers were called kills and towns bore names brought over from the old country.

He was surprised when the drive she pointed out led to a little bit of a farm. There were chickens in the yard and couple of penned goats outside a small barn. The house was an old two-story Victorian that had additions jutting out on either side. It had a wide, homey front porch with hanging pots of cascading petunias and begonias.

Will shut the truck down and gave her a long look that took in her sleek outfit and high heels. "Farm girl?"

She gave him a steady look back. "I can milk those goats." The next words were quiet, under her breath, but he heard them anyway. "If forced."

He chuckled and was about to take her mouth with his when he caught movement on the front porch. Cock-blocked by a mother.

She kept the look of a farmwoman about her, nothing of the citified glamour of her daughter. She wore a cotton tee, long sleeves pushed back to her elbows for work, with worn jeans, and covered it all with an apron that was dusted with flour. She had nearly the height, but was just a bit more rounded than Katherine. She appeared strong and in shape. Katherine had gotten much of her beauty here—the classic facial bones, the deep green eyes, the red hair.

Those eyes lit now as Katherine squeezed his hand and then opened her door and hopped out—maybe she hadn't needed as much help getting into the truck as she'd let on. The two women met on the walk and settled into a lengthy embrace, Katherine's heels exaggerating the bit of difference in their natural heights.

They exchanged kisses and a few quiet words as Will got out and slowly approached. This was a first for him, and important.

The women seemed to know it. They stood side-by-side, arms still linked, and wore twin looks of amused indulgence as he neared.

"Will, this is my mom, Darlene. Mom, this is Will Hunter."

He nodded, somewhat anxiously awaiting a signal about a handshake or something from the older woman. Then she took all awkwardness from it when she let go of her daughter to take Will into a good hug. He was enfolded in motherly warmth, a good, pure feeling.

She kept her arms around him as she kissed his cheeks. "Will, I'm so glad to meet you. Katherine cares for you very much. That makes you ours, too."

He caught Katherine's look as he kept the woman in his arms. He supposed Katherine could have told him he didn't have to worry about his reception—maybe she even had—but he wouldn't have expected this no matter what she'd said.

He was certain as he could be that Darlene was absolutely sincere in her welcome. And also certain that no one could blame him for sneaking a peek around for his woman's male parent. There was no sign of him, though, so Will figured he'd cross that bridge when he got there. Which would no doubt be entirely soon enough.

But he wouldn't look this particular gift horse in the mouth. He pressed a kiss into the top of her head. "Thank you, Mrs. Noble."

She smiled up at him as she turned to circle an arm around Katherine and walk them both toward the porch. "Oh, call me Darlene. Come in. I've got bread just from the oven.

And fresh butter."

Will said, "Fresh butter, like from...?"

"Like from a cow? Oh, yes."

She settled him at the big family kitchen table while Katherine left to go change out of her work clothes. Will started to get up to fetch her luggage, but she waved him back. Apparently there was an emergency supply of clothing still in her childhood bedroom. He should have guessed—she'd already taken over two drawers in his bedroom and a good part of his closet. Without any diminishment at all in the amount of luggage she toted.

Darlene put plates on the table, one laden with thick slabs of a hearty-looking bread—dark grained, rich with nuts and seeds—and a crock of pale butter. She filled three tall glasses with iced tea, and sat down just as Katherine came back in.

Skimpy cargo shorts, little cotton knit top with skinny straps over her shoulders, and another decent pair of hiking shoes.

"Where's Dad?"

"He's down at the college. They just finished up camp last weekend. He's been striking the set and cleaning up for the incoming students this week. He said he wouldn't be late."

Will knew the plan was for dinner this evening with the parents, then he and Katherine were going further into the Catskills for a couple nights at a mountain lodge. They'd be back for Sunday dinner that was supposed to include the two brothers and their families. They'd spend Sunday night at the house before Katherine went back to the city Monday afternoon.

It turned out fresh butter was nothing like any butter Will had ever tasted before. He kept from making a total pig of himself by just the smallest margin, not wanting to strain that welcome he'd been given, and thinking ahead to dinner. There was a pot of marinara sauce on the stovetop that was emitting a very tempting aroma.

Katherine, perhaps not as stunned by the awesome butter as he was, ate with a little more restrained appetite. She and Darlene chatted animatedly, catching up on the weeks since they'd seen each other, and making Will feel welcome to join the conversation whenever his mouth wasn't stuffed.

When they cleared the dishes, Katherine invited Darlene to join them on a hike she'd planned. She was taking him to Black Creek Forest, she said, to walk down to the Hudson. Will didn't even have to fake sincerity when he nodded that Darlene should join them.

They piled into his truck and spent two hours hiking through old woods, spotting lots of deer and little orange newts that had a tendency to dart suddenly across the trail, causing Katherine to give a little squeal. Midway through the hike, they rested on a log with their bare feet in the Hudson.

Will was very content as the women kept up their chatter. Katherine held his hand when the trail was wide enough for them to walk alongside each other and leaned into him while they sat at the river. Apparently, at least these limited PDAs were acceptable.

Darlene's uninhibited friendliness had taken the edge off his anxiety. That lasted well until shortly after they got back from the hike. The three of them sat on the front porch with another round of iced tea. Occasionally, one of the women would go in the house to "check the sauce." Will had walked off the bread by now and was beginning to think he could volunteer to do the next sauce check.

Any hopeful pleasure he took in that thought smashed to smithereens when a small hybrid pulled up to the house.

The tall, lithe man who moved with graceful ease from the car to the porch embodied an entirely male beauty and elegance. Here was the source, Will saw immediately, of Katherine's height and stylish flair.

He wore it entirely naturally and it suited him well. He eyed Will carefully as he strode to the porch, but he went first to his daughter and hugged her warmly. Then he went to his wife and kissed her. It was more than just a peck—he put some attention into it. Inside his head, Will lifted his brow. On the surface, the pair seemed ill-matched, but there was obviously some heat there.

Then the man faced Will and gave him a good looking-over before he extended his hand. Will nodded and put his hand out, not the least surprised by the testing strength of the man's grip, though determined not to be intimidated by it. "Mr. Noble."

"Will. I'm sure my wife has herself on a first-name basis

with you already, so you'd better call me Elliott else I'll appear stodgy."

Will nodded again and only just kept himself from saying, "Yes, sir, Mr. Noble." The man had a strong hint of British in his speech that Will hadn't known to expect. The careful, and not the least covert, challenging evaluation of him he had fully expected.

On some unspoken cue, the women moved together just before the more or less subtle male posturing got awkward. Darlene instructed Elliott to have a seat while she poured another glass of tea. Katherine prodded Will to a wood-slatted swing that was set at an angle at the edge of the porch. He felt substantially less comfortable holding her hand in front of her father than he had in front of her mother. But, with Elliott watching with hawk-like awareness, he wasn't going to let go either.

He briefly debated about whether Katherine's unguarded support of him was a sign that she was concerned about his ability to cope with the situation, even wondering if the fact that they'd stayed out-of-doors was a manipulation to keep things easy for him. But he hadn't any particular sense of scrutiny from her—she didn't seem to be carefully watching him—and it was very clear that this was an outdoors family. Certainly, the front porch was an oft-used extension of their home. And an end-of-day sit out here appeared entirely normal.

Mentally, he shrugged, figuring stressing about it was neither necessary nor helpful, and decided to relax—to the extent that he could. And if Katherine wanted to hold his hand in front of her father, well, he wasn't going to complain.

Apparently, Elliott wasn't one to change out of his work clothes, and Will suspected this—and loosening his collar— was as relaxed as he got. On another man, the clothes might have appeared casual. But the creases in the chinos were sharp, the button-down shirt was still, at the end of a day that had presumably involved some physical work, neatly tucked and wrinkle-free. The shoes were well-polished butter-soft leather and, at a guess, cost the equivalent of Will's entire year's worth of footwear. If not decade.

There was no sign of a farmer here.

Elliott watched his wife as she brought him the tea, and

Will saw a caress of fingers as she handed it over. When she sat next to him, their glasses were in their outside hands and between them, their free hands clasped briefly.

"You're police, Will?"

"Deputy sheriff," he answered, and settled in for the duration.

There followed an interrogation worthy of the Inquisition, if perhaps not *quite* so hostile. Darlene or Katherine would occasionally shush Elliott, but their admonishments never had a lasting effect. As far as Will could tell, the only things that made an impression on Elliott were his relationship to the artist of Fergus Weaves and reference to his grandmother's Georgetown gallery. It was only Darlene who got all hot about him being buddies with football star Leet Hayes.

Luckily, the inquisition had about wound down by the time they all got to the dinner table, and so Will was able to enjoy an extremely satisfying meal. As the mother of two sons, Darlene cheerfully took his appetite to be a testament to her cooking skills, which it was. He tried to ignore the way Elliott restrained himself, even going so far as to decline apple pie for dessert. The man might be brilliant in his way, but he was an idiot when it came to food.

In fact, Will would have had to struggle to find something to like about the dude, except that his wife and daughter obviously adored him, and the feeling was clearly mutual. Evidently, the two women conspiring to tease him out of a mood that threatened to be dour was nothing out of the ordinary. Darlene kept his wine glass filled as well, and that more than anything may have accounted for the increasingly friendly atmosphere as the meal progressed.

Nonetheless, it was a fine thing to have Katherine alone again, beside him in the truck as they drove up to their lodge. And even better when he got their luggage—his overnight bag, her three cases—into their room.

He kept a hard gaze on her as he put a match to the wood already laid in the fireplace. And still while he walked around the room, shutting off lights. When there was nothing but the fire casting dancing flames of light and shadow on the big bed in the center of the room, he slowly stepped to her. By this time, she'd begun to look a little nervous.

As she should.

Nervous and, he thought, hoping, a bit excited.

When he got to her, without touching, he backed her toward the bed. He stopped when he got her there, watching the glitter in her eyes, the pulse jump at her neck, the catch of her breath.

"Don't move," he said. "Don't move at all until I say so."

He took a couple steps around her and turned back the covers on the bed. Then he went back and stood in front of her.

He looked down at her breasts, covered just by a layer of cotton and the thin, clinging bra she wore under it. He'd checked that out several times during the day, though not too much in front of her father. Waiting, he stood and watched until, with a little catchy thrill in her breath, her nipples tightened for him.

He lifted both hands and put the backs of his fingers against her, making a vee of space for the hard little buds to poke through. Then he squeezed his fingers closed to pinch, and used this thumbs to rub her nipples. He pulled a bit, lifting her breasts up toward him while he continued to rub her.

Her breath shuddered out and then quickened in moaning little pants. He watched her eyes nearly roll back, glazing over a bit as he increased the stimulation, thumbing harder at her nipples.

She rocked just a little, steadied only by his hold on her. He gentled his actions a bit, loosening his hold on her nipples, caressing, massaging her breasts. Then he slid his hands to her waist, slipping his forefingers under her top to stroke her skin. When her breathing settled a little and her gaze cleared, he lifted the top to take it off over her head.

The bra was fine, translucent silk. He could see the hard, upthrust nipples, darkened by his use of them, and the dusky color of her areolas.

He took a good long look, muttering out a little hum of appreciation.

Abruptly, he pushed the fingers of both hands down the front of her shorts, just to either side of the fly. She startled a bit and he gave her a minute to feel the heat of his fingers against the smooth flesh of her belly. Without warning, he grasped the fabric and tugged up, pulling the thick seam up into her center. She gasped and swayed a little, a movement that increased the friction right where it counted.

Using the grip he had, he pulled her close, bringing her pelvis against his hard length. He held her there, then thrust his tongue into her mouth. She opened for him and he delved in, exploring her, tasting her, while he rocked against her.

After a very nice bit of that, he loosened his hold and set her back down. He unfastened the button of her shorts and lowered the zipper. He took a good look at the undies peeking out—a little swath of the same pearl silk as her bra— while he kept up a little tugging action with her shorts, rocking her against him, before he slid them along her hips to the floor. He had her step out of them, slipping her sandals— flats, but still strappy and sexy—off at the same time.

He filled his eyes again. The soft, translucent silk of her thong caressed her, giving little glimpses of heaven. He dropped his head nearly to her shoulder as he took advantage of the view and caught the scent of her skin, maybe even a little scent of her arousal.

Holding back his own shudder of desire, his gaze wandered back up—slowly—to hers. Keeping the contact there, he stepped closer until he could feel her breath mix with his. He cupped her ass with his right hand and squeezed, bringing her close against him again. Then he twisted his hand into the back of her thong and pulled up hard at the same time he went back to her nipple with his left hand and gave it a good pinch.

Katherine cried out. Will took her mouth and her cries turned to moans that mixed with his.

She was close to coming, just with tension of her panties against her center and sawing up her ass, and the pressure of his erection rubbing against her. He loved how hot she got, how responsive she was to anything he did to her.

But he'd been waiting for three weeks and he wanted to be filling her, sunk deep into her, when she came. So with a regretful moan and one last hump against her, he set her back. He slipped the straps of her bra off her shoulders, pulling them down her arms so the cups followed, catching at the tips and then letting her breasts spring free. He reached behind her, making sure to chafe his shirt against her distended nipples while he took his time releasing the hooks of the bra. He took it from her and dropped it to the floor while feasting his eyes on her bared breasts. Then he did the same with the thong, sucking a little bruise onto her hip before soothing with his tongue as he bent to slide it off.

He stood in front of her again, touching all his favorite spots with his gaze before he looked into her eyes. He took her hand, curled her fingers over his, and brought them to his mouth.

Katherine was working hard to steady her breath when he took her hand.

She'd almost come twice already and she knew that he knew it.

She loved his lovemaking. Any touch—his gaze, his mouth, his hands on her—could have her moaning. And wet. He played her like he knew every intimate potential for arousal, like he owned every one. He drove her like the pleasure he gave her was his too, every bit equal in measure.

And it was, she was sure. He loved driving her up and then sending her over or leaving her hanging, wanting. She knew he loved the power of it, the control he had over her. He ruled her passion, provoking and inciting, or restraining, toying with her as he pleased.

Her body belonged to him. It was gratifying to him, she was aware, that at least in this one realm, she was completely at his mercy. He couldn't control her commitment to her work, her life in the city. But when he touched her like this, she was his.

It made her breath catch at times. It put just a little fear into her. But when he looked at her with such wanting, such determination—well, there was love in it, too. His heart was there. For her.

She wouldn't be afraid.

He held her gaze as he took her fingers to his mouth. He kissed them, rubbing his lips over them, between them. He suckled and then scraped with his teeth. Then, still watching her, he used his tongue. He probed and delved, sliding into each little crevice. And his eyes told her he was thinking of touching her, tasting her in just this fashion in other places.

A shiver slid through her. Her nipples, already furled,

tightened further. The coil of heat that centered low in her core threatened to break free.

Will, watching her, clearly knew it. With one last stroke of his tongue, he let go of her hand then lifted her and laid her back on the bed. He stood looking at her for a long moment before her took her legs, bending her knees out, pressing open.

His gaze was centered there then, at her opening where she was wet and swollen. She saw his nostrils flare and was sure he had the scent of her.

Katherine was entirely vulnerable, exposed, as he stood there fully clothed. Her breath shuddered out and a spasm of excitement coursed through her. Of its own accord, her body writhed, opening itself more for him, summoning him.

He cast a hot look at her breasts and then her eyes before taking his attention back to her center. Staring only there, he lifted his shirt and pulled it over his head. He stood a moment longer, letting her look her fill of him—the sleek, hard muscles of his abdomen, the smooth swell of his pecs topped with flat, coppery nipples, the bulge of his biceps. The rapid lift of his chest that signified his own intense excitement.

Slowly, he unfastened his shorts and released himself. He was hard, hugely swollen, a glint of moisture already at the engorged tip. He held himself, stroking, as his clothing fell to the floor.

He crawled onto the bed, his knees placed to open her legs further, as far as they would go. Then he put one hand on the bed at her shoulder, holding himself above her. He leaned forward, using his hand to move himself to her wet opening.

He watched her eyes again as he stroked over her. Their moisture combined to make a slick path as he rubbed against her—at her opening, along the sensitive edges, then over that inflamed bud at her center.

Then back to her opening, where he pressed in, stretching her, forcing her to accommodate the full breadth of him.

His breath was harsh now, rapid. His eyes blazed. At her shoulder, his hand curled into her hair, pulling it tight until she arched up against him, tilting herself to receive him. He pushed into her, linked to her gaze, watching her eyes as he took her. They both let out a hoarse groan at the exquisite, almost painful balance of invasion and acceptance.

He filled her slowly, taking his time with every inch, pausing along the way to watch her reaction, relishing, savoring. Securing his claim, declaring his ownership.

His determined breach of her was deliberate body-and-soul-piercing torture. She was stretched, burning, giving way to his width and length. The friction as he pressed in caused her to shudder, the sensation acutely raw and gripping.

Tears filled her eyes, brought by the incredible sexual stimulation and nearly unbearable emotional tenderness. Her breath was unsteady, coming in broken gasps.

By the time he'd fully seated himself, by the time she'd accepted all of him, taken him deep into the keeping of her body, he'd come down onto his elbow. He held just over her. His eyes, heated and intense, searched hers, emitting the same extreme of passion and emotion that she felt. He brought a hand up and took a tear with his thumb. He rubbed it over her lips and then took it from her with his mouth.

He kept his mouth pressed against hers, open in a harsh grimace so their breath could ratchet in and out. He palmed her breast, rubbing, catching at the nipple.

Then he moved inside her once, flexing to stimulate her with one subtle, grinding stroke. That was all it took. She was already coming when he started thrusting, wild and lost. She lifted up to meet him, taking him. He curled over her, clenching all around her, his strength surrounding, containing her.

She couldn't come down from it. Her first orgasm rolled into the next, stronger yet as he pounded into her, possessing, pushing her to give over. She cried out, her body shuddering out the intensity of it.

Still he wasn't done with her. Hoarse, rough words of passion encouraged, demanded more. He slid an arm under to take her up, gripping her bottom to hold her, forcing her acceptance. He drove into her, fast, hard strokes.

She came again, flying apart. He was with her this time, spasming hard, emptying into her. He clutched at her, muscling her roughly against him. He growled his climax, long and brutal, into the mattress beside her head.

Katherine was just barely aware of it, soaring, taken as she was with her own ecstasy. But she heard him, felt the fierce shudders of his body, knew it when he filled her with his semen.

They were a long time coming down. Aftershocks continued to quake through them, surges of lingering pleasure. Their breathing eased, losing first the jagged edge and then the gasping urgency. She could feel his heartbeat and hers, the rapid pace of each gradually settling in union.

Will stayed over her even then, stayed inside her. His relentless stroking of her gentled to soft caresses. He turned his head, resting near her shoulder, and turned hers to face him. He slid his hand down to touch the backside of her hip, rubbing his fingers over the patch there.

"I want this off."

Katherine quirked a brow. Will watched her steadily, appearing undaunted by what her father termed her royal manner.

"No," she said. "Marriage first."

"Fine," he said, without a nanosecond of delay. "When?"

She had both brows up now. "That's a proposal?"

He lifted over her again, held her face with one hand. He was hard inside once more, though he didn't seem to pay any more attention to that than she intended to. "Katherine. I fucking love you. Where do you think I'd want to take this?"

She kept her gaze calmly on his. "Oh, good. The first man to offer a proposal and it involves the word 'fucking.' Be still, my heart."

Will's gaze was amused, but his thumb slid along her chin so he could hold her with more intent. "First and last," he said bluntly. "You going to bust my chops about this?"

"Apparently so."

He grinned widely then and flexed into her.

"Don't even think about it. Get off me, Hunter."

He chuckled and rolled off, but came back to tuck her against him.

He wasn't chuckling in the morning when she woke with his erection pressing against her bottom. He was rubbing moisture into her to ease his way. Only—not *there*.

His touch was just a little more stimulating than she'd have expected. "That's not going to happen, Hunter."

He pressed a bit into her, not just his finger now, and she didn't hold back a nervous moan. His breath was at her ear. "I think it is, Noble."

He went a little further and she gave a small shriek. "Will!"

"Trust me, sweetheart." He rolled them over so he covered her. Conveniently, he'd tucked his hand so his fingers pressed right against her center. He moved them a little and scraped his teeth along her shoulder. "Relax, baby."

He worked his fingers against her some and then said it again.

She took a shuddering breath and did what he asked.

He went in deeply. The yelp she gave, a mixture of panic and excitement, seemed to electrify him. "Christ, yes, Katie." He grunted, rough and eager, and brought his fingers hard against her.

She arched, moving a little away from the strong stimulation of his fingers. But that brought him further into her, an even more unnerving sensation.

He apparently liked that a lot. "Yes, Katie. Yes, yes. Do that. Do it."

And she did, pushed by his entreaty, driven by his sharp passion. She rocked her pelvis, the small movements making the most of his eagerly working fingers and giving just the tiniest bit of friction where he'd penetrated her. He stayed nearly still inside her, letting her control the motion there.

In just moments, they were in a frenzied craze. Katherine whimpered, panting hoarsely as he drove her up. She screamed when he brought her to orgasm, thrusting hard into her just twice as he joined her in release.

He slipped gently out of her, soothing with soft strokes of his hands, sweet brushes of his lips.

Katherine had sunk her teeth into a pillow. She still clutched it in her fist. "That's not happening again."

"I know," he said as he continued stroking. "I could tell you didn't like it."

"You shut up."

She felt the rumble of his chest against her back. But he did what she said.

They had a good two days, though to Will's mind their weekend had peaked just a few minutes before they left their bed on Saturday morning. He'd watched her carefully when they'd gotten up and showered. Not wanting to push his luck, he refrained from molesting her at all in the shower.

He could tell she was aware of his watching her and figured she knew he was a bit nervous about it. He hadn't exactly asked—or been given—her permission for that bit of morning experimentation. He knew not every woman was, uh, receptive.

He had plenty of time to watch, given the difference in their respective times from showered to dressed and ready for the day. He had no complaints, though—her rituals of girl stuff before and while she dressed made for easy entertainment.

Even better, when she was done, she came over to where he rested back in a big leather armchair, feet up on an ottoman. As he eyed her, still a bit uncertain, she climbed over him, resting a knee on either side and settling right down on top of his suddenly very interested, blind-stupid dick. She squirmed around a little, making matters worse. His head was pretty sure it was just a tease, but his dick was naively ever hopeful.

When she got him stirred up to her satisfaction, she leaned in for a long, wet kiss. Lifting up, she put her hands over his. Determined to prove himself smarter than his dick, he'd doggedly kept them on the armrests of the chair. She curled her fingers into his until their hands were loosely joined.

"You can trust me to tell you in a way you won't mistake if you push me to do something I truly don't want. Understand?"

He looked back at her. Nearly unable to speak, he nodded. "Thank you," he managed, grateful to his toes and unembarrassed by the gravelly catch in his voice.

She nodded too, and patted his shoulder before she got up. "I'll count on the same from you."

She grabbed a sweater and tied it around her shoulders, then leaned against the door waiting for him.

It took a bit. He closed his eyes and took several deep breaths while the wicked thrill her words had sent directly to his dick, totally bypassing his brain, dimmed down enough for him to stand.

He followed her out the door and eventually took charge. They shopped for picnic supplies then took a rental canoe across a high mountain lake, finding a secluded spot for their meal. They'd both brought books and they lay in the sun reading for a long while. Katherine rested her head against this belly and didn't entirely shoo him away a little later when he slipped his hand inside her bra to toy with her nipple. From outside her shirt, she simply pressed her hand against his to still the action of his fingers, keeping his hand there, filled with her breast. Apparently, she was pleased enough with that. Like he did, she figured out how to turn a page one-handed.

Her book lay on her belly and he thought she'd fallen asleep when she turned her face enough to press a kiss into his shirt. "Have you reconsidered then, about fathering children of your own?"

As he'd driven away from Maine, he knew he'd changed his mind. Eli Benson had given him hope. "I guess I have."

"That makes me very happy."

He set his book down too, and tangled his fingers in her hair. "I thought it would."

She patted his hand—the one still tucked under her shirt, like the conversation was over.

Leave it to her. "You understand why, don't you?"

"You trust me."

"To corral my crazy genes in our children? Yes, I do."

"You're very sensible." That, apparently, was all that needed saying.

They ate a quiet dinner at the lodge before finishing their day with a hike up the ridge behind it to watch the sunset. As darkness fell, he led her back to their room. By firelight, he made gentle, exquisitely tender, *traditional* love to her.

For Sunday morning, he'd found a local club that had an open racquetball court at eight o'clock. Katherine whined and moaned all the way there, then abused her girl-status on the court again. She was quick and agile and overall pretty good, but took unfair advantage of his unwillingness to risk hurting her. He'd pull a shot; she wouldn't. That made his victory over her the sweeter, though It was a perilously close finish.

When he got her to the shower in their room, he was not so gentlemanly about it. She watched the determination in his eyes with a certain amount of humor and trepidation, clearly seeing—and accepting—that it was payback time.

That bout, he won hands down.

Highly satisfied, he could hardly regret it when it came time to head back down the mountain. *Hardly.*

Will enjoyed the afternoon and evening with Katherine's family much more than he ever would have guessed. The brothers, Pierce and Chris, each had a wife and three small kids, all of whom were indulged and adored. It seemed the Nobles had a particular knack for cheerful, loving relationships. The single niece clearly had her father, uncle, and grandfather all neatly wrapped around her pretty little finger. He looked at Katherine, imagined the daughter she would give him, and all but shook with fear. She caught him looking, correctly interpreted his dread, and laughed in the face of it. And then again, out loud, when he mouthed the word, "*bitch*" at her.

He was more comfortable with the five boys and especially enjoyed the two who were near in age to Leet and Sadie's Tino. All the males save Elliott, who, Will figured, had too much dignity, joined in a rowdy game of what the Nobles called obstacle course croquet. Elliott and the women watched—and jeered—from the porch. Will was severely handicapped until he figured out that rules were meant to apply only to others, that those under eight years old didn't have to care about whose turn it was, and that it was never safe to turn your back on a Noble.

Great name, he muttered, for a bunch of untrustworthy, bald-faced lying cheats. But he said it with two or maybe three boys hanging off his back, and no one seemed to take him too seriously.

Elliott unbent enough to run the grill and did a truly masterful job of it. Over time, Will had to admit he came to enjoy Katherine's father. He was much more relaxed with his sons and grandchildren around. At the least it gave him something to do besides frown at Will for the things he was imagining doing to the man's precious daughter. Through it all, Darlene shone with maternal pleasure and pride that very generously included Will.

Aside from Elliott at the grill, the women had done all the cooking—Will noted with a heavy sigh that Katherine was given a pass on that—so the men got clean up duty. Much like the croquet, Pierce and Chris had their own rules about it, which pretty much meant that Will got the worst of every job. He stopped his knee-jerk objections after the second time Chris looked back at him and said, "Hey, you're doing our sister. You're lucky we don't just beat the crap out of you." Will had no response to that, and forbore even from inquiring which army would be involved. Very loudly anyway.

Will and Katherine and her parents finished the evening on the front porch, killing the last bottle of wine. The kids had been herded into their respective car seats by their parents and the young families had driven off to homes that were no more than twenty minutes away. To Will, it had been a remarkable family experience, one that had him hoping for just such a thing in his future.

There was just that one issue.

He broached it sidewise, and while Katherine was safely in the house.

"Darlene," he said, after they'd all just enjoyed the quiet for a while. "You're a stellar cook."

On the swing with Elliott, Darlene just smiled and hummed a little.

Will continued, picking his way. "I wonder if that's something—"

Elliott let out a snort, an undignified sound Will had to attribute to that last glass of wine. "Sorry, buddy. Katherine has no cooking skills whatsoever."

Will tried to take it like a man. "None? She made me—"

"Hollywood eggs? She's a one-dish wonder. It's not like Darlene didn't try. We finally had to accept that, in this one regard, the girl's out and out retarded."

Will would have laughed if it wasn't his gastronomical future at stake. And if he hadn't heard soft footsteps behind him.

"Will?"

Schooling his face into innocence, Will looked up over his shoulder. "Yes, darling?"

He didn't appreciate that next snort from across the porch.

"Is my father talking about me?"

"Uh, gosh, no. He was mentioning—and I don't even know why, 'cause really we were just talking about, uh, goats—but, anyway, he said one of your sisters-in-law, I forget which, isn't that much of a cook."

Elliott was doing such a poor job of smothering his laughter that Will silently cheered when Darlene swatted him.

"He said retarded."

"No, I think he said her cooking was not highly *regarded*."

"Um-hmm."

Will kept a straight face, but was highly relieved that he could see the twinkle in his woman's eyes. And then, right in front of her parents, she sat down on his lap. All he could do was circle his arms around to secure her.

He was speechless when she planted a long kiss on him.

"I made you eggs, didn't I?"

It took him a moment to find air. "They were delicious."

She kissed him again and would have used tongue if he'd let her in, which he didn't. "You have no complaints, do you?"

"Not one."

"Um-hmm."

She settled her head onto his shoulder while Will carefully met her father's eyes. All Elliott did was roll his eyes and shake his head in pity. Will thought he imagined the fake cough covering the word, "whipped."

There wasn't a lot more conversation, but still it was a relaxed, pleasant time as dusk came. Will enjoyed the cooling of the air, the night sounds, and the feel of Katherine in his lap.

When it was well dark, Elliott and Darlene got up. Darlene kissed both Katherine and Will goodnight then the two left the porch holding hands.

They were barely in the house when Katherine spoke. "They're going to have sex, you know."

Will so didn't need to know that. "Well, how long do they usually take? 'Cause we're staying out here until they're done."

"We can tell when the headboard stops banging. Though sometimes they go two rounds."

"Katherine Noble, you shut the fuck up."

The Nobles had made up the bed in Pierce's old room and, though Katherine insisted that was just for show, Will tucked himself in there nice and neat. There was no way he was sleeping—or anything else—in Katherine's room with her father just down the hall.

They'd had a whispered conversation about it outside his door. He won, telling her that when their own daughter was fifty years old, a married mother and grandmother, and came to visit, her husband was still going to sleep in the basement.

But he noted it wasn't a total victory when his door quietly opened and then closed. Katherine—for who else could it be?—climbed onto the bed. And onto him.

She settled over his thighs, then leaned down and ran her lips over his chest.

"Get out of here, Noble."

He worked his jaw as she ran her tongue over him—very near his nipple.

"Are you naked under there, Will?"

"Katherine, we are so not doing this in your father's house."

"Hmm."

She did something more with her tongue, and he was sure he could feel her naked breasts rubbing over him down a bit lower. His dick, covered just by a sheet and having no more sense than usual, celebrated.

"Katie, I mean it. Go away."

But she slid the sheet down and ran her tongue lower. Mind of its own, his dick cheerfully twitched up to greet her.

She lifted the sheet entirely out of the way and then paused—in admiration was what Will chose to assume. But the pause lasted, so he bunched up the pillow under his head so he could see what was going on.

She was waiting for him. The long lines of her body, the luscious curves of her breasts, and the intense glitter of her eyes were just visible in the dark that was broken by slats of illumination through the shutters from the yard lights out front. As he watched, she arched back and lifted her arms to slide her fingers through her hair, a movement that put her breasts on display for him. It sent a sensual, sexual thrill through him and pretty much ended any objection he had to what she had in mind.

Keeping her gaze on his, she leaned down and slowly slid her tongue along his whole length, ending with a curving stroke along the swollen head. Will's spine flexed, his hips lifting to seek more. A hard groan pushed through his throat. It was a hot turn-on to watch what she did with her tongue. But he thought better of it. He took the pillow over his head and pressed his face into it. This was no time to howl out his satisfaction.

It was its own kind of excitement to be blind, just waiting for what she would do next. She didn't keep him waiting long.

She took the head fully into her mouth, stroking with her tongue, milking him with suction. Then she slid down his shaft, wetting him and taking him further into her mouth. He took her head in his hands when he reached her throat, thinking to just hold her there for his pleasure. But she kept going, taking him deeper and, suddenly, his hands were urging her down further.

As deep as he could be, he flexed a little, withdrawing and advancing just the smallest amount. Her tongue stroked his shaft with the movement and her throat squeezed down on his head.

"Fuck, Katie." He held her, making small pumps into her mouth, his pace quickening. She made matters worse by doing all kinds of naughty things with her fingers. And thumb. In abject gratitude, he lifted his thigh up between her legs to give her something to ride.

It didn't distract her much. She kept working him, sending him over. His hips moved like pistons now and he growled out her name with every four-letter word he knew.

"Baby." He was so close, unable stop those lightning-quick small strokes. He tried to lift her head. "Baby, I'm going to come."

With her own passionate groan, she batted his hands away and took him. He groaned into the pillow as his body arched up, the strength of his orgasm nearly taking him off the bed. And, bless her, she stayed with him, even as he pulled out and took her into his arms, rolling over to pant out the end of it into the mattress.

"Katie." He rubbed his face into the bed, still clutching her close. "Fuck, Katie. I think you killed me."

Her head was in his chest, her arms tight around his waist, and he felt her chuckle. He couldn't believe what they'd just done in this house. "Fucking proud of yourself, aren't you?"

She just laughed some more, reasonably quietly.

"Fucking bitch."

She kissed his chest. "Are you about done using that word?"

He took a deep breath. "Not quite the fuck yet."

He rolled onto his side and slid down so they were face to face. They smiled at each other—she, proud of herself, and he in fucking humble gratitude. He stroked his thumb along her cheek. "How the hell do you know how to do that?"

"Advanced courses in human sexuality."

He *humphed*. "Where, in hooker school?"

"What do you know about hookers?"

He grinned. *His girl.* "Just things I've been told."

He held her some more, still grinning, no doubt foolishly. It didn't matter, though. His heart was as happy as it could be.

After a while, he turned her over onto her back. Being the man, he knew what he had to do. And knowing the woman she was, he started by putting his pillow over her face.

He noticed that she wasn't as careful with it as he had been. It didn't matter so much initially, when he was just getting things warmed up with little sucks and bites at her nipples. But when it got more heated, when he was sucking and tonguing and fingering her everywhere, she was entirely too careless about it. At the crucial moment, when his mouth worked her and he had one hand busily stroking fingers in and out of her, he reached up with the other to muffle her with a little more effectiveness.

She bucked against him as he drove her to a prolonged orgasm. When it finally ended, she collapsed back on the bed and he let her knock the pillow away.

She'd barely—or not even—caught her breath when she started bitching. "You nearly smothered me."

"I didn't do to you anything I didn't do to myself. It's not my fault you're a screamer."

She swatted him for that. "But you were in no danger of smothering yourself. You knew when you needed air. I could have died."

"I'll remind you. *Father*. Down the hall. Not a court in the land would convict me."

"Men or women on the jury?"

"The men would acquit me. The women would just be grateful and shut up."

She'd caught her breath enough by that time to laugh. But he noted that she did otherwise shut up. They held each other close, Will nuzzling into her, thanking the gods for his good fortune. He lingered on the edge of sleep until he felt her slip out from his arms and leave the room.

$\mathscr{C}$HAPTER SEVEN

September came and nearly went. Will was pretty happy with the progress Katherine and he were making in their relationship. They'd taken their last handful of weekends together down off the Hudson. It saved having Katherine making the drive all the way up to Vermont, and he'd come to actually enjoy the time they were with her family. They'd spent some time separately with each of the brother's families. Will had a good time hanging out with the men—football was involved, either playing or watching or, best, both. The wives treated him with a mild, innocent flirtation that annoyed their husbands and, much for that reason, entertained him.

They had a memorable weekend when the senior Nobles had gone down to the city, and Will and Katherine had their house to themselves. Will wasn't sure he'd feel comfortable making love there even when the parents were gone. So they worked up to it by starting out on the front porch swing. At first, he just rocked them lazily while Katherine, still in one of her hot little business suits, straddled him and he had her filled with his rampant hard-on. The sound of an occasional car passing by on the road—out of sight but for a couple quick glimpses through the trees—put a little edge of thrill to it. It wasn't long before there was nothing lazy about it. When it was done, Will was overcome with admiration and appreciation for whatever workman had gotten that swing so securely attached overhead.

After that, the only room that Will insisted was still off limits was Darlene and Elliott's bedroom. Will enjoyed the long, lazy times they had in Katherine's own bed, but what she let him do to her on the kitchen table brought him to his knees. He'd never eat a meal there again without thinking of it. And getting hard.

But now it was getting to be leaf season, so Katherine was coming up to his place. Will had gone into work early that morning and spent a couple hours with Jeff at the board. He'd set up a map of the lake and tagged it with identifiers of ownership back when Truman Hunter had come to town. Then they'd spent time on the phone—Will talked with his grandmother and a couple of friends of hers from back in the day. Jeff had talked with Justice, and the FBI, and a retired secretary who'd worked in the Senate office of a gentleman from Vermont.

As the hours passed, the two men were more and more certain they knew who had killed Truman Hunter.

Jeff called a halt. He knew Katherine was coming up, and he said both of them should take a spell to follow the trail again, confirm the facts, tease out the links. It had been thirty years, he said. Next week would be soon enough.

On another day, Will might have argued. But he had things to do.

Katherine enjoyed the drive up. The further north she'd come, the more lovely the leaves. Central Vermont's leaf season was two or three weeks ahead of the middle Hudson area and was well worth the drive. She was gratified by the way Will had been accepted into her family and happy that he seemed so comfortable with them. But she was more than looking forward to being with him again in his place, alone.

And was glad to see, as she pulled up behind his truck, that he'd beaten her to his home. She hooked her feet back into her heels—they looked very good with her skinny designer jeans, but they weren't great for driving in. She got out and stretched, taking a couple deep breaths of clean fall air. She made sure the skimpy silk top she wore settled just so over her breasts, then loosely draped her Fergus shawl over her arms.

She opened the gate and followed the path around to the side entrance to the porch. Will had been busy in the gardens, she saw. Compact, well-groomed mums abounded in cheerful color, Japanese maples were lit up in reds and oranges, and fall roses still added romantic touches.

She was surprised that Beowulf hadn't already bounded out to greet her. And was curious, when she got to the door, to see a sign saying, "*Come in.*" It was printed in a pretty font on rich, cream-colored vellum. A small satin ribbon of deep violet was tied in a bow at one side.

She opened the door and stepped inside. The stairs going up to Will's apartment were filled with flowers, a pot or vase on nearly every step. Streamers of ribbons, violets and lilacs and pinks, draped down from the ceiling, a kind of suspended fall of confetti. A few steps up, there was another sign, vellum, violet bow, with a single word printed on it, propped against the riser. Above that was another, and another, and another.

The first word was, "*Katherine.*" That was followed by, "*will,*" and then, "*you.*" After that, the word "*please*" was repeated up several steps. She took a few of the steps up, to the middle of the pleases. She stopped there and looked through the confetti forest up to the top of the stairs. Will stood there, dressed in a suit, looking handsome and serious as sin. He had his hand on Beowulf, who suffered the ignominy of a bow tied to his collar. When Katherine met the dog's eyes with sympathy, he whined out a little complaint.

Where she stood, a length of violet ribbon was suspended from a bouquet of ribbons and bows attached to the ceiling. Where it ended, just in front of her eyes, it was looped through a ring.

The ring was of white gold with a double row of diamonds circling the entire band. The stone was a large, round, radiant cut diamond. It was set within a square diamond halo that had a small emerald in each corner.

It took her breath away. She was almost afraid to touch it.

On a deep breath, she let her eyes follow the rest of the signs up the steps. Near the top, one sign said, "*marry.*" The next said, "*me?*" On the last step, the word "*me*" had been crossed out and a crudely lettered "*us?*" had been placed, with a dog paw print alongside.

Katherine laughed, though it was a bit watery. She looped a finger around the ribbon holding the ring—her ring—and brought it with her as she climbed the last steps.

Then she stood in front of Will, nearly his height in her

heels. He put his hands on her hips and held her steady while their gazes connected. When she smiled, his eyes lightened a little.

He reached out to take the ribbon and released the ring from it. He lifted her left hand then stopped to look at her. An eyebrow lifted as he waited.

"Yes, Will." She looked into his eyes, seeing his love, feeling nothing but confidence and endless happiness. "Yes, I'll marry you."

His eyes glittering just like the diamond, he slid the ring onto her finger and then lifted her hand to his mouth for a kiss. That gave her a good opportunity to see how truly excellently the ring sparkled on her finger before he wrapped his arms around her and drew her in to take her mouth. It was long and sweet and a really, really good kiss. When Beowulf whimpered again, they both reached down to pat his head.

Will's eyes were dark when he drew back from the kiss. "I love you, Katherine. You make me a very happy man. I promise I'll be grateful every day of my life that you let me make you mine."

Katherine slid her hand along his neck, savoring his heat and the strong pulse she could feel there. "I love you, Will. You make me very happy, too. I will love you every day of my life."

He smiled at her, a very powerful, satisfied maleness in his eyes. She was nonetheless distracted by the glitter of her diamond.

"I *love* this ring. And that was the best proposal I've ever gotten."

Will kissed her again. "I'm glad you like the ring. And, fuckin'-a."

They both laughed as he lifted her up in his arms and swung her around, much to Beowulf's noisy excitement. When he set her back down, he stroked his hand over her ass and gave her a good squeeze. "Love these jeans, but you need to dress up. We're going out to the Arlington for dinner. We have a room there for the night."

Katherine kept an arm slinked around his neck. "Oh, yeah? Any special room?"

He held her close, massaging her bottom now with both

hands. "Yeah. A very special room."

"Sweet. I'll need my luggage."

"Of course you will." He enjoyed watching the process as she pried her fingers into the pocket of her painted-on jeans to retrieve her keys.

"I want to shower. I'll be in the bathroom."

"I'll find you."

He did find her. And watched her, first as he stood at the bathroom door and then when he sat in the easy chair in his bedroom while she readied herself for him. About a dozen times he figured he could take her without having to do anything more than open his fly and let nature take its course.

But it was a very, very satisfying thing just to watch. Knowing that she was his—tied up and committed now, promised. Knowing that she was thinking of him—he saw it as she glanced at his reflection while she applied totally unnecessary stuff to her eyes, as she touched herself with dabs of equally unnecessary scent. In places he never would have thought of, but wouldn't *stop* thinking of now. As she faced him and stepped into a little strapless sheath of gleaming copper—with absolutely nothing on underneath.

As she turned around to show off that slit in the back that she'd know would drive him crazy, flaunting it when she propped her feet, one at a time and lingeringly, on the bed and leaned over to fasten the straps of her heels. He didn't miss her siren's smile when the urge to stride over and shove some body part up into the piece of heaven that was no more than a millimeter from view tore a pained grunt from his throat.

It was wicked, feminine foreplay and he loved it.

And he would pay her back for it soon.

Finally, she stood before him, apparently ready but for the strand of sparkles she dangled out toward him.

He took a good long moment, looking her over.

Then he stood and stepped close. He took the necklace and circled his finger. She turned around and lifted her hair, sending a waft of that sexy perfume his way. He draped the jewelry around her neck and worked the tiny clasp. When he was done, he moved closer and slid one hand around her front. He ran it under the top of her dress, slipping in to cup her breast and then tease her nipple. With his other hand, he found that ever-loving slit and pushed through it. He pressed his middle finger into her core, tight and just a little moist so he had to work his way in. Her breath caught as he diddled her a little, chafing inside until she heated up and his finger moved easily.

Then he slipped both his hands out and patted her ass. "Ready to go, babe?"

"Uh, sure."

It took her a moment, and her first couple steps were unsteady. Payback was sweet.

Then, sherpa-like and totally unashamed of it, he grabbed his tote and her three bags. There was absolutely no point in asking her to lighten it up.

Their weekend passed too quickly, as usual. Will was entirely satisfied with the success of his proposal and their night at the Arlington. They'd had a great dinner with champagne and violins—he thought Katherine had been pretty charmed. He knew the memory of his finger inside her had stuck with her through the dinner. He could see the heat in her eyes, and she did things to him with her heels under the table that were against the law in several states. He blessed her when she'd asked their waiter to have her selection for dessert— some chocolaty sin deal—sent to their room later.

It was a close enough thing as it was. As he rushed her up the stairs to their room, his hand was not all that discreetly under her dress, readying her. Then, the moment he had the door closed behind them, he had her up against it, lifted so he could fill her. She wrapped her legs around him, he tore the bodice of her dress down, and they both had what they wanted.

Later, they took their time about it, a number of times, on that big bed where they'd first had each other. There was more champagne, and chocolate, both of which played feature roles as they pleasured each other.

Their lovemaking was needy and hot, edgy as it always

was. But there was more, too. Their gazes held until those last exquisite, ravaging moments. Their touches were warm, gentle until driven to rough by brutal need. Their coming together was tender until it clenched into frenzied tumult by mad passion.

Through it all, the gazes, the touches, the coming together were all laced with promise, with commitment. Will held her, joined with her, and knew the meaning of being one with her. He touched her face, brushed the smile of her lips, lifted the diamonds of tears from the corner of her eyes, and worshipped her. Owned her, and was owned. Felt both in his soul.

They had Sunday breakfast with Elyse and Jeff and announced their engagement. They called Katherine's family and shared the unsurprising news. Before she left that afternoon, they spoke with Will's grandmother, agreeing to spend their next weekend together with her in Washington.

Letting her go, watching her drive away, was no easier than it had ever been. But he knew she left thinking about their future and committed to it. He knew she would start disengaging from her clients in the city, making a plan to settle them with other therapists, finding replacements for her at her volunteer jobs, looking into possibilities for work nearby.

She and her mom had talked engagement party and wedding plans. He let them have at it. He had what he wanted. She was his, and she'd be here, living with him, by the first of the year.

"The old man had a stroke. He's at Washington Hospital Center. I'm guessing it doesn't look good."

Will turned his eyes from the board to look at Jeff. It was Wednesday, and they'd had nothing but bad news all week.

Jeff and he had talked with FBI Special Agent Tillison out of Rutland in Jeff's office on Monday afternoon, laying out their case. Will had hovered, increasingly frustrated, pointing out documents, shaking papers in front of the man's face. More than once Jeff had stood and, with a hard hand on his shoulder, directed Will back to his chair.

Tillison had oozed skepticism. It was what Jeff had warned Will to expect, but it rankled nonetheless. He'd take it back to his supervisory agent, he said, and that guy would take it to the SAC in Albany. If he bought it. Then to the Director—if the SAC bought it. That would be in Washington and would take time.

On Tuesday, against Jeff's advice to refrain from nagging, Will called Rutland. Tillison wasn't in the office and, *no*, he'd learned, rudely, after the third call, he hadn't seen his chief yet. And wasn't sure when he would get around to it.

"Shit," Will said now. "They had a big party for his ninetieth this summer. He's not likely to outlive a stroke."

"Or be able to talk to us if he does."

Will looked at his soon-to-be stepfather. He and Katherine hadn't been the only ones to have an announcement to make on Sunday. Jeff had beamed and Elyse had smiled shyly, looking comfortable if slightly embarrassed with Jeff's arm around her. Will had lifted his mother from her feet in a hug while Katherine had hugged Jeff. The awkwardness when they'd exchanged hugging partners and Will faced Jeff was, *well*, passing at least. All in all, Will was very happy about the arrangement. He liked Jeff without qualm and was grateful to him for the happiness—and move toward normalcy—he'd brought Elyse.

"We'll have to go directly to Simon."

Simon Carlson was the son of Theodore Carlson, a downstate New York Congressman who had parked himself on the House Appropriations Committee for fully half a century. Old Teddy was the one in the hospital now.

Thirty years ago, the Carlsons had owned a house on Lake Fairlee.

Jeff sat and propped his feet on Will's basement desk. He shook his head. "We can't do it yet, or maybe not at all. We have to let the case work its way to FBI headquarters. It's going to be theirs to manage. If they buy in, they'll be the ones to interview Simon, and they probably won't invite us."

"Oak Mill Basin had a kidnapping, rape, and murder. It's our case, too."

Jeff nodded. "You're right, and that will get us something. But it's going to be a freaking political hot potato and, trust me, we're gonna want to stay out of that mess."

"Simon's got money and he likely has some of his father's connections. He could hear about this and be gone before it even makes it to D.C."

Jeff met his gaze steadily. "That could happen. You should be prepared for this not ending the way you'd like."

"Shit." Will leaned back and propped his own feet, looking at Jeff across the desk.

"You should think about that." Jeff's gravelly voice was quiet, his dark eyes searching Will's. "You need to think about what would satisfy you."

Will was pretty sure that Simon Carlson had tortured and raped his mother, had tortured and killed his father. What would satisfy him? The man's very slow, very painful death. Short of that? Will really couldn't imagine it.

"I don't want a long, ugly trial." Will could imagine that, and he knew he wouldn't be able to stomach it. Aside from all else, he wouldn't want his mother to have to survive one more bitter, ugly thing.

Jeff had told Elyse that they'd opened the case again.

It was more than Will could do. He knew she knew what Jeff and he were doing, but he couldn't talk to her about it. He figured she would understand the need in him—that it was about himself as a law officer, himself as a son.

He just didn't see how she could understand, as a mother, his doing something that was likely to be very painful to her. When she'd suffered enough pain in her life.

As always, she was stronger than he gave her credit for. When he'd seen her next after Jeff had talked to her, she'd held him in a particularly long hug. He knew, in that, she'd given him her blessing for the work he was doing. Still, they never spoke of it, and Jeff said he hadn't talked to her any further about it either. She was fine, she'd said. She didn't need to hear any more.

Will looked back at Jeff a bit longer. By rights, given his history with the case and his current relationship with Elyse, Jeff could claim the lead on this. He was letting Will have it. That was a thing Will appreciated.

What would satisfy him, what would satisfy both men, remained unsaid.

Friday night Will was to work the midnight shift. He spent

the morning working out and taking a good run along his favorite river path. Then he chatted with his landlady, Mrs. Dern, over lunch on the front porch. They'd come to an agreement that pleased them both about his gradual purchase of the house. They had only to have the lawyers put it to paper now, and then weather the storm her children would stir up when they got wind of it.

He spent most of the afternoon working in the gardens, following instructions laid out by Mrs. Dern that they both knew he no longer needed. Then he drove up Fergus Mountain, planning to give Beowulf a run with the dogs and himself a couple hours with Elyse.

He knew it wasn't right as soon as he got there. Beowulf's mother, Lucy, ran anxiously to the truck as Will pulled up. Spinner sat hunched on the front porch, showing nothing of the jubilation he usually displayed when his brother came to play. And Elyse, as reliable in her practice of greeting her son in the yard as Lucy was, was nowhere in sight.

Will took a careful deep breath after he shut down the truck and felt the silence. Before he got out, he unlocked the glove box and took out his side arm, checking it and tucking it into his belt at the small of his back.

All three dogs had run around back to the dog door off the deck and were in Elyse's living room as soon as he opened the door. They surrounded Elyse, who lay on the couch facing the TV that was playing some afternoon talk show.

Elyse watched a couple hours of news nearly every day, beginning with the national news, then the BBC broadcast, and finally, the late local news. It was her main way of keeping up with the world off the mountain.

But she never had the TV on during the afternoon.

And she would never lie on the couch, apparently unaware of his presence, unless something was very, very wrong.

"Mom." He went to her, pushing past the worried dogs, and crouched before her. She was pale but warm. She breathed and her heartbeat, when he palpated her neck, felt normal.

But she was unresponsive.

"Mama."

Her eyes were open, but even when he put his face right in front of hers, eye to eye, she didn't see him.

Will looked at the TV for a minute and used the remote to identify the channel it was set on before he flicked it off. He held his mother in his arms and settled onto the couch, holding her against his chest. Then he called Jeff, using his cell number.

"Yeah?"

"Are you in the office?"

"Yeah."

"I need you up the mountain. Tell dispatch to send an ambulance."

There was a short pause and Will heard the breath Jeff took. "She's alive?"

"Yeah."

Jeff came, looking with sad and worried eyes at Elyse as Will held her. He crouched down, took her hand in his and stroked it, speaking quietly to her, calling her his love. After a minute, Will exchanged a look with him then got up to let Jeff take his place. He left his mother in Jeff's arms and wandered a bit about the house. When he came back from the kitchen, he sat on the far arm of the couch.

"She fed the dogs yesterday, but it doesn't look like she changed their water today. The coffee pot is cold—usually she leaves it on for a cup to take into the studio in the afternoon. She cleans up the day's dishes after dinner. That job was done. But there's no sign that she was in the kitchen today." Jeff spoke, but he kept his jaw pressed against Elyse's hair. "So this happened late last evening. She feeds the dogs before she sits down for the evening news, then has her own dinner."

"Yeah. The TV was on when I got here."

"Congressman Carlson died yesterday afternoon. It would have been on the evening news."

"Yeah. But this didn't happen then. She finished her dinner, did the dishes."

"I didn't think to call her, Will. I talked with her yesterday morning, said I wouldn't see her last night because of the town board meeting. I didn't think about it later, Will. It didn't even occur to me she'd know who Carlson was."

"It's not your fault, Jeff."

It wasn't exactly Will's fault either, but he knew that wouldn't keep them both from feeling responsible for it. And guilty. Will stirred just a little as he heard the rescue vehicle in the drive.

"She saw Simon," he said. "The late local news must have made the connection to the lake house. They might have interviewed him, or shown an old photo."

"Goddammit, Will."

"She'll come back. She's stronger than we think."

Will met the EMTs at the door. It was Denny Rendeau, whom he'd known since high school. Denny had been a tackle on the football team and was still an occasional drinking buddy. He'd last seen him at Leet's wedding.

Denny's partner on the rescue truck was the driver, a guy named Nielson whom Will had run into at a couple of MVA sites. He nodded the two men in. Jeff took over as Denny approached Elyse.

"The event was unobserved. We believe it was a psychological trauma that occurred last night, related to experiences from her past. You know her history. As a young woman, she was in a trauma-induced comatose state for several months."

Denny took her blood pressure, got an oxygen sat reading, and listened to her heart with a stethoscope. "Her vitals are okay." He looked from Jeff to Will. "We'll take her into the med center, let them evaluate her."

Will nodded. "You ride with her, Jeff. I'm going down to Channel 8 in the Junction. Then I'm going to Rutland. I'll find someone to cover my shift."

Jeff nodded. "Try Dick Nolan. His mother-in-law is in town. He'll probably be happy for an excuse to get out of the house."

Will stayed with Jeff and Elyse until they had her secured in the rescue vehicle. After the truck had turned and started its way down off the mountain, he went back to the kitchen. He left enough food and water to last all three dogs a couple of days. Then he got in his own truck and called Katherine.

"I need you," he said. "My mom's in the hospital."

"The medical center?" she asked.

"Yeah."

"I'm on my way. I'll call you from the car."

Katherine found Jeff at Elyse's bedside. She'd been admitted to the psychiatric observation unit. She was in a bed, curled on her side while Jeff held her hand.

She looked peaceful and at rest. There were no tubes, no IV lines. Katherine knew such things would come later, if it came to it.

Jeff looked older by a decade as he stood and kissed Katherine, looping an arm around her even as he kept hold of Elyse's hand. "Thanks for coming, Katie."

"You're welcome, Jeff," she said. "Has there been any change?"

"Not really. I spoke with the doctors in the emergency room. They decided it was best to rule out physical causes, so they did an MRI. That was normal, they said. So, based on her history, they're calling it a dissociative disorder, in response to acute stress." He paused and leaned into Katherine. "That's not the same as a coma, right?"

She wrapped both arms around Jeff's waist. He was an attractive man—smart and caring and, at the moment, lost. "No. A coma is a neurological condition. She wouldn't respond to pain or sound. This is different. This is psychological, a defense mechanism, a way for her to escape a thing that is too frightening, too painful to face."

It was similar to the dissociative disorder often referred to as multiple personality, which was most commonly a response to childhood sexual abuse. But instead of building another personality to help the victim cope, in this case, Elyse just—went away.

"Her doctor said that—that she responds to stimulus. That's good, he said. She walked. A nurse came and walked her to the bathroom. Elyse went with her. But it was still like she wasn't there."

"She'll come back, Jeff. She has you and Will. She won't stay away."

"She can hear us? She hears me when I talk to her?"

"Yes."

"Does it matter? Will it mean anything to her?"

"Yes. It means something, Jeff. She'll know that you love her, that you need her back. That will help her. It will help her be brave."

Jeff let go of Elyse for a moment and used both arms to give Katherine a hard hug. He pulled a chair over for her so they could sit together near Elyse. He scrubbed his hands over his face before he took that still hand again.

"We shouldn't have done this," he said. "We should have left the case alone. There was nothing about it that would help Elyse. We weren't thinking of her."

"Will said the same thing."

He had, stressing about it over the phone as they both drove—she on her way to Vermont, he heading to Rutland to talk with SA Tillison and the chief there. A phone call later, he was going south to Albany. He had the same guilt about it that Jeff expressed.

"You're both wrong," she said. "You didn't make this happen. Will said Channel 8 ran the story last night and brought in the local connection. They showed an old photo of the Congressman and his son taking a boat out on the lake. She saw it, Jeff. She saw a picture of the man who raped and tortured her. She'd have seen it whether you were working the case or not.

"Think of it. If you hadn't been pursuing it, if you hadn't learned what you have about Simon Carlson, you'd be here not knowing what happened. It's better to know—for you and Will, and for her. You'll be able to help her better when she comes back."

Jeff took her hand, too, and brought it over with his to rest on his knee, propped by his ankle on his other knee. "I never know whether to trust you shrink people. I think you'd say that whether you believe it or not. I think you'd say what you thought would make me feel better."

Katherine squeezed his hand. "I would say what I thought would help you feel better, but I wouldn't lie either. I believe Elyse is strong. It's clear she's not as sick—not as withdrawn—as she was thirty years ago. She knows that you and Will will be there to help her face down what Simon did to her. She trusts you—she'll be back soon."

They sat together quietly. A night nurse came, introduced herself, and checked Elyse's vital signs. When she heard the local church bells strike midnight, Katherine nudged Jeff. "One of us should get some sleep." Neither Jeff nor Will had said it, but she knew they would be sure that someone Elyse knew and loved—and who loved her—would be there with her whenever it was that she woke up.

Following her thoughts, Jeff nodded. "Thirty years ago, Elyse's parents and Truman's mother kept a vigil so she was never alone. It lasted for months back then. We'll do the same."

"Will said his grandmother is flying in about noontime. I told him I'd pick her up if he's not back from Albany. I don't think he will be. Do you?"

Jeff squeezed her hand. "My guess is when he leaves Albany, he'll be headed to D.C."

"Because he won't be satisfied with the way the guy in charge there wants to handle it?"

"The Special Agent in Charge. Yeah, I think Will won't be happy with his response. The SAC knows that no one in FBI headquarters is going to want to crash the Washington pomp and circumstance of Theodore Carlson's funeral with an arrest warrant for the man's son. Nobody who wants to keep his job is going to do that."

"Does it matter now, Jeff? Is Simon still hurting women, do you think?"

Jeff watched her for a long moment, thinking about his answer, Katherine figured. Will had not been entirely willing to talk with her about the case. She knew he wanted to protect her from the ugliness of it—and protect himself, too, from the speaking of it. She met Jeff's gaze squarely, letting him know she wanted to hear more, and letting him make the call.

He came to a decision and started speaking slowly. "Serial killers have a kind of natural history if left to it—if their work is not interrupted by arrest or death. Their chosen path is not without risk. Generally, their first kill is unplanned, a spontaneous response to some event that caused humiliation, frustration, or anger. In Simon's case, we think this was Elyse's friend Melissa, who, we guess, rejected him. They get a taste for it then. They think about the sense of power they got from the experience and, often, the sexual thrill. If killers are smart and organized, they begin to develop a pattern that lets them boost the thrill.

"If they're not caught—or killed or maimed by a victim or someone defending or avenging the victim—then they go through a period of time, often a decade or two, that's kind of their heyday. It's their glory days—they've honed their skill, established their pattern, and maximized the pleasure they get from it.

"Then, *whatever* happens—something. They get bored with it. They get older and their testosterone drops, maybe they just would rather lie on the couch and watch TV. Anyway, the theory is, the natural course is that they come to have fewer and fewer kills until they stop. We don't know, but that may be what's happened with Simon. He's been living in the family's Long Island mansion for years now—he appears to be pretty reclusive and entirely law-abiding. All we can say that's suspicious is there's a high turnover of housemaids. I'd enjoy having a chat with a couple of them."

Elyse made a little movement and Jeff leaned forward to stroke her forehead. After a minute, he picked up his story.

"When Truman came up here and met Elyse, the Carlsons owned a house on the lake. It had been in the family for a couple generations. The whole family would come and spend a few weeks in the summer. For the three years before Truman's investigation, Simon started spending time alone there—he'd come up with the family but then stay a while after they left. Eventually, he came up entirely on his own. He spent at least one winter there.

"During that time, after Melissa, it looks like he picked up several girls and young women from around the state. Probably, he brought them to the lake house. Certainly, he killed them. After he took Elyse and then killed Truman, it appears that Simon left the lake house and never came back. About five years after that, he left the country."

Jeff sighed and leaned toward the bed, bringing his hand and Elyse's to his forehead.

"We suspect that he was responsible for some deaths in the D.C. area, and maybe his father realized Simon hadn't given up his hobby. Based on what Will learned from Eli Benson in Maine, specifically his suspicions about the aborted FBI investigation, we figure Theodore Carlson got at least a hint of what his boy had been up to at the lake house. What we know for sure is that Simon moved to Thailand and got set up in a shipping and supply firm that cashed in big on the construction boom there. And his daddy bought him a yacht that he kept harbored there. It was a powerboat, big and luxurious, but not so big that a man couldn't sail it on his own. In a place where the sex trade thrives virtually unmolested, especially back in those days, a man with a good boat can cover up a lot of sins.

"About the same time Simon was exiled, the Carlsons sold their land on the lake. I say land, not home, because they razed the house before they sold. I shudder to think what got buried when that happened." He ran a thumb along Elyse's brow, no doubt thinking of the horrors she'd experienced at that site. "We'll be doing some digging there now." He straightened and looked at Katherine again. "The man is nearing sixty. Maybe the worst he does is peek down the tops of maids in their little black uniforms, or pinch their fannies. But I'll devote the rest of my life to seeing that he pays for what he did here."

Katherine nodded slowly. She knew Jeff wasn't alone in that commitment. And she wondered if he, like Will, expected her to—*oh*, not defend the man, but to look for the explanation, the history behind the man's pathology that might provide some kind of excuse or, at least, an understanding.

They were right to a small extent. Surely, the man had suffered some abuse and it was probably wicked. Such twisting of a personality didn't just arise spontaneously, accidentally. It was made to happen. That was nearly always true.

But they were wrong to think she would be sympathetic to Simon. A person chose his or her behavior. To Katherine's mind, that was the basis for humanity. And for the progress that humans could and should make in the world. One overcame bad experiences. One rose above. The resilience of the human spirit was one of life's miracles.

Jeff seemed satisfied by what he saw in Katherine's eyes. He spoke slowly, intending that she see his meaning. "This is unlikely to end in Simon's arrest. It's more likely, when it's done, that Simon will be dead. It's the only way to be sure it's over."

Katherine understood. At best, bringing a legal case against Simon, even if successful, would cause more suffering. Elyse and possibly others—the families of his victims, for example, would pay a cost. And with the man's wealth and connections, the outcome of even the most solid case would not be certain.

While he lived, they could never be sure that Simon's potential to cause pain—even torture and death—had truly ended. They couldn't be sure that the man would pay for the evil he'd done.

Jeff's telling her this was not a small thing. And, she noted with a twinge in her heart, it was more than Will had done.

She gripped Jeff's hand and kept her gaze hard on his. "If you or Will suffer for how this ends, however it happens, then that gives Simon Carlson one more chance to cause hurt, to destroy lives."

Jeff broke from her gaze to look back at Elyse.

"I mean it, Jeff. Elyse would say the same. She wants you—happy and healthy and *with her*—much more than she would ever want vengeance against Simon. If he's not hurting anyone now, if you can be sure of that, then nothing that happens to him could be worth any risk to you or Will."

"I understand." He looked back to Katherine but didn't quite meet her eyes. "It's a thing we may not agree on. The man lives in a mansion and takes a cruise on his damn yacht every weekend. It's entirely possible that this could end with his sailing off to a content and smug life some place U.S. law can't touch him. I couldn't live with myself, couldn't feel I'd honored my love for Elyse, if I allowed that to happen." He lifted a hand to stop her interruption. "I get that you don't agree, that Elyse wouldn't agree. You're women. There are certain things that men will always see differently."

Katherine took her hand from Jeff's and gripped his shoulder until he faced her fully, eye to eye. "Then you'll have to make sure that neither you nor Will is put at risk in this. However you have to make it happen, you be sure of that, Jeff."

"I'll watch out for Will."

She pushed his shoulder, hard, with anger. "Not good enough. Elyse can't speak for herself now, so I'm speaking for her. You, too, Jeff. You make sure you come out of this okay. Or I'll find a way to stop you."

He lifted a brow, scoffing in a minimalist way.

Katherine refused to stand down. "Isabela Hunter will be here soon. I suspect she's a woman to be reckoned with, and with substantial connections. What do you think she'll make of your stupid, *you're-a-woman-you-wouldn't-understand* argument?"

That brow went up again, though not scoffing now. "You can be tough, Noble."

"And mean."

"I'd rather not go there."

"You certainly would not."

He sighed and watched Elyse for a moment. "I'll do my best. That's all I can say. I'll do my best to keep both Will and me out of trouble." She didn't answer and, after another long pause, he looked at her. "That has to be good enough."

She leaned over and kissed his cheek. "Okay."

"I'm not gonna sleep. You should go to Will's and hit the sack. Bring Isabela here in the morning. Maybe by then I'll be tired enough to fall asleep."

"All right."

Katherine slept for a few hours, waking a little when Will crawled into bed beside her.

Yes, he said quietly. He was going to go to Washington. But it was Saturday. He'd spoken with Jeff and his grandmother and they'd all agreed there would be little to be gained by pounding on doors down there until Monday.

He'd go, but now, he just wanted to sleep with her.

He brought her close against him, flexing his arms strongly around her, nestling his head into her until, she knew, he was breathing in her scent. Katherine dozed while he slept soundly for two or three hours. She knew he was waking when she felt that certain twitch against her bottom. She turned over, pushed him a little onto his back, then climbed up and slid down onto him before he was even all the way awake.

He hummed and brought his hands up to gently grasp

her waist. "Will you marry me?"

She ran her lips over his chest. "Asked and answered."

He lifted his head a little to look. "Oh, Katherine. It's you."

She chuckled but nonetheless punched his arm.

A little laugh rumbled through his chest and she felt it everywhere. She raised her head and waited until he lifted again to meet her lips. It was a warm, slow kiss and she felt the way it stirred his interest deep inside her.

"I love you, Kate," he said when he broke away for just a breath. "Can I wake up this way every day?" His touch grew stronger, both hands on the small of her back, pressing her down a bit to receive him as he flexed up into her.

She wrapped an arm around his neck to hold him to her mouth and felt the friction of his chest against the sensitive points of her nipples. He was filling her, stretching her now, making her body weep with need.

"Yes," she said, tightly gripping him. "After every night you come home to me."

He missed one stroke and pulled back to look at her. His eyes searched hers as he began moving again, more gently for a few strokes. He watched her and she looked back at him, waiting for him to see her meaning.

He moved in long, slow strokes now, deliberate, making the most of each movement. He grasped her hips, grip bruising hard, and held her against the strength of his thrusts.

Her breath was scattered, whimpering out when he pushed roughly into her and held. "Not one day of my life," he said, eyes just as hard, just as determined as the way he held her, penetrated her, "will I fail to do everything humanly possible to come home to you. Never. I will never fail in that."

He arched then, flexing up off the bed as he began thrusting hard and fast. Her knees lifted from the mattress so her own weight added to the force of his grip to bring her down on him, to permit him maximal access, full penetration, the complete taking of her body.

Katherine arched too, flexing back to accept all of him, opening herself to the overwhelming stretch and stimulation of her most sensitive tissues. With his grip on her hips, he ground her against him at the peak of each thrust. She began to come, moaning and shuddering, seizing and crying, as he drove himself into her.

When she'd reached her limit, when she thought she could take no more, he rolled with her. Up on his knees, spreading her legs impossibly wide, he pounded his orgasm into her with harsh, urgent, commanding breaths. She wailed as she peaked again, a hoarse, pleading sound that had him gentling, soothing even as he finished flexing and emptying into her.

Still filling her, he sank down next to her shoulder and held her head in his large hand so they were face to face as their labored breathing slowly settled. He watched her for long minutes. "I'd give my life willingly, darling Katherine," he finally said, "for you, for our children. But I want the life we have together, the life we'll make." He shook his head. "I won't give that up easily. I won't let go of it without the worst sort of fight."

"You're going to try to stop Simon."

His hand on the side of her face pressed against her. "I *am* going to stop Simon. And when I'm done, I'll be coming home to you."

He kissed her, gently, with love.

He leaned back to watch her a little more. "And I'll expect you to wake me up in exactly this same way."

Katherine took some breaths, trying to give him the faith he was asking for. After a while, she managed a small nod.

"Say it."

"I'll wake you up just like this."

"Fucking-a." He grinned through another kiss. And, hard again, he pushed into her a little too. "My girl."

Katherine was to spend Sunday morning with Elyse. She and Will had met his grandmother together and then the three of them sat with Elyse while Jeff finally slept Saturday afternoon. He'd come back and taken the night shift again.

It had been a great pleasure to get to know Isabela, and to watch her and Will together. Isabela was an elegant woman, flawlessly dressed in a classy ruby-red, tailored, feminine suit. She was trim, petite with perfect carriage and a surprising strong, no-nonsense demeanor. She spoke loudly and bluntly to Elyse, informing her that she would need to come back from the little "break" she was taking quite soon. The woman clearly adored Will—her gaze and her voice softened when directed at him—though Will appeared completely un-aware of it. And she said Katherine's name with a lovely, sexy French accent.

She seemed to have taken Katherine's measure quickly and given her unspoken blessing. Katherine knew that was no small thing.

In the morning, Will and Jeff were to meet Isabela for brunch at the Arlington. It was a strategy session to develop Will's game plan for his trip to Washington. After the meet-ing, Jeff would sleep and Isabela would sit with Elyse while Katherine and Will had some time together. Then Will would leave in the evening, overnight at Isabela's home, and start tracking down his quarry on Monday morning.

Before he and Jeff left for their powwow, Will made the suggestion that Katherine should go home later in the day, go back to work. She rejected the idea immediately and would have even if his reluctance about it had not been so transparent. His relief at her refusal was obvious. She'd ap-preciated the hug he gave her for it, but that didn't save him a small lecture about how counterproductive it was to ask her to do something he really didn't want her to do.

"Relationships 101, dude," she'd said, and she felt his grin against her temple.

"Just so I have this straight," he countered. "I shouldn't ask you to do what *I* don't want you to do, but I can ask you to do something *you* might not want to do? 'Cause I've no-ticed sometimes that turns out all right."

She lifted her head to look at him, feeling a bit of a blush, and mostly suppressing her own grin. "Yeah, *for you.*"

He nipped at her lip. "I'm sure there's some rule in your relationship manual about not acting like you weren't satis-fied when really you were."

She shook her head. "I've never seen nothin' 'bout that," she drawled.

He kissed her goodbye while they still chuckled.

She spent an hour pleasantly enough with a novel, and another, better one visiting with Sadie, who took a break from her shift on the labor unit downstairs. When Sadie left, she opened her phone to catch up on her e-mail.

Katherine looked up sometime later when she heard the

door to the room softly close. A man stood there, his back to the door. He looked at her and then beyond to Elyse.

Katherine understood who he was and stood to place herself between him and Elyse.

He was a big man, nearly as tall as Will. His frame was large but not noticeably filled in with muscle. His face was tanned, handsome, smooth. There was no shadowing of beard. His hair, slicked back from his forehead, was thinning and, to Katherine's eye, expertly, expensively colored to hide any hint of gray.

His gaze came back to Katherine. She made no effort to disguise that she knew who he was or why he might have come.

"I saw the sheriff leave with Isabela and Will. I thought I might have a moment alone with Elyse." He spoke softly, almost gently, in the best well-bred tones. "I must admit I'm disappointed."

He wore a skillfully tailored double-breasted navy jacket that aimed, she thought, for debonair but landed barely short of making him look like he was a captain just stepped off a cruise ship. Either way, the effect was ruined when he eased his hand from his pocket enough to let her see a small pistol. It was sleek and silver. Like him, an unsettling juxtaposition of elegant and lethal.

His hand slid back into his pocket and he left it there, the threat hidden but not gone. "If you would be so kind as to step away from the bed. If I thought that hand behind your back was searching for the nurse's call light, there would likely be unfortunate consequences."

Katherine stayed where she was, but she brought her hand forward and crossed her arms at her chest. Inwardly, she cursed. Next time she had to defend someone against a psycho, she was going to make note ahead of time which button would bring help.

"An acceptable compromise, though you'd do better in the future to follow my instructions more precisely. Now, my dear." He spent a moment appearing to consider his options. "I believe we can safely allow you to leave this room. Why not step out for a cup of coffee or take a moment to use the restroom? You can say you let your guard down for just one unfortunate minute. I'll never gainsay you."

"Alternatively," Katherine said, "I believe we could allow you to leave. You can pretend you were never here, and I will never gainsay *you*, Mr. Carlson."

"Ah, I see you have the advantage on me. That does change the nature of our relationship, Miss...?"

His eyes had darkened when she used his name. His displeasure was a small victory for her, and one she couldn't regret. But she knew how to deal with psychopaths. They always liked thinking they were the smartest one in the room.

"Noble," she said. "Katherine Noble. It won't help you to harm her now. They know who you are. They've taken the case to the FBI."

"Oh, I'm woefully aware." He waved the concern away. "It's unfortunate, but so much a likely eventuality that I am fully prepared for a life lived well elsewhere. Given my, shall we say, colorful history, such a need has not been unanticipated. So, Miss Noble, you are, perhaps..." He made a point of noting her left hand. "Deputy Hunter's fiancée?"

She nodded.

"How charming. It appears he has a better discrimination for diamonds than I'd have given him credit for."

"I'm sure he'll value your good opinion when I tell him of it."

He looked at her, assessing. "Very clever. The hint of mockery in your words was barely noticeable. You appealed to my ego, at the same time planting in my head an image of a future moment when you and the deputy will be together again. Almost masterful."

Dammit. The trouble in dealing with psychopaths was that they often *were* the smartest one in the room.

Carlson took a long moment sliding his gaze along her body. It made her skin crawl and she just held back a shudder. "You've hardly the look of law enforcement about you. What's your training?"

"I'm a midwife." A good lie, she thought. It came quickly to her, she could remember it, and it brought with it an expertise that would not threaten him.

He lifted an eyebrow and kept it raised as he studied her.

He was reconsidering now, she thought. He was wondering if he'd read too much into her comment about Will. Maybe it had been simple sarcasm. She'd do her best to keep him thinking that, keep him expecting less of her.

His gaze finally left her for Elyse. "She's looking right at me. Does she see me, do you think?"

In her head, she chided him. That was too unsubtle. He was a man who would always assume to know more than others. He didn't rely on someone else's opinion for anything. So he wasn't asking for an opinion, but trying to elicit a professional assessment.

He wouldn't get it from a midwife.

"She looks the same all the time. If you stand in front of her, it's like she sees you. Sort of like the photo of Elvis my older sister kept on her wall. No matter where you stood, it seemed like he was looking right at you."

Her adversary let out a little snort. "What is your sister's name?"

"Sadie."

"That sounds a lot like the midwife, Sadie Benjamin, who recently married Leet Hayes, the deputy's best friend since high school. I understood her to be an only child."

Shit.

"How about you tell me who—*what*—you really are, and I promise I'll walk out of here without hurting Elyse."

Shit, shit, shit. But, okay. "I'm a PhD psychologist. And you mean without hurting Elyse anymore."

He shrugged—the distinction was of no consequence. "Forensic?"

"No."

"Too bad. That would have made this more fun."

This? She was pretty sure she didn't want to know.

"Well, it appears that Elyse is gone from me again. You mistake my intention, thinking I mean to harm her. I can't even really say why I came. It's just I've always kind of enjoyed the thought of her here, damaged and yet thriving in her own little way. I take credit, you know, for her success as an artist. It was I who brought them into her life, after all—Truman Hunter and, through him, Isabela. Without me, she'd still be obscure, with her back bent by the farm work her crazy parents had her doing."

He moved closer to the bed, circling in such a way that, when Katherine took two steps back to keep her distance, his body was between her and the door. He spent a long moment gazing down at Elyse.

"Anyway, I had an urge to see her before I left." He looked up at Katherine. "Unfortunately, I find I must leave my home, my country. I thought, maybe, to..." He looked at Elyse again with a kind of yearning that made Katherine shiver. "She was such a tender innocent, so unsullied. She was mine before he came. I watched her. My love for her was pure, chaste. She disappointed me gravely once Truman Hunter walked up Fergus Mountain. My love turned dark then, though still it was pure. Not chaste any longer, but wicked, depraved, even. I had no idea of the exquisite pleasure waiting once she turned from me. I almost could think she'd done it purposefully. That maybe she knew what her faithlessness would unleash. That it was what she intended after all, what she wanted.

"I suppose it was foolish to think I'd find some trace of her essence today, of her love."

It was several moments before his gaze came back to her, and Katherine hoped she'd contained the shakes his words had generated. She forced her eyes to meet his, but she knew her face was pale. She felt cold, despite the way she gripped her arms around herself.

She shook her head. "Elyse knows what love is. She knows it has nothing at all to do with the perversion you inflicted on her. The torture."

"She knows what love is? You mean—ah. The sheriff, perhaps?"

Katherine mentally kicked herself, but couldn't take back what she'd given away.

"Yes, I can see it. Young Jeff Anderson poked around so ineffectively while I enjoyed testing the limits of my passion with Elyse. It quite added to my amusement. Still—" He reached down and stroked Elyse's hair, forcing Katherine to suppress another shudder. Then he spoke sadly. "She disappoints me yet again." He spent a long moment looking out the window on the far side of Elyse's bed before he brought his attention back. "I'll need you to come with me, Katherine."

She shook her head.

"I'm afraid I must insist." He moved his hand in his pocket again.

"Where?"

"Well, to the parking garage, to start. I have a perfectly hideous rental car there."

She watched him, silent.

"Ah, and then where? Well, we have a bit of a drive. I brought my yacht up the Hudson. It's a lovely day for a sail. By nightfall, I'll be out of U.S. waters."

"Good," she said, with emphasis. "Enjoy your trip."

His face hardened, losing all its false affability. "You'll come with me, my dear, and cooperatively so. Otherwise, I'd have to put an end to Elyse's latest betrayal right now, and you would be of no further use to me either. Come."

Little choice, Katherine meant to take a step forward, but dread weighed her down, cementing her feet to the floor.

"Come," he said again. "I haven't hurt anyone in years. Not to speak of anyway."

That qualifier really didn't help.

He lost patience. Stepping close, he took her jacket from the back of her chair. Though it was warm out, she'd brought it in anticipation of the likely unevenness of hospital air conditioning. He used it against her now, putting her arms through it, and then placing his hand under it on the small of her back. His hand with that sleek, menacing pistol.

Simon Carlson, serial killer, rapist, and torturer of women, gripped her elbow with his other hand and pushed her toward the door. She made a grab for her purse—cell phone within—but he deliberately blocked her movement. Her feet were working by the time they reached the door and he waited, nudging cool metal against her back, until she opened it.

He walked her through corridors, into and out of an elevator—during which time he politely greeted staff and other visitors and referred to her as "darling"—and out of the hospital. He pushed her into the rental and went around to sit behind the wheel. Leaning toward her, he ran the gun softly along her neck then used it to turn her face to his.

"This car is equipped with door and window locks. The windows are tinted. You're obviously a bright young woman. You may find some opportunity to signal for help or try an escape. I advise against it. There is a small chance that, in the next several hours, I may find it of benefit to have you alive. I weigh that against the potential nuisance it is to keep you with me. It's a fairly delicate balance. Keep that in your thoughts when you consider your behavior."

"I should believe you'll let me go once you've secured your escape?"

"Most likely, to be honest, it will be a matter of expediency. I'd get no, shall we say, *thrill* from killing you. Mind, when I can consider myself safe, we'll be in international waters. How well do you swim?"

She turned away from the sick smirk he gave her. That was okay. He'd let her know she should take whatever chance she found. She watched out of the corner of her eye as he tucked his pistol into the cubby by his left knee.

As he drove—out of town, along the highway—he spoke grotesquely, though he seemed to mean to reassure her. He'd stopped taking his pleasure from women sexually, he said, several years ago. He'd gotten careless once in Thailand. The brother of a girl he'd been "enjoying" had found him and, with a knife, had removed his ability to achieve "ultimate satisfaction" from women. He'd been "gelded," he said. He'd tried, he assured her, to find comparable pleasure by employing other means. But he'd never achieved true "fulfillment." After a time, it no longer seemed worth the cost and effort. These days, he said, he was forced to settle for small thrills.

"I assume that explains why you can't keep your house staff."

He looked at her, a malicious flicker lighting his eyes. "Ah, Katherine. You are so sweetly judgmental." And he related then, pridefully, his little ingenuities. A crack discreetly placed in a wine glass so it shattered when it was removed from the table, blood and red wine staining white linen. An accidental pinch of fingers when he asked for help searching in his desk drawer, and the drawer unexpectedly closed. A chance bump or brush of bodies that involved a squeeze of the breast or thrust of his finger up under a skirt, so fleeting, so innocent seeming that it could almost have been imagined. His pleasure in watching as suspicion developed, awareness of the purposefulness behind the little "accidents," the gleaning of his twisted gratification. The cultivation of nerves, a jumpy, fearful anticipation of his next subtle strike. Always watching, pushing, to see when the limit would be reached. To see how many times abject, if insincere, apologies could reassure. And then to guess how big a raise of an already magnanimous salary it would take to overcome a bit of self-centered squeamishness.

Katherine watched out her window as he spoke—the fall color that surrounded them as they drove south through central Vermont the smallest bit palliative to the horror of his words. She thought of Will and wondered what the chances were he'd be able to help her. He would move heaven and earth. Would that be enough?

Will's grandmother had a long history in Washington and she brought to the table—an elegantly set one at the Arlington Inn—ideas and connections that never would have occurred to either Jeff or him. Nonetheless, as the three of them spoke, it became more and more clear that there would be no satisfactory solution coming from that direction. Will knew it, he knew Jeff knew it, and Isabela was beginning to understand it.

At one point, she just stopped in the middle of a sentence and looked at the two men. "You have no hope, do you, that this monster will be made to pay for what he's done?"

Jeff looked to Will to answer, and Will hesitated. His grandmother was from a different time, an age when the government and its institutions accomplished good, sometimes nearly miraculous things. Her outlook, her kind of admirable, optimistic faith would be lost to her if he answered honestly.

While he considered, she drew herself up. "Don't think to coddle me, young man. We are talking about the man who killed my son, unspeakably tortured his innocent young wife, and left a dreadful legacy for my only grandchild."

That set Will back. A warm kind of soldiering on was the feeling he'd always gotten from Grandmère. She'd survived a war that had destroyed the family, home, and dreams of her childhood. He'd always gotten the sense that a life lived without a father, with a pathologically reclusive mother, and hampered by a somewhat limiting psychological handicap was nothing to garner particular sympathy.

Who knew?

She took a breath, conscious, no doubt, that her voice

had risen to an unladylike pitch. "It also has not escaped my notice that he had protection. Someone—likely more than one someone—abused his power to shield a villain of the worst sort. That man, those men—they're from my town." She sipped from the delicate china that held her tea. "That particular travesty was no doubt instigated by Theodore Carlson. If there is any justice in the hereafter, he already burns in hell. But there were certainly others who bent to his will, unethically and criminally so."

A neat, tastefully polished nail traced the pattern of the white damask that covered their table.

After a few moments, she looked directly at Jeff and then at Will. "I shall leave it to you two men to determine the proper disposition for Simon Carlson. I think my energies are best spent sniffing out some dirty linen in Washington." She delicately patted her lips with her napkin, tidying up her thoughts as well. "I always liked Eli Benson. He was a good friend to Truman. I'd enjoy a chat with him. It's been too long already."

Jeff and Will exchanged a look across the table. Jeff's face very likely mirrored his own. There was no mistaking the implications of Isabela Hunter's words regarding the "disposition" of Simon. That didn't mean they weren't shocking.

They left the inn together. Will had borrowed Leet's high-end sedan—he hadn't been about to transport Grandmère in either his pickup truck or Jeff's sheriff's unit. Jeff would look in on Elyse then go home to sleep. Isabela would stay with Elyse while Will took a couple hours with Katherine. She'd insisted when they'd laid out a plan for the day. A newly engaged couple needed time alone, she said. They had plans to make, after all. That last was said with a distinct twinkle in her eye.

Plans. *Yeah*. He and Katherine would make plans.

Will stood in the door of Elyse's room. Isabela and Jeff had walked in ahead of him and their sudden silence, but for his grandmother's quick, audible intake of breath, stopped his next step, nearly stopped his heart. He put a trembling hand out to steady himself against the jamb and closed his eyes. He was entirely certain that what he saw when he opened them would shatter him.

He forced himself to look, taking in the whole tableau with one single scan, in that hyper-processing mode that cops frequently described. And knew relief and despair in a single flash.

There was no sign of harm to his mother. She lay in her bed much as they'd left her. The room held no blood, no evidence of struggle.

Just—no Katherine.

Isabela, face pale, stepped close and put her arms around him. Jeff looked at him for a moment, his jaw grimly grinding. As if from a distance, Will watched as Jeff turned away and scanned the room, slowly now.

And could do nothing but keep watching as Jeff went to sit in the chair that Katherine had pulled close to Elyse's bed. He bent to retrieve Katherine's purse from the floor and rifled through it. Grim-faced, he looked up at Will when he pulled out her cell phone. He followed the movements and knew in a corner of his mind that Jeff was checking her phone for recent activity.

Then Jeff came and stood in front of him. "Can you work?" he asked, and wasn't gentle about it.

Will straightened and took a deep, bracing, and not entirely steady breath. "Yes."

"She sent out an e-mail about two hours ago. She hasn't been on the phone since early this morning when she talked with Sadie."

Will nodded. They'd just gotten out of the shower. It had been a long, very satisfying shower. And even then, he'd nearly succeeded in talking her back into bed. "Sadie's scheduled to work a shift today. She was going to come up when she was free, spend some time sitting with Katherine."

Jeff stepped away and pressed a couple buttons on Katherine's phone. "Missing," Will heard, and other words he didn't want to listen to.

Grandmère put her hands on his cheeks and brought his face down to hers. "Talk to your mother, Will," she said. "Ask her to tell you what happened."

Will stared back at his grandmother, but followed her with his eyes when she turned away. She went to Elyse.

"Elyse, dear," she said. She spoke brusquely, with no

sympathy. She took Elyse's hand and patted it firmly. "Will needs to talk to you. Your son needs your help. Sit up, dear. You're safe here."

Tougher than she looked, Isabela sat at Elyse's head and started pushing her up. Jeff watched for a moment before he went to help, bringing Elyse around so she was curled into his lap.

"Elyse, sweetheart."

Will stood, stunned, as Elyse lifted her hand to twist her fingers into Jeff's collar.

"Mama. Mom." He went and knelt before them, putting his fingers onto Elyse's cheek, turning her toward him. "What happened, Mom? Where's Katherine?"

She looked at him, seeming for a change to actually see him. Then she closed her eyes and pressed her face into Jeff.

"Mom," he said, louder now. "Did he come here? Simon? The man who hurt you?"

She moaned, a pitiful sound.

Will and Jeff looked at each other in silence. Finally, Jeff stroked his hand over Elyse's hair. "Sweetheart, tell us. You can. You can tell us."

Tears streaming down her cheeks, she lifted her face to Jeff's. After a moment, she looked at Will and grasped his hand. "He had a gun." In words whispery soft, she spoke to both of them, looking at one then the other. "Down the Hudson, he said. Lovely day for a sail."

"Elyse." Jeff took her face gently in his hands and kissed her.

"Go," she said to him. She looked at Will and squeezed his hand. "Go."

Sadie was there then, dressed in blue scrubs. She took hold of Elyse while Jeff stood and then settled in next to her. She nodded, asking no questions as Will fired instructions at her. "Call Leet, tell him to get my pickup down to the sheriff's office *now*. Then Canaan. Tell him to gear up."

She had her phone already in her hand when he glanced back from the door. The three women sat there, his mother propped between Sadie and Isabela, holding hands on either side.

CHAPTER EIGHT

Will drove the sheriff's unit while Jeff used the radio to contact the office and put people to work there. As they sped, lights flashing, to the Basin, they learned that the Hudson was navigable up as far as Albany. To go any further north required the use of the canal system and locks. They got the model of Simon Carlson's yacht, its hull identification number, and its name. They learned that the *Indulgence* was moored at a private marina just south of the port of Albany. It had been there since early morning.

Will was busy with his own calls. By the time they got to the office, Canaan, gear loaded, was already on his way to Albany. And he'd used Katherine's phone to have her brothers getting ready to launch Pierce's speedboat into the water near the Mid-Hudson Bridge.

It was a three-hour drive to Albany. Katherine and Simon could be as much as two hours ahead of them, or as little as a few minutes. There was no way to know how much time had passed between the moment Simon took Katherine and when Elyse brought herself to tell them about it.

Simon would keep his vehicle at or near the speed limit. Will had a flashing blue light; he wouldn't have to. There was a chance he could beat them to the boat. Was there a way Simon could get there faster? "Plane?" he asked loudly. "Helicopter?"

Jeff paused and glanced at him, interrupting the report he was receiving from staff in the office. "We can get there just as fast by car. It would take too much time—making the arrangement, pre-flight check, transportation to and from airports. We can run hot, travel faster than—"

Will waved his hand to cut him off. "No. I mean Carlson. Could he have air transportation waiting, already set to go?"

Jeff nodded and pointed to a deputy to a check the local airport. Then he looked at Will. "You head out when you're ready. I'll call Albany and get them to the marina. I'll be right behind you." He turned and started taking the stairs to his office two at a time before he stopped. "Wait!" He came back down and met Will. He put both hands on Will's shoulders and faced him, looking hard into his eyes. "You be careful, Will. Katherine is smart and strong. We'll get her back and she'll be safe. Don't take any chances. I'll have to face your mother when this is over. No chances, you hear?"

Will turned his head away. "He's got Katherine. I'll do what I have to do."

Jeff shook his shoulders, pretty tough for a smaller guy, and nudged Will's chin back, not gently. "Not good enough. You remember your mother, and the harm this guy has done. Don't let him hurt her more. You're not alone, Will."

"Katherine is."

"We'll get her. She's strong. We'll get her. You hear me?"

Will heard, but didn't have it in him to answer. He nodded once and stepped back. He went out the door and nearly ran into Leet who was on his way up the steps. Leet put his keys in Will's hand and turned to walk with him back to his truck.

"My rig's got more power," he said. "I almost brought it, but I figured you'd have gear in your lock box you'd want."

"Yeah," he said. His handgun. His shotgun. His Colt AR-15. "Thanks, man. I left your keys with Sadie. One of the deputies inside will drive you to the hospital."

"I can go with you."

Will opened the door to his pickup, but took a deep breath and then looked at Leet before he climbed in. For a man with social anxiety, he was blessed with some damn fine friends. "Thanks, Leet. But no. If you'd check in on my mom, that would be good."

"Sadie and your grandmother are still with her. Sadie says your mom wants to go home. Your grandmother has the doctor coming in. If he says it's okay, I can take her and stay with them until you get back. That all right?"

"Yeah, man. Thanks. Jeff's inside. Will you let him know?"

"You bet."

He gripped Leet's hand and clapped his shoulder. "Thanks, bro," he said, in a heartfelt acknowledgement of real fraternity.

Leet heard it. He met Will's gaze hard, nodded, and then motioned him on. He stood back and watched as Will pulled out.

"We're not going to the Hudson, are we?"

Simon had stayed on I-91 through southern Vermont and most of Massachusetts. He wasn't making any move to turn west toward the Hudson.

He gave her an approving little grin and Katherine wanted to slug him. Like his approval of her "cleverness" would ever mean anything to her.

"So you're a liar in addition to a self-indulgent, sadistic rapist and murderer."

Now he wasn't so approving. His happy face fell and his pouting meanness shone through. "I said my yacht was on the Hudson." His tone was snide, biting, and superior. "I said it was a lovely day for a sail. Both true."

"Ah," she said. "Then just a deceiving, self-indulgent, sadistic rapist and murderer."

That might have been too much. His face was grim now. He reached into the cubby and came out with his pistol. He switched it to his right hand and pressed it against her temple. "Don't speak again."

They drove that way in silence for fifteen miles until they reached a rest area. He exited the highway and pulled over along a curb at the margin of the parking lot, far from other cars. With the gun, he motioned to her door. "Put your forehead against the window," he said.

Katherine complied. She heard him move, then felt the gun press against the back of her skull. In her mind, she whispered a litany of apologies. To her parents, her brothers, her niece and nephews, her friends. But mostly to Will. This would hurt him the most. He would feel responsible.

"Are you sorry for your words now? For your smart mouth?"

"Yes," she said. "I'm sorry." She was, in fact. Endlessly

sorry. Not for offending him, but for carelessly baiting him. Tears slid down her cheeks.

"What will you do, hmm? What would you offer to keep me from blowing your brains out right here? Right now?"

Katherine took a quivering breath. "Anything, Mr. Carlson. I'll do anything you want."

"It's a bit late to pretend respect, isn't it?"

He was still talking and that gave her a glimmer of hope. She tried to think rationally about what words, what attitude would feed his ego and keep him satisfied. "I apologize for taunting you. I've been foolish because I'm—I'm afraid. I will do anything you ask."

"Will you kneel over me and take my dick in your mouth, let me push it down your throat?"

Katherine closed her eyes and eased out her breath against a shudder. "Yes."

"Will you spread your legs for me, let me rub you with my fingers, let me push them up your cunt until you come?"

She thought of Elyse and what she had endured. "Yes."

"Ah, Katherine. You will let me do whatever I want with you? You have lost all pride?"

For her family. For Will. To save them from standing at her grave, *yes*, she would do anything. She made herself say it. "Yes."

"I'm sad to say I don't believe you. Put your hands behind your back, Katherine. Make sure your left hand is around your seat belt."

The pressure of the gun on her skull lifted and he clasped her wrists tightly, painfully, with a sharp-edged strip nylon. Moments later, she felt the prick and burn of an injection into her arm.

"Sit back now."

She fell back against the seat, her arms wrenched awkwardly behind her, the seatbelt cutting painfully across her neck. "What was that?"

His happy face was back. He was enjoying the power he had. "Morphine. Just a little something to help you sleep. Have a nice nap, Katherine."

Morphine was not so strong a sedative that it would necessarily knock her out. And with an injection into the muscle, it would be twenty minutes or so before she began to significantly feel the effects. Nonetheless, Katherine closed her eyes and leaned back against the headrest. Sleep was probably the safest way to pass whatever time there was until they got to where he was taking her. At least it would keep her mouth from getting her in trouble again.

She was handcuffed. Simon had a gun. There was little else she could do.

Will, she said, in her mind. *I will wait for you. I am stronger than this man who has me. I will survive whatever happens, and wait for you to find me. Unless he gives me a chance to hurt him myself. Then all bets are off.*

Will took several calls in the first hour as he drove south and west. Jeff let him know that the SAC in Albany had agreed to get a team out the marina where the *Indulgence* was moored. Photos of Katherine had been faxed. In the next call, he said he was on the road and then asked who Canaan was. "Who?" Will answered. Jeff sounded a little pissy about that, just before Will hung up on him.

Grandmère called and told him the doctor had agreed to discharge Elyse and that Leet would take them to Fergus Mountain. She said she'd spoken to Jeff, but that might have been something Jeff didn't get around to mentioning before Will had cut him off.

He drove—fast—through all those calls. Then he opened his phone to an unidentified caller.

"Deputy Hunter." The voice was soft-spoken, male.

"Who is this?" Will asked brusquely, but his foot was already hitting the brake and a chill skittered down his spine. He screeched to a stop off the side of the road, much to the annoyance of the driver behind him, whom he'd just passed.

"I have the lovely Katherine here with me."

"I want to talk with her now."

"She is resting. I am loath to disturb her."

Will closed his eyes. The man's speech was cultured, formal, and filled with subtle menace.

"Don't hurt her, Carlson. I will do whatever you want. I'll help you get whatever you want. Just don't hurt her."

"I want you, Will. I want you to come, entirely alone, to

my home on Long Island. It's long past time we met."

"I will. I'll come."

"You know the address?"

"I do. Don't hurt Katherine."

"She will be safe if you follow my instructions exactly. I want you to come to us, you and no one else. I want no one with you, no eyes watching. No FBI, no sheriff friends out of their jurisdiction. I want no one to even know that you are coming. Can you do that?"

"There are agents already on their way to your boat. I'm not sure I can stop them."

"Let them go, Will. They will be too late. The *Indulgence* has already sailed."

"Are you and Katherine on it?"

"No calls, Will. I will know if you use your phone. You have five hours to join us on Long Island."

"I can't make it in that time. Sunday afternoon, getting across a bridge will take at least an hour."

"Three hundred minutes. Or I'm afraid it will end badly for Katherine."

"Carlson—"

But Will knew the line was dead before he even got the man's name out. He took a minute to program the Carlson mansion address into his GPS system and thought about his options. He supposed it was possible that Simon could track the calls he made. It was more than likely a bluff, but not one he was willing to chance.

He made one stop. He filled his tank and bought a cup of bad coffee. He had Katherine's cell phone to his ear when he turned south and drove like hell.

A little less than two hours later, Canaan called on Katherine's line. Will had ignored several calls on his own phone. Jeff could not be happy.

"I'm on *Indulgence*," Canaan said, speaking so quietly that Will strained to hear. "She's not here."

Will cursed—long and loudly, given that there was no one to hear.

"There's one man driving it," Canaan went on when Will

marginally quieted. "No one else is on board. What do you want me to do?"

"What's the guy look like?"

"Muscle. Young and stupid. Armed, and he's got a phone and radio."

"Does he know you're there?"

"Nah," Canaan said, sounding offended to be asked.

Despite the circumstances, Will smiled. "How'd you manage that?"

"Came down behind him, by rope from the Mid-Hudson Bridge. Katherine's brothers did a good job of maneuvering him into range for me and slowing him down." Will heard his grin. "Those Noble boys are a little wild."

Will would have enjoyed seeing that. "They can fish you out if you go quietly over the side, yeah?"

"Sure, no prob."

"All right, do that."

"Why don't I put this guy out of play now? Or just disable the boat?"

"Cell phone and radio. Simon thinks he's getting out of this. I need him to keep thinking that."

"Until you have Katherine."

"Yep."

"Okay, man."

Will could hear the sigh. "Think you can beat the boat to Carlson's place?"

"Maybe. The damn thing is fast. And he doesn't have to worry about bridges onto the Island, which are going to suck. It'll be close."

"I'll see you, then. Thanks, man."

"Yeah. I'll be about an hour behind you."

"Cane, be careful when you get to Carlson's place. If he has a man on his boat, he may have more at his home."

"Stop wasting your time insulting me and go get your woman."

Will huffed out a breath. "Will do. Enjoy your swim."

"Don't piss off Carlson too much before I get there."

"Got it."

Sunday afternoon traffic into the city thickened as Will pushed closer. It didn't improve any as he cut over to Long Island. He managed to avoid getting boxed into it, but sometimes only by using his lights and taking to the shoulder. Still, there was nothing he could do about the hour wait at the Throgs Neck Bridge. A couple of times, he started to feel a bit edgy and used his deep breathing, but mostly he just didn't notice it.

It was three hundred minus just a couple minutes when he approached the Carlson home. The population density of the city had diminished gradually, with the size of properties increasing until the houses became mansions and the grounds would pass for public parks in most towns. High stone walls and iron gates ensured that no one would mistake them for public land, though. These pricey estates, and the little bit of shorefront attached to them, were obviously, arrogantly, privately owned.

A horseshoe drive, iron gates open, led up to the Carlson place. Will took it and pulled right up to the entrance. He smirked as he climbed out, enjoying the thought that most pickup trucks of his sort—utilitarian and more than a couple years old—in this neighborhood were no doubt service vehicles to be directed around to a substantially less majestic side entryway. The waterfront was close—the air had the taste and feel of salt.

The entrance to the mansion was indeed grand. Wide steps rose to a gray stone terrace that extended along the whole front of the house. The balustrade was heavily ornate, pretentious to the point of pomposity to Will's mind, but still a remarkable feat of stone craftsmanship.

The house was lit up like a party rocked, making the silence that emanated from it seem eerie. Will raised his hand to knock at the double doors, more over the top baroque carving, this time in aged wood. But he saw one door was unlatched, so he put a couple fingers on it and pushed it open.

Silence, still, and more tasteful ostentation. Polished marble floor, a curved, double staircase leading up, and a magnificent crystal chandelier adorning the half-acre of entrance hall. Will stepped in and met the gaze of the man standing at the center of the second floor balcony.

Simon Carlson. Master of his universe, if one were to take

seriously his carefully choreographed pose. One hand, understated ring glittering, rested on the burnished wood rail to establish ownership, in case of doubt. The other was tucked oh so casually into his expertly tailored jacket, presumably meaning to convey self-assurance, a complete confidence in his ability, his power, to manage this little denouement.

Will sincerely hoped there were some unhappy surprises in store for the elegantly dressed, murdering, psycho thug.

Find Katherine first, he thought. *Then get this asswipe his just deserts.*

Asswipe made a show of checking his Rolex.

"Perfect, Will," he said with grating and false sociability. "Just in time to join our little party. Close the door, if you would. Though don't lock it—we're expecting one more guest."

Keeping his gaze fixed on Simon, Will kicked his foot out behind, connected with the door, and slammed it shut. Carlson wouldn't know about Canaan, so who else did he think would join them? Presumably the driver of the yacht. Will's back itched as he moved, unarmed, into the lion's den.

"Where's Katherine?"

"Up here," he said, gesturing a welcome with his hand. "We've been waiting for you."

Simon disappeared into a room off the balcony while Will took the stairs two at a time. When he got to the doorway, Simon was standing in the middle of the room, facing the door. In front of him sat Katherine, alert and *alive* in a chair where she was secured wrist and ankle. The chair faced a desk at a right angle to him, but she looked over her shoulder to meet his gaze.

Will just kept from having to steady himself against the doorframe, just kept from whimpering out a thankful moan. His eyes drank her in. She answered his gaze directly—no sign of injury, no sign even of being cowed, despite the seriously lethal handgun Simon held to her head.

"Baby," he breathed out, moving toward her until Simon nudged the gun harder against her. He stopped and lifted his hands, looking at Simon.

"Naturally, I'd consider that you might be armed," Simon said with a little lift of his brow.

"I have weapons," Will said. "They're in my truck."

"I regret, truly, that I cannot at this time accept your word. Lift your shirt up and turn around." He circled one finger and Will did what he said, doing a little twirl with his shirt held above the waist of his chinos.

When Will raised his brow back at Simon, he motioned to his feet. "Lift your cuffs."

Impatiently, Will complied, brusquely demonstrating that he had nothing concealed in an ankle holster. Then unilaterally deciding they were done, he moved to Katherine. Watching her eyes, he knelt in front of her. He checked the cable ties that held her wrists to the chair, sliding his fingers along the ties where they bit into her flesh, now scraped red. There was little give and, clearly, she'd made matters worse, chafing her skin trying to work her hands free. She wore a long-sleeved slinky tee so he tugged the ends of her sleeves down under the ties to protect her skin. Then he put his hands along her face and gently touched her lips with his before he rested his forehead against hers and spoke in a whisper. "Baby, are you okay?"

"Will." Her voice caught and she bit down on her lip, fighting for control for just a moment. "I'm so glad you're here. I knew you would come."

His heart ached, weighed down by the sense of responsibility that she was here, and lightened by her faith in him. He kissed her again. "Hold on, sweetheart. We'll get you out of this."

"Us," she said, and nudged back against his forehead, staring into his eyes. "We'll get *us* out of this."

Will nodded, touching her lips once more, but made no further commitment. He had only one priority.

Simon had taken a couple steps back when Will approached, but kept his gun aimed at Katherine. Will looked up at him, keeping his hands on hers. "If you hurt her any further, I'll kill you. What is it you want, Carlson?"

"Ah, now, there's a question for the ages. What do I want, and, more to the point, what can I have? Right now, I'll have you in this other chair here."

The furniture was classically traditional tufted oxblood leather, brass nail heads, and polished wood. A chair that matched the one Katherine was in sat a couple feet away. Both faced the massive, stately, leather-topped oval desk.

The desk chair was the same plush leather but deeper, and wing-backed. A Boston rocker with a distinguished university seal engraved on the cherry wood of its crown was off to the side, with a small table and reading lamp.

This was Theodore Carlson's study. Over decades, it had no doubt been the site of thousands of negotiations, deals, and compromises that had helped shape the country—often for the good, Will knew. Now it was being used for the perverse entertainment of his twisted son. The man hadn't made it to his grave yet, but he was no doubt rolling over in his coffin.

Four long, black cable ties lay open on the seat of the chair that was to be his. Will knew what Simon meant for him to do. He spent a minute looking at the man, psychopath and killer, evaluating whether to just rush him now and be done. Simon might shoot him, but Will would make damn sure the bastard would be the first one to fall. And he wouldn't be getting back up.

He was stayed only by the fact that the gun was pointed at Katherine, not at him. And Simon watched him with knowing eyes. "I won't hurt you," he said. "And I haven't hurt Katherine, out of respect for you. But I will, if need be. It's up to you."

Will had to believe the man. He went to the chair, but lifted its heavy ass up and hefted it over so the armrest snugged against Katherine's. He sat and bent forward to secure each of his ankles against a front leg of the chair. Then, with a challenging look at Simon, he put his left hand on top of Katherine's right, and started to put the third tie around both of them.

"Stop." Simon stayed Katherine's side, gun intractably aimed at her. "The other hand first, if you please."

Will hid his frustration. He'd have been more than happy for Simon to come around to secure his right hand. Or try to.

Instead, he reluctantly tied his right hand to the chair then had to sit passively as Simon wedged one end of the last tie under Katherine's wrist to stabilize it while he wrapped the long end around both of them. Then he pulled it tight, securing them together with no slack at all. The gun was pressed hard against her chest through it all. Will knew there would be a bruise there, between her breasts—another offense for which Simon would pay.

Giving an unwarranted, gloating tug on the tie, he walked around the desk and sat back, admiring this little tableau of his making. It put Will in mind of a small boy trying to play grown-up.

Which was a lot better than letting his mind wander to the sense of restriction he felt with his hands and feet bound. That was a feeling which could grow like a tight band around his chest, bringing suffocation. He ignored it, focusing instead on the warmth of Katherine's hand under his own.

Her fingers moved in response, and when he looked over, she was looking back. Her green eyes searched his and the trust and support he saw there steadied him. Without words, they both leaned toward the other until their lips met in a soft, lingering, binding kiss. It was an unspoken expression of their love for each other, accepted as well as offered, and Will knew that nothing was truer. When he drew his head back, he looked into her eyes for a long moment before turning to face Simon.

"What are we doing here, Carlson?" He was grateful his curt question wiped the smarmy grin off the man's face. It was replaced with a hurt little pout.

Simon tried too late to recover his air of false composure. "Relax, Will, my boy. I mean you no harm. Your lovely Katherine either." He pursed his lips, pressing his fingers against them, contemplating. "Does she please you well enough, Will? Is it in her nature to allow you to explore the darkness in your sexuality? Does she derive pleasure from it? Some women do, you must know. Even if they pretend otherwise. Like your mother, for example."

Will spoke through a clenched jaw. "You are begging for me to kill you."

"I loved Elyse, you know. I already told Katherine. And yet I am disillusioned once again. I hear she has taken up with the sheriff. Honestly, do you suppose she has allowed the man into her bed? Quiet, innocent little Elyse?"

Will bared his teeth and lunged against the bindings, scraping his chair along the hardwood floor, moving closer to Carlson.

Simon waved away his reaction. "Forget I mentioned it. Even adult children abhor hearing about the sexual lives of their parents. Still, the issue must be addressed." He leaned back in his chair, calmly watching Will. "I'm ready to leave the country. Indeed, I would be gone already if not for what Katherine ingenuously let slip. You must understand I really can't go just yet. I cannot expect to live with any contentment knowing Elyse is giving herself to another man. She is mine, you understand. She always was. The sheriff has sullied her, and will pay for such an insult with his life. I have invited him to join us—I expect he'll arrive any moment now. Once we've taken care of that matter, I'll be on my way. My yacht will be here shortly as well. Katherine will accompany me initially. I'll take good care of her, I promise. Unless—have you tired of her, Will?" He shrugged. "It's your call. She can disappear once I'm well off shore, if you wish. No questions asked."

Will didn't answer, just stared hard at the monster who sat behind the desk.

The monster stared back. "You have my darkness in you. Perhaps you haven't admitted it yet, but you do. Don't you feel it, when you take her? Don't you revel in the fact that she is yours, that you can do with her what you will? Have you hurt her, Will? Even just a little? Did it feel good, that power? Did you want more? You can have it, you know. There is no need to hold back. Take what you want. Men like you and I see women for what they are—vessels for our pleasure, our amusement. Ours to enjoy, to use as we will. It's what they want, and what they deserve."

The evil in the man's words sent a shiver down Will's spine. The grip of Katherine's fingers steadied him. And her words even more so.

"You're a fool if you believe Will is your son, Simon. He doesn't have your darkness. He is not of your blood. His father was Truman Hunter, the man you killed."

Simon's temper flared and he took his pistol back from the desk and pointed it at Katherine again.

"Is that what Elyse would have you think, Will? She lies to you, as a woman will. She was mine, nine months before you were born. I planted the seed that made you. I had her, again and again."

Will fought the despair that the ugly words brought raining down on him, drenching him, drowning. But the defense against them came not from him, but from behind him.

"You raped her. But you weren't the one who fathered her child."

All eyes turned to the door, where Jeff Anderson stood, his fingers wrapped around the grip of a gun.

"Ah, Sheriff. Welcome. Do tell. I am curious to hear what you know of it, you who were not there. It was entertaining to watch your ineffective search for her, to think of it while I plundered her delectable young body. While I fucked her."

Jeff's fist tightened around his gun, so much so that his fingers turned white. His voice was hard, edged with hatred and anger that no doubt matched Will's own. Purer, though, than Will's. Without the burden of guilt, the weight of responsibility, the awful specter of shared blood. "Put the gun on the desk and push away, Carlson. You speak one more word and you'll die with it on your lips." He'd lifted his weapon, aiming directly at Simon's head, making the meaning of his words entirely clear.

Silently, Simon let his pistol hang on his finger by the trigger guard. He lowered it to the desk and then, using both hands, pushed his chair back.

"Stand, and put your hands behind your head."

The man complied, watching Jeff with a complacent grin. He hadn't lost his confidence, making Will sure there was more to come. "He has an armed man coming in on the boat. He may have others here."

Jeff met his eyes and nodded as he walked to Simon, covering him carefully with his gun. "The boat's docked but looks empty. I haven't seen anyone on the grounds."

Simon looked from Will to Jeff, still appearing confident, even triumphant. "It wasn't rape, you know. She loved what I did to her. She moaned and screamed with the ecstasy of it."

Jeff had moved behind him, shoving the chair away. "Put your head down on the desk." And he helped him, clouting the back of his head with the grip of his pistol. Then he circled one of Carlson's wrists with a handcuff, pulling both hands back to complete the job of securing him. He kicked at Simon's ankles to spread his feet out. He spoke bitterly as he worked. "It was rape, you sick fuck. She hated everything you did to her. She saw you for the freak that you were, and she despised every moment she was forced to spend with you. She never, ever enjoyed one thing you did to her. She hated you so much she disappeared inside herself rather than have to know all that you did to her. Rather than have to know you. Because you're a pathetic, sick fuck, and she knew it."

"That's a lie!" Carlson cried, almost crowing.

Jeff leaned over him, pressing his pistol into the man's skull.

Undaunted, Simon's words still held a chilling giddiness. "She opened herself for me. She wanted me! And my child. She could have gotten rid of it, but she didn't. She kept him—for me!"

"You sack of shit." Jeff pressed with the gun and spoke right into his ear. "Truman Hunter fathered Will. She begged him. You raped and tortured her and made him watch. And when you left them alone, she begged him to make love to her. You'd chained them so they couldn't touch, but their bodies could reach. He didn't want to hurt her, but she insisted. She wanted to be his. And she wanted to have hope that, if she conceived, the child would be his. Truman's. Not yours."

"No!" Simon screeched now. "They were never together. I put them in the same room to taunt him. But she was out of his reach. I would never have let him touch her."

"They managed," Jeff said. "The first night you left them together. The next day, you raped her again—"

"Not rape! She wanted me!"

Jeff spoke over him. "You chained her to the bed in your chamber of horrors. You raped her, and Truman was forced to watch it happen one more time. That night, when you left them alone again, Truman smashed his hands against the cement wall of your basement, until the bones were broken enough to wedge the cuffs off. Then he freed her and took her away from you."

"She didn't want to go with him."

"She did want to. He carried her as far as he could, nearly to the point of collapse. And when he meant to leave her, safely away, in the woods, when he meant to go back to find you and kill you, she made him make love to her one more time. It was as though she knew she'd never see him again."

Jeff was looking at Will now. Will swallowed, hardening himself against the painful details he'd never heard before. Jeff lifted away from Simon and loosened a knife from a sheath on his belt.

"Elyse didn't want him! Not after she was with me."

"She loved him. And she despised you."

"Shut up!" Simon lifted his head and yelled, "Now! Now!"

A gun fired twice from the doorway and Jeff fell. Will lunged up, scraping his chair over the hardwood floor. But the cable tie that held him to Katherine's wrist and chair limited him. Katherine struggled, too, crying out Jeff's name. He could only glare with helpless fury as a man—doubtless the young and stupid muscle from the boat—smirked on his way by.

Simon stood, a gloating look on his face, and used his foot to roughly push Jeff over. "Here, James. The key is on his belt, do you see?"

The thug nodded, bending to retrieve the key before releasing the cuffs.

Simon rubbed his wrists while he looked down at Jeff. "Is he dead?"

"He will be soon. He's sucking air into that chest wound."

He was right, Will knew. From the other side of the desk, he could only see Jeff's head and shoulders. But he could the wet gurgle of his breath. With a bullet hole into his chest cavity, his lung would collapse and then fill with blood.

Simon crouched over him and gripped his jaw to bring his face around. "You won't ever have Elyse," he said. Then he stood and kicked his foot hard into Jeff's abdomen. Turning away, he faced Will. Sitting on a corner of the desk, he crossed his arms over his chest and studied him for a long moment. "What do you say, Will? Do you recognize yourself in me? Are you my son?"

Will looked back at the horror of a soul, the hideous specimen of a human being. He felt his blood rage, imagined horrifically satisfying ways of seeing this man to hell. And he considered for a moment that it could be true. A gritty nausea rolled through him, an insistent denial. Then he thought of Katherine's safety, and the small chance of saving Jeff. And he met the monster's gaze squarely.

"I've always believed it to be true."

"You've feared it was true, you mean. It's why you've never done the DNA testing, isn't it?"

"No, Simon," he said, choosing his words carefully. Words that might be their only hope. "I've never done the testing because of my mother. Elyse is—weak. She relies so much on her fantasy of lost love. She's really not strong enough to face the truth, is she?"

Simon searched his eyes skeptically. Then he walked around the desk, took a ring of keys from his pocket, and used one to open a drawer. He drew out a manila envelope, still sealed. He held it with his fingertips, twirling it by its corners.

"My father arranged testing," he said. "He wanted a legacy, I suppose. It had become clear that he had no other chance for a grandson. He requested it once he learned his cancer was terminal. But the end came too quickly—the stroke was a surprise. He never saw the results. What do you say? Shall we look now?"

Will stared at the envelope, only vaguely aware of the subtle tightening of Katherine's grip on his hand. Was this something he wanted to know? He looked up at Simon's expectant expression.

"Hmm? Well, your choice." Simon carelessly tossed the envelope on the desk. "I don't see a lot of father-son activities in our future either way, eh?" He motioned to James. "Cut the woman loose and bring her with us." He looked again at Will. "I don't care if you have to hurt her."

James moved over to stand in front of Will and Katherine. The message that Will sent with his eyes, that if he hurt Katherine, he was dead, didn't seem to register. Watching Will, he closed his hand into a fist and struck her, hard, against her temple. She was stunned, her head rolling toward her shoulder.

While Will yelled viciously, cursing and vowing deadly vengeance, James cut Katherine free. He saved the binding that held Will's wrist too for last. As he cut it, he kicked his foot into Will's chest, sending him over backwards in the chair. From his back, struggling to roll himself and the damn chair over, he could see James take Katherine up over his shoulder and follow Simon out the door.

They were gone by the time Will got to his knees, still bound to the chair, its weight and bulk inhibiting his ability to move. Awkwardly, he wrangled his way around the desk to Jeff. He found the knife that had fallen from Jeff's hand and cut the three ties that still bound him. Finally, he was able to shove the chair off his back and move.

Jeff was still alive, though he was pale and breathing rapidly. Blood had pooled underneath him. Will was sure more filled his right lung. He pulled the phone from the desk and dialed 911 as he worked on Jeff. "Code ten double zero." *Officer down*. He gave the address. "Two armed men with a female hostage. Additional law officers on site."

He hung up as the dispatcher was instructing him to stay on the line. He tucked Jeff's right arm and rolled him so his body weight pressed the area of the wound against the arm flexed underneath him. That put pressure against the wound, and put his left side up, hopefully leaving him better able to breathe from the uninjured side.

He spoke to Jeff as he worked, telling him what he was doing, that help was coming, and that he had to leave him to go after Katherine. He prayed it wasn't just his desperate imagination that had him seeing Jeff's small nod.

He was gone then, tearing down the stairs. He'd seen that double doors at the back of the entrance hall opened into another large space and he ran there now, shattering glass panes of the doors when he slammed them open. As he'd hoped, the next room had more doors opening onto a terrace that ended at a long, well-groomed lawn. Beyond that were the quiet waters of the Sound. And a dock, where the *Indulgence*'s engines were firing up.

Will ran full-out across the lawn. With a single bark, Beowulf joined him. Canaan must have brought him, and the presence of both, man and animal, gladdened his heart immeasurably. He didn't see Canaan, and he didn't slow his pace, but he hollered as he ran. "Jeff's hurt! Upstairs!"

He could see James at the helm up on the high bridge of the *Indulgence*. Simon was on the deck below, pushing Katherine toward the cabin. He could smell diesel exhaust as engines dug the propellers into water and started the sixty-footer moving.

The port side of the yacht was halfway down the dock when Will's foot hit the first wood plank. In a half-dozen long strides, he reached the end and leaped off the far corner. He caught the portside rail with his hands and held, then pulled himself over. Beowulf jumped a half-second later, scrambling onto the swim platform at the stern and then up over the transom.

James had seen him coming and stepped astern. He gripped a handgun, but as he lifted it to aim at Will, two shots came from behind. Knocked back, James fell out of sight. On deck, Will rolled to his feet, facing Simon.

Simon had his gun too, and yet again held it against Katherine. Backed against the starboard rail, he pulled Katherine in front of him and met Will's gaze squarely.

The powerful engines caught momentum and they were moving fast now into the Sound. As Will straightened to look hard at Simon, Beowulf streaked past him. James, lying prone on the deck of the bridge, peeked over the edge. He'd stretched out his arm, pistol still threatening. As he brought it around toward Will, Beowulf leaped, capturing James's forearm in his jaws.

Ferociously growling, Beowulf clung to his objective. Panicked, James fired wildly, repeatedly.

Time slowed in the next moments so that Will saw them in single frames. He watched in horror as blood splattered over Katherine. She cried out at the same instant Simon did. Blood spouted from a wound on Simon's right shoulder, rapidly staining his jacket. His arm hung uselessly at his side, the pistol gone.

Even as he gathered himself to leap across the cockpit deck, Will was aware of calculation in Simon's eyes. Even as he was in the air, arms stretched out reaching for Katherine, he knew it was too late.

Still holding Katherine hard against him with his left arm, Simon went backwards over the side. Unable to stop his flight, Will slammed into the bulwark. He tumbled to the deck. Finding his feet and shoving up, Will leaned over the gunwale, crying out Katherine's name. He searched the water for a moment before he saw her right beneath him. As she'd gone over, she must have grabbed at a dock line. She had her hand wrapped in it now and was being pulled alongside. Water churning off the side of the boat splashed over her head.

Securing himself with a grip on the rail, Will went nearly all the way over to reach for her. He got her wrist and pulled her up enough to relieve some of the tension where the line bit into her skin. But the force of the water pulled her down and he couldn't get her any closer. Then he swore out loud when he realized she had her other arm wrapped around Simon. It was Simon's weight that pulled her back into the water, away from him.

"Let go of him, baby. I can't get you up."

Simon's head lolled off his shoulder and bobbed into the water. Will couldn't tell if he was still alive and didn't fucking care. He'd seen it in Simon's eyes when he went over—the man had made his choice.

"Katherine!" He jerked at her wrist, commanding attention. "Let go of him! I can't pull you in."

She turned her head to look up at him, fighting against sharp spray as the boat cut through water. He leaned further over the water, getting as close to her as he could.

"Sweetheart, he went over. That was his choice," he said. "Let go. No one's driving this boat. We're not safe."

Katherine closed her eyes and turned her head away.

Will held her, his grip on her wrist like an iron shackle. This woman was his life. He'd go over with her before he let go. All he could do was beg her, cursing in his mind, urging her to let Simon loose. Will knew Simon had seen death as his best choice. And Will fucking agreed. Only Katherine would think that man should be, *could* be, saved.

Simon could go to hell, and, by God, should. But he damn well wasn't taking Katherine with him.

For long moments, he concentrated only on keeping his hold on her. Finally, she turned her face back to Will. Keeping her gaze on his, she loosened the arm she had around Simon. The second she was free of him, Will pulled her up into the boat. They fell in a wet heap onto the deck.

Beowulf nuzzled them with an anxious whine. Will lifted his head and saw that James lay unmoving, half fallen from the bridge, dripping blood from the torn flesh of his arm.

Will wanted nothing more than to curl Katherine into his arms and cling. But the boat was moving fast and he couldn't see over the bow to know what was ahead. He pressed a kiss into Katherine's sodden hair and crawled up onto his knees. He gave Beowulf a good rub and told him to stay.

Then he got to his feet and lumbered toward the bridge. He bent over to pick up the handgun James had dropped to the deck and secured it at his back. Then he pulled himself up the ladder and went to the helm. He throttled down, knowing just about that much about piloting a big boat. He looked at the lights over the bow and saw that they'd reached nearly halfway across the Sound. There was a wheel, and he figured he could handle that, so he started them on a wide turn to circle back to the dock they'd left.

Full dark now, he was saved the trouble of having to make out which was the Carlson estate by the flashing lights of a multitude of emergency vehicles. He pointed the boat in their direction and sped things up a bit.

Amidst those activities, Katherine came to stand with him, and Beowulf, too. Katherine had wrapped herself in a blanket and shared it with him as she snuggled into his arms. It really wasn't cold, but the warmth of the blanket and their body heat was a mutual comfort.

They held each other in silence for long moments while Beowulf nudged himself in between. Finally, Will lifted his head, held Katherine's face with one hand, and looked into her eyes. "Are you okay?"

His voice cracked, roughened by the salt air, the yelling he'd done, and emotion. He watched her carefully as she nodded. He nodded back and then kissed her soundly before he turned her to face the helm. He put her hands on the wheel and pointed ahead to the lights. "You can keep us headed there, yeah?"

She nodded and he kissed her again. "I'm going to see what needs to be done for James."

Will grabbed James by the belt and pulled his body back fully onto the bridge, rolling him over to assess. He'd lost a lot of blood. Most of it was from the two closely spaced bullet wounds in his chest—upper right, most likely to stop an armed man without killing him—and from the exit wounds on his back. Comparatively little was from the canine bite injuries on his right arm. Still, the man was alive, which Will thought was maybe more than he deserved.

Somewhat begrudgingly, Will hobbled down to the head in the main cabin and came back with towels and a first aid kit. He managed to get some pressure bandages over the leakiest of James's wounds, aware that it was more than he'd done for Jeff. Then he left him, knowing that he needed fluid replacement. That would have to be done by the first responders on shore.

Katherine turned into him as soon as he got back to her. He held her with one arm while he took over the wheel with the other. She burrowed into his neck and took a few breaths. Then she lifted up to look at him. "Jeff?"

He kept his eyes on the dock, closer now. "He was alive when I left." She burrowed in again and clung. She would understand, he knew, what it cost him to leave Jeff there alone and maybe mortally wounded. She would get that he couldn't have stayed, and that Jeff wouldn't have wanted him to. But it would be a burden to her that it was for her sake that Jeff had been left untended.

"Canaan was there," he added. "He'll have done what he could for Jeff." She nodded against his chest, but he knew her eyes would look bleak. He tightened his grip. "Jeff's strong," he said into her hair. "But he'd give up his life for you if he had to. He wouldn't hesitate or regret it."

But Katherine would, he knew. It would be a burden to her for the rest of her life. All Will could do was hold her close and pray for Jeff's survival.

CHAPTER NINE

Katherine pressed her face into Will's shoulder. He'd been nearly as drenched as she, so his shirt was cold and smelled of seawater. It warmed only when she stayed there unmoving for a while, capturing their body heat between them. She had her arms around him, and he clenched her close against him with the one free arm he had.

None of it was enough. However close she burrowed into him, it wasn't enough.

She couldn't stop the wracking shudder that shredded her control. Her mouth opened and a raw, broken wail scraped her throat. Each breath quaked, not quite a sob.

She felt the movement of Will's body as he leaned forward. The roar of the powerful engines ground down to a quiet rumble and the forward motion of the boat fell to a slow drift. Then he had her in both his arms and, as her legs collapsed, he lowered them to their knees.

"James," she managed. "We have to—"

"I don't care a rat's ass about James. I care about you, Katherine."

"Will—" There were tears now, a river of them she couldn't stop.

"I'm so sorry, baby. I'm so sorry."

She shook her head against his chest. "This wasn't your fault."

"It was. All of it."

"No. It wasn't." Compelled by this need, the necessity of reassuring him, she sat back on her heels. This was the thing that could stop the tears. She put her hands alongside his head, looked into his eyes, and spoke plainly. "You saved me. I knew you would. I knew I could survive whatever he did to me—" She felt his tremor and gave him a little shake. "Whatever he did, because you'd come for me. I believed that, without a shred of doubt."

She saw it in him then, too. The need to comfort her, to care for her, was greater than his own suffering, his sense of guilt and self-blame. He held her just as she held him, his big hands cupping her head. "You're strong, Katherine."

She nodded. "And I have you."

"Yes."

"He didn't hurt me, Will. He used words, horrible, ugly words, but that was all."

"He hurt you, Katherine. I know him. It wasn't just ugly words. It was twisted pleasure in manipulating you. It was evil mind-fu—" He paused and took an unsteady breath. "He hurt you, Katherine. Please, don't, for my sake, pretend that he didn't."

The tears started again, even as she nodded. They weren't tears of horror now, but of grief, and relief, and the beginning of healing.

He took her in his arms again and rocked her. He kept it up for a good long time even after the tears came to an end. Finally, he lifted her face up to his and, when she nodded, he got back to his feet and started the boat moving again.

Beowulf took over Will's place beside her and Katherine was content, sitting on the bridge of Simon's horrid yacht, resting her shoulder against Will's muscular leg, solidly supporting her in an I-shall-not-be-moved kind of way, warmed by slightly wet and smelly dog. Life was okay.

Implausibly, Katherine might have dozed a little. She came to awareness as Will killed the boat's engines. Flashing lights formed an eerie strobe-like effect. They came from shore as well as from a patrol boat that now accompanied the *Indulgence*. The noise from a helicopter lifting off added to the weird welcome.

Which wasn't very welcoming at all, Katherine realized, as Will let the boat drift slowly and bump against the dock. "Stay down," he said, crouching over her. He lifted her face up to his. "They're going to separate us, so it will be a while before I can be with you. Answer all their questions truthfully." He stroked his thumb along her jaw. "If you can avoid mentioning Canaan, that would be good." He leaned in to kiss her. "I love you, Katherine Noble." He patted Beowulf and told him to stay with Katherine. Then he stepped out into the light—multiple spotlights, from shore and the patrol boat. He raised his arms and held his star out in one hand. The gun he'd taken from James was tucked into a cubbyhole at the helm.

"I'm Will Hunter, sheriff's deputy out of Sussex County, Vermont." He called out the words loud and clear. "I have the man who shot Sheriff Jeff Anderson. He's on the deck here. He's wounded and needs medical care ASAP. There's a Glock up here in a cubby that belonged to him. There may be more guns on board that I don't know about. I also have a woman who was taken hostage. She has minor injuries and psychological trauma."

Katherine *humphed* to herself, but understood that Will was trying to assure that she'd go first into medical rather than law enforcement hands.

And that was what happened. Will was instructed to have everyone stay put as the local authorities—also mostly county sheriff department, Katherine saw—boarded the boat. They went to him first, one man patting him down before he lowered his arms, another taking his ID from his hand and inspecting it under flashlight. Then he was directed off the boat, apparently pointed to the man in charge.

The second round of law enforcement went to James and her. Two deputies, one female, helped her to her feet. Katherine nodded as the woman matter-of-factly informed her she would do a pat down. As Katherine stood still for that, she watched Will leave the boat, a deputy at either side. He met her gaze for only a brief moment before he was gone.

Around her, deputies secured the boat, searching the cockpit and below decks. One officer took the gun from the helm and shouts from below indicated more weapons had been found.

EMTs came next. She directed them to James, apparently reassuring them enough about her own status that they left her to concentrate on the one in obviously greater need. They worked fast on him, starting two IVs and pushing fluid into him. She heard one call for another airlift.

After several minutes, he was carried off the boat and up to the grounds. One rescue worker, a young man with ginger hair twisted incongruously into dreadlocks, stayed back to evaluate her. He stopped at Beowulf's low growl and didn't come forward until Katherine spoke to the dog and he settled again at her feet.

The EMT greeted her then. "I'm Sam," he said.

She nodded. "Katherine."

"How are you doing, Katherine?"

"I'm fine. How is Jeff Anderson? Is he—"

"He was alive when they put him on the helo. I heard you had minor injuries."

Frowning, she held out her wrists. Between Simon's stupid cuffs and the boat line she'd managed to wrap around her wrist in a desperate grab as they'd gone over, she was pretty torn up. Sam took her hands, gently turning them, and inspected.

Then he touched her chin, tilted her head to the head to the right. "You've got a contusion here, on your left temple."

"I got hit."

"Did you lose consciousness?"

"No."

"Anything else?" he asked.

She shrugged a little. If she really paid attention, pretty much everything hurt. It had been a long day. In terms of how her body felt, it would be worse tomorrow. "I could use some ibuprofen."

He smiled at her. "So, you're tough, eh, Katherine?"

"Apparently I am."

"You want to talk about the psychological trauma to me or someone else?"

"Someone else. No offense."

He smiled again soothingly. "None taken. But nothing physical I should know about?"

She shook her head.

"Nothing that needs evidence taken?"

"No."

He looked at her calmly. "You weren't assaulted in anyway? You weren't raped?"

"No."

"Good. Cool. Come on then." He took her elbow and turned her to the ladder, taking a couple steps down before waiting for her, keeping her in the circle of his arms as she descended. "We'll get you the ibuprofen, get you warm and dry, and then dress your wrists."

She was somewhat pathetically grateful for the way he hovered as she walked off the boat, Beowulf at her other side.

The *Indulgence.* She looked back at it before she turned away, toward land, toward Will, toward her life.

The yacht was Simon's secret place, his floating house of horrors, where he *indulged* his sick cravings. Where he committed his vile sins.

She wondered if he knew the other meaning of the word—a remission of the time to be spent in purgatory. No doubt he had, with his bright, wasted mind. No doubt he'd thought it a clever little play on words. She was sure it wouldn't help him.

Will had been right to force her to let him go into the water. She wasn't even sure why she'd grabbed for him, why she'd taken even the smallest risk to try to save him. There was no saving him. And no even brief stay in purgatory. Nothing but hell awaited him.

It was nearly two hours before she saw Will again. She worried for him, but she herself was in good hands. A lovely surprise waited as Sam walked her off the dock—her brothers were there, arms open and warm. They'd stuck close as Sam had taken care of her. He'd tried to send her into the mansion to change out of her wet clothes, but she'd refused. It was her full intention to never step onto the *Indulgence* or into the Carlson home again. So she'd clambered into the warmth of the rescue truck, stripped down, and donned the unglamorous but warm and dry something-more-than-paper jumpsuit that Sam had given her. She might look like a convict, but her fashion standards had, for the moment, sunk just that low. Warm and dry was enough.

Sam bandaged her arms there, while she sat on the back step of the truck with Chris and Pierce on either side. She'd seen that Will had waited, watching from the stone terrace at the back of the mansion, talking with the sheriff. He didn't follow the man inside until he'd been sure that she was there, getting care, safely tucked between her brothers.

While he worked on her, Sam's partners gathered up and stowed their equipment. One truck had left already by the time he was finished with her. He nodded his driver into the cab as he finished.

He glanced at her two brothers before he took both her hands. "Is that all I can do for you then? I can safely leave you here?"

She nodded. She'd already declined more than once his suggestion that they take her into the ED. "Thanks, Sam. I'm good."

He squeezed her hands and she was warmed by the little suggestion of flirtation there. This was a man who had an excellent, ah, truckside manner. "Cool. It was a pleasure to meet you, Katherine."

She knew Chris and Pierce were exchanging a look as they stood and brought her up with them. The three of them saw Sam off and then wandered the grounds, avoiding going too close to either the house or the dock. Finally, they settled into an ornate ironwork gazebo, an eccentric two-story affair. The whimsy of the second story made perfect sense when they climbed up and took in the view. In the dark, they saw the far lights of the mainland and limitless stars.

Sam had left her a blanket and she sat wrapped in it, warmed even further by the body heat and solicitous concern of her brothers. They told her Will had called them, said she was in trouble, and got them headed down to the Hudson with Pierce's speedboat. With the giddy glee of the boys she remembered so well, they described how they'd laid a trap for the *Indulgence*. Lurking between the bridges, they'd waited until the yacht had passed under the Walkway Over the Hudson. Then, putting on an act of drunken revelry, they'd torn across the water, maneuvering the *Indulgence* to the spot under the Mid-Hudson Bridge where Canaan had hung suspended, ready to rappel down and board.

They had great admiration for that feat—and Katherine heard the sub-text. They were fishing around in their minds for an adequate rationale for them to try the same thing. It would have to be good enough to pass muster with their wives. And since those two women were eminently sensible, Katherine trusted she didn't really have to worry about it.

They continued their story. Canaan had dived off the yacht into the water and they'd pulled him out, disappointed to learn Katherine wasn't aboard. Canaan had them take him to his truck and then they'd followed him to the Carlson estate.

Canaan had slowed, but drove past the gates and didn't pull over for another half mile. He climbed out and gave Pierce and Chris hell and told them to stay put. They'd watched from Pierce's SUV as Canaan had geared up. Camo clothes and face paint and—great excitement here—assault rifle. He'd given them a hard look through the windshield, then disappeared into the dark, Beowulf at his side.

They'd stood it as long as they could, Chris said. When the waiting became intolerable, they got out and walked along the road to the estate. By the time they reached the open door of the mansion, they heard sirens in the distance. They found Canaan working over Jeff Anderson. He instructed them on the first aid needed and bade them say they'd followed Will in search of Katherine. If they could fail to mention Canaan's presence, he'd be grateful.

Then he disappeared again, and they hadn't seen him since.

Chris nudged Pierce at this point, nodding his head toward the house. A man in casual dress strode toward them. The three held their silence as he approached. He took the winding stairs up to the top level of the gazebo with the vigor of a much younger man. That, his bearing, and his buzz cut all had Katherine figuring ex-military.

He introduced himself as Sheriff Clay Rodier. He asked how Katherine was and apologized for intruding. He assessed Chris and Pierce, nodded as she introduced them, and seemed to accept that they weren't going to leave her alone with him.

"I understand you know Will Hunter," he said.

"Yes. He's—we're engaged."

Rodier nodded. "What instructions did he give you with regard to this questioning?"

"He said to tell the truth."

"About everything?"

"Yes."

"Who shot James Hanson?"

"The man on the boat?"

He nodded again.

"I don't know."

"Did Deputy Hunter have a weapon?"

"No."

"Why were you in the Carlson mansion?"

"Simon Carlson brought me there. At gunpoint." She held out her bandaged arms. "With my wrists bound behind my back."

"Where's Simon Carlson now?"

She gestured with her head. "Out there. In the water. He fell in after James shot him."

Rodier took a deep breath, considering her. Then he sat across from them, leaning back against the wrought iron. She thought he was trying to give the impression he'd rather be back in his den, feet up in his easy chair, a beer in one hand and the remote in his other.

She didn't buy it. This man was sharp and, while he might have a beer once in a while, she figured he could pry the cap off the bottle with his teeth and spit it out with enough force to dent concrete.

It went on for more than an hour. He'd ask a question, then circle around to ask it again, another way, and another. She was yawning and drooping against Chris's shoulder when she felt Pierce's arm lift. She'd been aware when Will had come out on the terrace. He'd paced there while a deputy stood stoically with him. At Pierce's gesture, he halted. Then, ignoring his guard's objection, he came down onto the grass. In seconds, he was there in the gazebo.

He crouched down in front of her and lifted his hand to touch her face, studying her. She knew he saw the fatigue. He stood and faced Rodier, physically blocking him. "It's enough, Sheriff. I'll bring her to your office later if you want. But she's finished now."

Rodier stood too, slowly, just short of menacing. There was a tense silence until he nodded. "I'm done with her for now, though I may need her to return. She's free to go, as long as I have phone and address."

Katherine sighed out in relief and stood, propped a bit between Chris and Pierce. She reached out to touch Will's back and he circled a hand around to grasp hers. She felt him stiffen when Rodier continued.

"I'll need you to stay here, Hunter. We've got a couple bunks down at the station. You can sack out there if you like. We'll give you a ride. I'd like the keys to your rig."

Katherine felt Will take a couple deep breaths. "They're in the ignition. And I'll spend the rest of the night at the hospital where Jeff Anderson is. Your men can drop me. I'll be there until you need me."

The sheriff took a moment before nodding in reluctant agreement. He stood back while Will led Katherine and the brothers down and away from the gazebo. When they had some distance, he stopped and pulled Katherine into his arms, holding her tight. He spoke over her shoulder. "How'd you guys get down here?"

Chris spoke. "We've got Pierce's SUV. We followed Canaan."

Will huffed. "Bet he didn't like that."

"Probably not that much," Pierce said. "He looked at us in a disgruntled manner, but he didn't try to beat us up or anything."

Katherine felt the rumble of laughter in Will's chest. "'Try?'"

She could hear the grin in Chris's voice. "Okay, so yeah, he wouldn't have had to try hard."

Will nodded, still chuckling. "He said you guys did good." Then he was serious. "Thank you for your help."

Pierce was serious right back. "We're her brothers."

Will nodded again. That, apparently, was all that needed saying.

Tilting back to look at Katherine, Will brought her face up gently with his fingers. "I have to stay here, baby."

"I'll stay, too. I want to see Jeff. And I want to be with you."

He kissed her softly and then pulled her close again. "I'd feel better if you were away from here. Could you let these guys take you to your place in Manhattan? Or to your parents'? I'll come get you in the morning. I promise."

Katherine wasn't sure that was something he could promise. Rodier might have an opinion about it, and the man appeared to have some teeth. She burrowed in, not wanting to let go.

Will stroked her head and rubbed his hand over her back. She suspected there was some kind of communication going on over her head, because Pierce spoke next.

"Katie, Mom's going to need to see you. Dad, too. We

called and said you were okay, but they need to see you."

She was outnumbered, and they were right. She sighed, then lifted her head to look at Will. "I don't want to leave you alone."

"I'm good," he said. "I'm fine." He kissed her again, lingering. "I love you."

Katherine had seen the officer who'd been dogging Will step close. He stood waiting, clearly sent to fetch his charge. One more heavy sigh and she straightened. "I love you, too. Call me about Jeff."

"I will. Your cell's in my truck. If they won't let you have it, I've got Chris and Pierce's numbers."

"Come, Katie. Let's go get it," Chris said. "Pierce, you go and get your rig. Bring it to the gate and we'll meet you there." He leaned in and spoke clandestinely, their ears only. "You might have to maneuver it around to get back on the road. Back and forth, back and forth, you get what I mean?"

All four of them exchanged looks. Chris was instructing Pierce to cover Canaan's tracks. Katherine figured Canaan would have taken care of it himself, but she was amused by Chris's concern. That little moment of the four of them together, mirth in their eyes, felt good, *normal*.

Pierce, saluting in a rolling his eyes kind of way, walked off.

Will put his hands on Katherine's shoulders, studying her. "Can you guys take the dog, too?"

She nodded. "He can stay at the farm until we go back to Vermont."

"'We?' I like the sound of that."

Katherine took a big breath, let it out slowly. It had been a long day. "Me too."

"You're a hell of a woman, Noble."

"Damn straight."

"And only you could look so frigging hot in a paper jumpsuit."

That felt good too, backed up as it was by his slow perusal of her.

"I think I make it work. I haven't fully accessorized yet."

He smiled and kissed her once more. "Gotta work with what you have. I'll call you from the hospital, then I want you to get some sleep. I'll see you tomorrow."

"Okay. Will, call your mom and grandmother."

"I will." Then he handed her off to Chris. "Take good care of her."

Deputy Dawg—okay, his name was Ulysses Washington, and he was decent enough—drove while Will borrowed his phone to call Elyse and Isabela. He gave them all the reassurance he could and promised to update them as soon as he learned Jeff's condition. They wouldn't be sleeping, they told him, until he called again.

In his mother's voice, he heard relief, worry, and love. That she was speaking at all, and facing with bravery her fears for Jeff's life, nearly moved Will to tears. When he told her Simon Carlson was dead, she simply said, "Good," and moved on.

Closing the phone, he rested his head back, grateful that he was riding up front alongside Washington. A little afraid he'd be shown to the backseat when Washington had walked him to his unit, Will had taken a good look at it. It was cleaner than some he'd seen—maybe the drunks on Long Island were better behaved than most—but every cop knew what happened back there, and none wanted to personally experience it.

He opened his eyes sometime later and realized by the road signs where they were headed. He looked over at Washington. "Manhattan?"

"They flew Anderson into Presbyterian," he said. "Level one trauma."

Will nodded. He spent a moment thinking about sidewalks dense with people and concrete canyons. Then he closed his eyes again and slept.

He woke up several times in the next few hours. The first was when Washington dropped him at the hospital. He'd gotten report then about Jeff—nearly out of surgery. Again, when they moved Jeff to SICU. He sat with him there—creeped out just a little by the units of blood they dripped into his arm, and dozed to the hum and beeps of his respirator and monitors.

He woke to talk with Elyse. And then with Sheriff Rodier. A chat with the FBI had worked wonders on the man's attitude. He no longer treated Will as a potential bad guy. Will, in fact, was free to do as he pleased, if he would just check in with Rodier sometime later in the day.

But his favorite time of waking up was just after noon.

He was in Katherine's bed and he'd heard her come in to the apartment.

He'd spoken with her last at six. Jeff was coming out of intensive care within the hour and, wonder of all wonders, Elyse and Isabela were on their way to be with him. Isabela had somehow managed to arrange a chauffeured limo. He'd told Katherine he'd get his truck back and drive up to get her. Then they'd come back to the city to be with Jeff and his family.

Katherine had a better idea. Within the hour, Kyle/Thor was at the hospital. He had a taxi waiting. They had a couple awkward moments in the back of the cab. Kyle waved away Will's attempt at an apology for his murderous thoughts when they'd first met—to the extent they had. And then, as they drove through the thick Monday morning traffic of the city, Will was aware of Kyle's careful monitoring of him. He seemed to expect him to go lunatic at any moment.

Will gave him a look that didn't seem to quell him much, then took a peek around at the city. Some of it was kind of pretty, he had to admit. But you'd have to actually *be* a lunatic to want to live there. In another minute, he had his head back on the seat—grimier, he guessed, than the squad car—and slept.

Sometime later, Kyle let him in to Katherine's apartment. Mumbling his thanks, Will walked in, making quick note of the living area as he moved through to the bedroom. He stripped and showered, then dumped about a thousand throw pillows off her bed and slept.

He heard her key in the lock and, by the time she got to the bedroom, he was already on his back. She'd promised, but there was no reason not to make it easy for her.

He listened as she undressed and he didn't need to open his eyes to have the image of that bringing his body to full attention. Since she had eyes, she was going to be aware of it, too. He was certain of it when he heard the little hum of her breath.

She peeled the covers back and climbed aboard, straddling him so their very critical body parts rubbed against each other. Then she leaned forward, took his head with her hands and his mouth with hers.

He did the same.

Hands gripping, they mated with their mouths. In seconds, their breathing was harsh, needy. She lifted just a little and he let her, looking up at her. They watched each other, love and blazing need in their eyes, their hands clenched in each other's hair. She rocked just a little, and tilted, until the tip of his throbbing hard-on was poised at her moist entrance.

His breath shook, his body quaked as she lowered herself, impaled herself. She was hot and wet and, oh, so fucking tight. And right, so fucking incredibly right.

"Love," he said. "Love." It was how he thought of her. What he felt for her. What he wanted, needed her to do. All of those things.

And she understood. "Yes," she said.

Still grasping each other, still watching, they moaned as she lifted up and then slid back down. He arched up to meet her, thrusting, pumping to her rhythm.

Sounds came from his throat—not words, but still exclamations of love and need. And she answered, softer, feminine, but every bit as urgent responses.

He held her, hard, and thrust, hard. Every muscle in his body clenched. Fiercely, he kept her face close to his so their eyes were lost in each other's, the air of their shared breaths churned around them, and their mouths collided.

He arched off the bed, lifting her up, as he strained to reach her very depths. Flexing then, he worked into her, agitatedly pushing her to climax. He fucking needed her to come. And he told her so bluntly, grinding out the words, urging her to submit.

And she did, blessedly, intensely, harshly, and loudly. She cried out as her whole body spasmed, shaking and seizing. Inside, her muscles clenched and squeezed and ripped from him a wrenching orgasm. He came hard and long with a guttural roar. Searing spurts of semen tore through him, filling her, making them both slick and hot.

He couldn't stop thrusting into her, couldn't stop clench-ing her to him. He gave in only when exhaustion took him, when she'd already collapsed against him. He fell to the bed and rolled, disengaging so he could hold her, comfort her and find comfort in her.

They lay facing each other, nuzzling into one another as their breath and pulse, feeling like one, settled. After long minutes of it, Will moved back so he could see her, search her eyes.

They were soft and glistening with tears that filled but didn't overflow. She swallowed hard and he knew that she, like he, was thinking of the day they'd just passed. Of the horror of it, the threat of devastating, crushing loss. The de-termination to endure, the will to survive and prevail. The steadfastness of their love that had seen them through it.

He knew if he'd been standing, he'd have gone to his knees. Or maybe even prostrate on the floor. He'd nearly lost her. The risk of that, the bone-chilling menace of it, had sat like a solid mass, like a growing, malignant cancer that took his breath and his heart.

It let go now. For the first time since he'd looked into his mother's hospital room and seen that Katherine was gone, he felt like he could breathe, like his heart could beat unre-stricted.

He put his hand to her face and stroked with his thumb, like he was smoothing away the tears she refused to let fall. He took her into his heart, the all of her. Her beauty, her strength. Her openness to love, her trust in it. Her spirit that withstood, that stayed pure even in the face of evil.

She'd tried to save Simon Carlson. *Only Katherine.*

He might not deserve her, but he fucking wasn't going to let her go.

He stroked his hand down her arm, her side, to her hip. Around back, he rubbed his finger over the little patch she wore there.

He kept his gaze on hers, watching. She watched back. He started to pick at it, loosening a little corner from the ad-hesive. She took a deep, steadying breath, but made no ob-jection.

Reading her acquiescence into that, he pulled the patch

off. Then he rolled them, so he was on top of her, settled between her legs. His dick, by all rights down for the count,
rose to the occasion.

He set himself at her entrance, just barely pressing in,
eased by the shared moisture that still lingered there. He
held himself over her, lifted on one elbow. Then, with his lips
and his hand, he began to worship her just as she deserved.
Touch, and words, to express what was in his heart.

Stroking his hand over her face, through her hair, he
gripped her head. He rubbed his thumb into her lips. His
gaze over her breasts had them tightening for him, lifting up,
her nipples peaking, seeking. Obliging, he leaned forward to
take one in his mouth. The action brought him a little more
deeply into her, breaching her opening, drawing moans from
them both.

He quelled the urge to let go and thrust into her, taking
her, claiming, owning. The pleasures offered by her breasts
were enough. He stroked and tongued, chafed and suckled,
gently pinched and bit. He couldn't get enough—of the sight,
the feel, the taste of her.

She liked it, too. Her eyes darkened, her gaze compelling
his. Her body arched, pressing her breasts harder into his
mouth, his hand. Her pelvis flexed, asking for more.

He resisted. Lifting up again, he watched her as he
moved his hand lower. He circled her where their bodies
joined, moistening his fingers. He slid them over her, stimulating her little bud. He caressed and rubbed, circling with
slow, drawn out motions, then sliding over her with quick,
urgent strokes.

Her breathing became needy, a bit plaintive. She rocked
closer, silently demanding more.

He gave her some of what she wanted. He pressed deeply into her, filling, stretching. But he held there, still fighting
the urge to ransack.

Instead, he gripped her little bud, taking it between his
thumb and one knuckle of his forefinger. Then he tugged. He
pulled and held her, then wrenched a little, tweaking. Again.
Again.

She tossed her head, clasped her hands on his arms.
"No, Will," she cried. "No!" Then, "Yes. Yes!"

She climaxed roughly, her body spasming, her spine

arching to grind down on him. Buried deep inside her, he felt the clenching, milking contractions of her muscles. He rode it out, reveling in her frantic pleasure.

She'd dug her heels into the bed in order to bring herself up to him. The moment she began to subside, breath still ragged, he grasped her ankles and brought them up to hook her legs around his back.

Then he fell on her, collapsing his weight onto her. He pressed his head into the bed beside her, breathing her in. He worked his hands between their bodies, covering each breast.

Holding her then, massaging and squeezing, he did what he'd been dying to do. He started lunging into her determinedly. With each long thrust, he took all of her, reaching her depths, grinding against her.

He gripped her nipples, tweaking hard. He arched over her, pressing his teeth into the crook of her shoulder.

His strokes into her came harder, faster.

She thrashed under him, complaining again. "No, no." She should know by now that wouldn't work.

He was beyond words. But his rough breaths, his rough strokes, told her what would be. He'd have her again. He'd have her coming in desperate, urgent need. In convulsive, compulsive pleasure.

He wouldn't have it otherwise. His own need grasped and clawed. He leashed it, in bare control, skimming the edge of his own brutal orgasm while he drove her back into it. His breath came in harsh, guttural commands. "Come," he bade, swearing. "Katie, come."

It was fucking close. He'd already started to feel it gather, the wrenching climax that would rip through him. But he felt her bow, arching to take him, receive him. He felt the quiver of the screams that were to come, the pulsation, the throb of that hot, wet cavity that he plundered.

Then they were in it, together, a maelstrom of quakes and shudders, screams and roars, urgency and ecstasy. He filled her, pouring life and love into her. He held her, a vow of commitment and devotion.

It was almost painful, almost anguish. Altogether staggering.

Long minutes passed while they were still held in the clutches of it. Long minutes until the convulsions of their bodies stilled, the rasping breaths eased, the aftershocks of pleasure, little mini-orgasms, finished shuddering through them.

He groaned when she nudged his shoulder. She probably needed to breathe. He gathered himself, gently lifting off of her. She mostly squelched a little whimper of complaint—no doubt she was tender.

He lay on his side beside her, watching, a bit uncertain of her.

Moving slowly, a little wobbly, she turned to her side to face him. Then she wrapped her arms around his neck and brought him close.

They'd laid there for a long time, not quite dozing but in a little twilight consciousness. They'd stayed in each other's arms, grips tight despite their semi-comatose states. They had each other; they didn't want to let go.

It was so very much better than the day before.

The spell finally broke when one of them—it wasn't him—had to get up to the bathroom. When she came back, she held her hand out to him and he reluctantly left her bed. He looked back at it as she pulled him away. It was worthy of bronzing. At least a plaque. Damn fine sex was had here. Unbelievably fine. Bring-you-to-your-knees fine.

They showered together, close, still holding each other. But there was no more sex. There were a number of her body parts he didn't get to touch, not even in an entirely in-nocent, let-me-help-you-wash kind of way. She wasn't above slapping at his hand, or swatting him when he chuckled.

He wasn't sure how to express how much he adored her. But they kissed—just sweet, sweet kissing—before they tow-eled off. He thought maybe she got the idea.

His wonder woman had shopped, so he had a clean change of clothes. She rustled around in her two—okay, he forced her to admit—*three* closets until she found just the per-fect thing for herself. They walked out of her apartment, flagged a cab, and headed to the hospital. He held her hand every minute of it. And never needed to even think about tak-ing deep breaths.

$\mathcal{E}$PILOGUE

Thanksgiving was celebrated at Isabela's. It was to be a long weekend, with a wedding on Friday. Will and Katherine were present, and Elyse and Jeff.

Eli Benson and his wife Tammy came just for Thursday dinner.

Mother and son had come a long way, separately and to-gether, in vanquishing the demons that had limited their lives. When Will and Katherine had walked into Jeff's hospital room, Isabela and Elyse were already there. Other than when she'd been hospitalized herself, it was the first time Will had seen his mother away from Fergus Mountain since he was a child. But she was there, holding Jeff's hand, and worried, to all appearances, for him but not for herself.

Will had spent most of that week in Manhattan, visiting Jeff, finishing up the Carlson case with Sheriff Rodier and a whole herd of FBI agents. He'd stayed with Katherine that week, traveling to the hospital and the federal building with her or, when she was working, alone. When he was with her, he held her hand. But after a while, it became clear that was pretty much because he wanted to, not because he needed to.

There was no doubt it was a relief to go back to Vermont. He felt very much more comfortable in the hills and open spaces and clean air of home. But that meant Katherine and he were back to just weekends together, and that sucked more than the relief was worth.

Jeff had looked like hell when they'd first seen him, but he was alive and aware, and pretty much clung to Elyse's hand as Will had clung to Katherine's. His recovery was un-complicated and remarkably speedy. He liked hospitals the way Will liked crowds. Within the week, he was also back in Vermont—and staying with Elyse.

It was their wedding that would take place on Friday. They'd discussed adding on to Elyse's cabin. Jeff had thought Elyse wouldn't want to leave the home that had been her safe haven since she was a child. Unexpectedly, Elyse objected—she'd been confined there for too many years already. They had a plan to build a new home on the mountain, one that would have room enough for an office for Jeff, and for family gatherings with grandchildren. Even the chiropractor could come, Jeff said.

Will was pretty sure there would be a grandchild from the Hunter side of the family by summer. Katherine wasn't talking yet. He knew she hadn't had a period—even when they were apart, that was something he wouldn't miss. She'd tried half a dozen times to convince him that, interrupting her body rhythms the way they'd done, removing her patch midcycle, they had to expect it to be a month or two before things got back on track.

But this weekend, she'd left the table in a hurry a couple times, and she'd come back giving the evil eye to his smirk. He'd start being sympathetic just as soon as she let him in on the news. And then he'd strut only behind her back.

They'd make it all right in another month, when their Christmas wedding was planned.

Simon Carlson was dead and so a lot of open cases, from Vermont to Washington to Thailand, had fallen closed. The arrogant psychopath had left records in a file tucked into a safe on the *Indulgence*. His body had been found a couple weeks after they left him there in the water. James Hanson would be tried, and both Will and Katherine would have to testify. But neither of them cared much what happened to him. Will would have liked a couple minutes alone in a cell with him—the man had hurt Katherine after all—but since that wasn't going to happen, he'd settle for a good long jail sentence. He figured anyone who would hit a woman would surely piss off someone in prison and get what was coming to him.

A month after Simon had been declared dead, Will got a call from Theodore Carlson's estate attorney. He excitedly shared what he assumed would be good news—the old senator had left his very substantial fortune to Will.

Will dropped the phone, called to Beowulf, and went outside and ran. Two hours later, he collapsed on his front porch, but he still hadn't outrun the meaning of that bequest—he was Theodore Carlson's grandson. Simon had been his father.

The sealed envelope that Simon had taunted him with must have been a duplicate report. Theodore had known the results.

When Will had run out of the room, following Simon and Katherine to the boat, he'd left the vile envelope there on the desk. He supposed it had been picked up in the search of the mansion that was part of the investigation that followed. Will had never asked.

He tried to make a case that Teddy's gesture might simply have been a sort of apology for the harm that his son had brought down on Will and his family. It wasn't the kind of thing for which you'd just send flowers or a box of chocolates.

But a multimillion dollar apology? Not bloody likely.

He'd considered keeping the news to himself. He spent a couple days not telling Jeff, and determined that he would never tell Elyse. But Katherine came up for the weekend and wormed it out of him in about twenty seconds flat. Apparently, she had, like, radar for drama. Or he wasn't the least bit skilled at hiding from her something that was weighing on his mind.

So he guessed that was a good thing to learn early on. They spent a good part of that weekend together thinking about what to do with the money.

In the end, it was simple. They knew each of Simon's victims—all they had to do was read the list he'd left. They would set some of the funds aside for programs that helped vulnerable women. But the bulk of it would be divided up and given to the families of the victims.

He still hadn't told Jeff, though he figured he might, someday. And he still figured he'd never tell Elyse.

Inevitably, he worried some about that little bun that Katherine had in the oven. She had, indeed, won that argument, and he couldn't truly say he was sorry. He trusted that the Nobles were good blood, and he knew Fergus blood was true. The Carlson genes were getting gradually filtered out. He assumed Katherine would cop to his anxiety about that issue as well and knew she'd have confidence in their ability to avoid raising any little serial killers. It would be good to talk to her about it, if she ever got around to the big reveal.

All in all, he was a happy man, sitting at the head of his grandmère's table, surreptitiously drinking Katherine's share of the wine. There was a lot of love at the table, even where there wasn't blood.

He grinned as Eli lifted his glass. There had been a lot of toasts, and, with a significant amount of wine drunk now, the mood was pretty cheery.

"To Isabela," he said. "As lovely and generous of heart today as she was more than thirty years ago when I first sat at this table." He lifted his glass to Elyse. "To the girl of the long braid and pure heart, who brought a true and deep happiness to my good friend. To Truman, our fallen soldier, the finest man I've known." He turned then to Will. "And to you, Will. He'd be proud of you, as I am just to know you."

Will's hand wasn't steady, but he lifted his glass in acknowledgement. He set it down carefully, grimly suppressing the urge to throw it.

He took Katherine's hand and held tight, but when he looked at her, her attention was across the table.

Will turned to his mother. Tears streamed down her face. She seemed shrunken, closed in on herself. Like she would go away again and not come back.

"Mom," he said. He shoved his chair back and stood. "Mama."

Jeff reached for her, too. But when Will got to her, she rose and fell into his arms. "I'm sorry, Will. I'm so sorry." Her words were choked, all but sobbing.

Will was ready to cry himself. "It's okay, Mama. It's not your fault."

All around the table people stood, concerned and questioning. "What is it?" Isabela asked.

Will rocked his mother, aware of her tears through his shirt. With her tight in his arms, he turned to Katherine. Comforting his mother, shushing her tears, he nodded a go-ahead to her.

She walked the length of the table and put an arm around Isabela. She gave her a squeeze and then looked around the table.

"It looks like maybe Will's father wasn't Truman, but Simon Carlson."

There were murmured objections from around the table, but one voice spoke loudly.

"I never believed it!" Elyse lifted her head and looked at her family. Then she put her palm on Will's cheek and spoke to him. "I was always certain in my heart that Tru was your father. I never doubted it. Not once. But then...then that lawyer called." She looked around again, meeting eyes. "Theodore Carlson's lawyer called, looking for Will. Will is his beneficiary." Tears fell as she looked back at Will. "I'm so sorry, Will. I couldn't bring myself to tell you. Even if you knew, I couldn't talk to you about it."

"But, Elyse," Isabela said. "Surely you know Truman was Will's father."

"Yeah," Eli said. "He's got the mark."

Everyone looked at Eli. But it was Isabela who spoke. "Yes, the mark. Elyse, you must have known."

"The Durak Archipelago?" Now everyone looked at Katherine. She raised her eyebrows. "The birthmark on his, uh..."

Eli nodded. "On his butt, yeah. Truman had it, too, just the same. But what's the Durak Archipelago?"

Will felt he was on another planet while Katherine answered. "The Gorbachev mark—on his forehead. It's shaped just like an archipelago off Siberia. It's a big tourist attraction now."

Jeff had Elyse by the shoulders, so Will lifted his hands. "Wait," he said. "Will somebody explain what we're talking about?"

Isabela spoke up. "You were born with a birthmark, Will, in the, uh, diaper area."

Will snorted. *Diaper area.*

Isabela gave him an arch look, like only she could do. *Well,* maybe his soon-to-be wife had something like it, too. "Your father, Truman"—she said the name with a clear emphasis—"had exactly the same mark. Surely you saw it, Elyse."

Elyse's tears had halted while her interest was drawn by this conversation. "On Will, yes, of course. But Truman..." Her words trailed away. She tried again. "I never..." She shrugged, still at a loss.

"She never saw his ass, guys."

Will snorted again and shook his head at Eli's blunt words.

Isabela walked around to hold Elyse. "It was just the same, even from birth. It never occurred to me that you didn't know, Elyse, that you wondered. I'm so sorry, my poor dear."

"But..." Elyse was at a loss. She looked around to Will. "Did the lawyer find you? Did Theodore Carlson really name you in his will? Why would he do that?"

Will rubbed her back. "I don't know, Mom."

Katherine looked down the table at them. "Simon said that Teddy ordered DNA testing, that he wanted a legacy. But Teddy died before he got the results. He knew that Simon had been—that Simon was sterile. Maybe he just...maybe he just hoped it was true."

Will sat and was grateful when Katherine came to stand beside and slip her arms around him. He wrapped his arms around her waist and leaned into her. He didn't know what to think.

He caught Eli's gaze from across the table. "I told you," Eli said. "You're just like your dad. And the mark—it's exactly the same."

Isabela looked from his mother to him. Will would swear she blushed. "Your grandfather had it, too."

That seemed to close the deal for everyone in the room. Smiling, most of them returned to their seats. Jeff still held Elyse, and Will kept his arms around Katherine.

She leaned down to give him a kiss. He held her to it a bit. "I'm sorry, baby," he said. "I'm afraid we're going to have a little Gorbachev."

She put her hand over his, where he'd placed it on her abdomen. "Mikhail." She grinned, trying the name out. "Nothing wrong with that."

Will realized their words had fallen into a well of silence. He thought what followed might be called a pregnant pause. Then they were all on their feet again with laughter and, this time, happy tears.

ABOUT THE AUTHOR

Rebecca Skovgaard is a midwife in Rochester, New York. She and her husband are raising (yes, *still)* their three children, who give them great pride. She believes that if you live in Rochester, you can never have too many spring bulbs in the garden or Christmas lights in the trees.

Under the pen name Rachel Billings, she has published several erotic novels.

www.ingramcontent.com/pod-product-compliance
Lightning Source LLC
Chambersburg PA
CBHW020059180626
46812CB00006B/2390